"I will not share your bed, Wyldehaven."

He raised his brows and gave her a cool smile. "Who asked you to?"

She crossed her arms over her chest. He should have been irritated; instead he was charmed.

"If that kiss was an invitation," she said, "consider it declined."

"It was a kiss, Miss Fontaine, not a proposition."

"Better if it is said. I will have no misconceptions between us."

"As you wish."

"I am not here to be a companion for your convenience."

"Miss Fontaine, I believe you protest too much."

Outrage flickered across her face.

He wished she would let go of that control of hers, let her passion lead her back into his arms . . .

Romances by **Debra Mullins**

Debra Mullins

To Ruin The Duke

AVON

An Imprint of HarperCollinsPublishers

This is a work of fiction. Names, characters, places, and incidents are products of the author's imagination or are used fictitiously and are not to be construed as real. Any resemblance to actual events, locales, organizations, or persons, living or dead, is entirely coincidental.

AVON BOOKS
An Imprint of HarperCollins*Publishers*
10 East 53rd Street
New York, New York 10022-5299

Copyright © 2009 by Debra Mullins Welch
ISBN 978-0-06-157785-7
www.avonromance.com

First Avon Books paperback printing: June 2009

Avon Trademark Reg. U.S. Pat. Off. and in Other Countries, Marca Registrada, Hecho en U.S.A.
HarperCollins® is a registered trademark of HarperCollins Publishers.

Printed in the U.S.A.

10 9 8 7 6 5 4 3 2 1

To Esi Sogah,
who gave me chances
when I really needed them.
Your belief in me
made this book possible.

To Ruin The
Duke

Prologue

The tiny attic room stank of sweat and blood. The midwife had opened the door to ease the stifling heat, but the ensuing draft barely made the flame on the single stubby candle flicker. The mewling and fidgeting of the newborn babe in the midwife's arms broke the heavy silence and added burden to the grief that weighed on them all.

By the doorway of the closet-sized chamber, the vicar waited and watched, as patient as death. Miranda tried not to look at him, tried not to be reminded that Lettie would not live to see the sunrise.

She sat on the floor beside the pallet under the eaves, holding Lettie's limp hand in her own. Her friend looked so pale, so weak. Not at all like the vibrant, brilliant Lettie who had returned from London only months before, bursting with health and expectations for her unborn child. Oh, the plans she had spoken of, the grand schemes for raising her

1

baby and seeing that he or she took his or her rightful place in society.

Gone now. They would never come to pass.

Miranda swallowed past the lump in her throat, then leaned closer as Lettie slowly turned her head on the pillow. Her blue eyes, always so stunning, no longer sparkled with life. The roses had gone from her cheeks, leaving them waxen. Her lovely blond hair was dark with sweat and clung to her scalp.

Lettie's fingers fluttered in Miranda's, and she opened her mouth, but no sound came forth.

"Hush now." Miranda swept a hand over Lettie's damp brow and tried to summon a reassuring smile. "You need to rest."

Lettie gave a knowing chuckle, half laugh and half sob. Her voice came finally, thready and frail. "Liar. I am dying, Miranda."

"No." Panic streaked through her veins. To speak of death so easily—that made it all the more real. There had been too much loss in Miranda's life already. She could not accept more. *Would not.* "You must get better, raise your son."

"A son." Lettie's lips curved ever so slightly. "Wylde would have liked that."

"Shhh." Miranda brought her friend's hand to her cheek. So cold. Already Lettie's flesh took on the aspect of death. She struggled for the strength to maintain her composure. Falling to pieces would

2

not help Lettie. "Do not speak of that man. He does not deserve a single thought from you."

Lettie curled her fingers around Miranda's. "You must take care of my son."

"Nonsense. You will be here to see that he grows up properly."

"Miranda." Lettie's voice strengthened, and just for a moment she seemed to be her old self, all confidence and dazzling ideas. "Listen now." The sternness faded from her tone, and she took a shaky breath. "I am dying. I can feel the life slipping away from me."

"No." Miranda shook her head in vehement denial. "I cannot lose you, Lettie."

"Be practical." Lettie's voice faded to a whisper. "Take care of my son, Miranda. Take care of my James."

"James." Tears stung her eyes, and she blinked them back. "A lovely name."

Lettie's eyelids drifted shut. "My father's name."

Lettie's fingers weakened their clasp, and Miranda bit hard into her lower lip, holding back the sob that threatened to choke her. Lettie was fading before her eyes. In a moment she would be gone.

Just like everyone else.

Miranda bowed her head over their clasped hands and let the tears fall at last, streaming down her cheeks in silent tribute to her friend.

Lettie's fingers tightened again. "Mira."

Miranda jerked her head up, met Lettie's gaze. The nickname nearly tore away the last of her self-control. "Lettie. I thought—"

"Soon." Her lips curved again. "So impatient, Mira. Even rushing me to the grave."

"I am not, of course I am not! I do not want you to go, Lettie." The sob finally burst from her throat, smashing the dam of her restraint. Grief flooded through her, stealing the strength from her limbs. "Whatever shall I do without you?"

"You will take care of my son." Lettie's gaze never wavered. "Make certain he gets what he deserves. A place in society with his father. Swear to me."

"Yes, yes, I swear." Miranda nodded, willing to promise anything, do anything.

"You will go to London. Collect the dowry your mother left for you with Thaddeus."

"I will."

"Use it well. Make a life for yourself."

"Yes, Lettie."

"I can count on you to do what is right, my dear Mira." Lettie smiled again, and her lips were still curved when she closed her eyes and breathed her last.

Miranda sat frozen by her bedside. She waited for Lettie to open her eyes again, to laugh at the joke. But Lettie remained silent and peaceful in her death, and the fingers Miranda continued to hold grew lax.

4

She heard a rustle of clothing and then the vicar was beside her. He laid a hand on her shoulder. "She is gone."

"No." The sound was more croak than word. Miranda clasped Lettie's hand tighter. "She cannot be gone. Not so quickly."

"She is at peace." He took Lettie's hand from Miranda's and laid it gently across the still body of the deceased. "I am sorry. You must let me see to her now."

Miranda nodded, her shoulders slumped, watching as the vicar bent his head and prayed. For a moment it felt as if she again sat at the bedside of her mother, gone just over a year ago now. She supposed she should feel comfort from the familiar rituals of death, but the truth was, she hated them. How was it she always lost the people she loved?

She had never known her father. He had gotten her mother with child and then, upon hearing the news of her condition, dismissed her with a healthy financial settlement. Her mother, once the great actress Fannie Fontaine, had lived the rest of her life in obscurity, and once the money ran out, had no choice but to eventually become a prostitute at the tavern where Miranda still lived—until the drink finally killed her.

Lettie had also worked at the tavern, but as a barmaid, not a whore. Before her death, Fannie had seen potential in the girl and sent her to her friend

Thaddeus in London, who arranged for a career on the stage. Months later Lettie returned to the tavern, having enjoyed some success as an actress but abandoned by her lover when she had gotten with child. Hoping for advice from Fannie, who had suffered the same fate, Lettie had instead discovered Fannie was dead.

With Lettie having nowhere else to go, Miranda had offered to her a place in her tiny attic room at the tavern until the child was born. Even though Miranda now had to serve ale at the tavern to pay for the extra food—in addition to her long days writing the memoirs of wealthy Mrs. Etherington, and her evenings ciphering the tavern's accounts—she felt she could not do otherwise. She could not escape the thought that if someone had helped Fannie in her time of need, maybe her own life would have been different.

But now Lettie was gone, and Miranda had no idea what she would do next. The burial, of course. And then back to her solitary life. Always alone.

A wail rent the air, jolting Miranda from her memories. The midwife jiggled the howling baby. "There, there, little man," she cooed. "We'll find something for you to eat."

With the baby cradled in her arms, the midwife came to stand before Miranda. "You'll be needing a wet nurse for this one," she said. "Or goat's milk. But the lad has to eat." She leaned forward and placed the squalling infant in Miranda's arms before she could think to protest.

"Will you be raising the boy then?" The vicar turned from Lettie's bedside. "With his mother dead, I expected to take him to the orphanage."

"Not the orphanage." Her arms tightened around the child, and she instinctively rocked him, calming his cries. "I promised Lettie."

The vicar raised his brows. "It will not be an easy path, with no husband to provide for you."

Miranda glanced at Lettie's pale, still form, then down at the baby. His little face was scrunched up in fury, fists clenched as he wailed his displeasure. He was so tiny. So helpless.

And hers now.

She looked up at the vicar and braced for an objection. "I intend to do what she asked of me."

To her surprise, he simply nodded, his face solemn. "Very well. I will pray for you."

"I will manage." *I always do.* She glanced down at the child again, her heart already unfurling with love. "Do not fret, little James," she whispered. "Miranda is here to make everything right."

Chapter 1

He had carried Michael out of many a tavern, but he had never expected to be carrying him to his grave. Not so soon.

Thornton Matherton, Duke of Wyldehaven—called Wylde by the few who knew him best—shouldered the coffin of his dead friend as it slid from the hearse. As the personage of the highest rank, he had been given the post at Michael's head, with Wulf—Edwin Warrell, Earl of Harwulf—on the other side. Kit and Darcy, a viscount and an impoverished earl, respectively, bore the burden in the middle. How fitting that the four of them, friends since their school days, should be the ones to bring Michael to his final resting place. Michael's younger brothers, William and Peter, hefted the foot of the coffin.

They began to walk toward the entrance of Michael's parish church. Every step Wylde took, every crunching footfall on the dry earth, echoed like a drumbeat in his head. The scent of burning wax and flowers wafted from the doorway of the church and reached his nose before he had ascended all the steps. Sickly familiar, memory struck him like a staff across the knees, and his booted foot caught on the top step. He caught himself just in time to prevent the coffin from sliding back down the steps. Wulf steadied the box, then sent him a warning look.

Wylde inwardly flinched from the unexpected censure but took pains to assure that his expression of solemnity never wavered. A duke never revealed weakness—or his emotions—to anyone. And the fact that his heart screamed in grief was no one's business but his own.

But death, and the trappings of it, slid through his defenses like a well-placed dagger through the ribs, tearing at his insides and leaving him bleeding. It seemed only moments ago that he had stood by Felicity's elaborate coffin as she had been laid to rest in the family crypt at Wyldehaven, though he knew nearly two years had passed. And now he walked his best friend to his entombment in this tiny parish church just outside London.

An elderly woman swathed in black sniffed into her handkerchief as they walked down the aisle. She threw Wylde a look of contempt and hissed, "Drunkard!" as he passed. Wylde blinked in surprise but then pushed the moment aside, focusing on balancing the coffin and then lowering it with the other pallbearers to its place near the altar.

The ceremony passed by in a blur. He heard the words of the vicar through a dense fog of unreality. He was conscious of Wulf, Darcy, and Kit sitting in the hard pew beside him, of Michael's mother wailing unceasingly from the front row, comforted by her younger sons. He stared at the ornate wooden box, unable to conceive that Michael was really in there. It was all a nightmare from which he could not wake.

He should have done something. He should have stopped him.

But no, he had been so engrossed in his grief over his own losses that he had refused Michael's invitation to go on that trip to India. Perhaps if he'd gone, if he had let Michael lure him from the gloom of mourning back into the vibrant colors of life, maybe then Michael might still be alive. They could have watched out for each other, as they had since childhood.

But he had not gone, preferring his darkened rooms and the perpetually unfinished opera he was composing over spending time laughing in the sun with his dearest friend. And now the shadows of grief stretched even longer over his life. First his wife and unborn child had been taken from him, then his closest friend. Everyone he loved, it seemed, suffered by association with him.

Before he knew it, the ceremony was over and he was out of the church, away from the cloying smells of death and mourning. His coachman waited nearby, the black-swathed coach with its ducal emblem on the door a fitting testament to Michael. He headed toward it like a bullet, his careful walls crumbling beneath the grief that waited to claim him. He had not been anywhere near London since before Felicity's death and had no idea how to even talk to people anymore. How he longed for the isolation of Wyldehaven, for the peace to be found in his own music room as he worked on his compositions.

Forty-eight hours was his limit for staying in London. Twenty of those hours had passed already. By tomorrow he expected to be on his way home to Dorset, leaving London and its rumor-mongering, busybody citizens far behind.

"Say there, Wylde! Wait!"

Wylde halted just as the footman jumped down to open the door of the coach. He gave a longing look at the welcoming interior, then glanced back to see Darcy dashing over to him. "Darcy, good to see you."

"Blast it, Wylde, you barely said three words to me today." Darcy came to a halt, clutching his hat in one hand after the quick sprint and smoothing his curling black hair back with the other.

"Apologies, Darcy. I just . . . funerals."

Darcy nodded. "Too painful after your wife."

"Yes."

"Understood." Darcy flashed his famously charming grin. "I would be glad of a ride, Wylde, if you can spare the time."

"Certainly." Wylde waved a hand at the coach. "Just give Goodman your direction."

"Splendid!" Darcy leaped toward the open door, calling his destination to the coachman as he did so.

Wylde sighed, then climbed in after him. It appeared he would have to wait a bit more for his treasured solitude.

Once they were seated, the coach lurched into motion. "I thought you arrived with Kit," Wylde said.

"I did, but your coach is finer." Darcy gave a quick laugh, but the eyes he turned on Wylde were serious. "Truly, I wanted to speak to you and did not want an audience."

Wylde frowned. "Is something wrong?"

"That is just what I was going to ask you." Darcy settled back against the squabs, his handsome face creased with concern. "I understand that you needed time alone in the country to grieve for Felicity and your unborn child. Wulf, Kit, and I all tried to let you be, assuming you would contact us when you were ready."

"I appreciate that."

12

"But I cannot believe you returned to London and never even told us," Darcy continued. "And I especially find it difficult to comprehend how you could even think of going to a gaming hell like Fulton's without asking me to join you."

Wylde frowned. "What are you talking about? I only arrived in London last night."

"I'm talking about the incident three days ago. I wish you had asked me to go with you. I could have helped." Darcy's brow creased. "I worry about you, Wylde. You seem to have gone a bit mad after your wife's death, sorry to say."

"You will be even sorrier if you do not explain yourself. What is this about Fulton's?"

"Come now. 'Tis common knowledge that you lost a small fortune there three nights ago. But what disturbs me is the fight afterward. 'Tis not like you at all to beat a man bloody because he was cheating."

Wylde stared at his friend with growing confusion. "Darcy, are you foxed? I was not at Fulton's three nights ago, and there was no bloody fight. As I told you, I only arrived in London late last night."

Darcy's jaw tightened. "I am trying to be a good friend to you, Wylde, but we will get nowhere if you continue to deny the facts."

Wylde's eyes narrowed, his affection for Darcy icing over like his garden pond in winter. "In the twenty years of our acquaintance, my dear Lord Rywood, when have you ever known me to lie?"

"I can't say that I have. But now I have done it, eh? You only become formal with me when you are vexed. But I am just trying to help. You have always been the epitome of propriety, Wylde, and this sudden burst of disreputable behavior is simply not like you. The talk is all over Town."

"Talk?" Wylde leaned forward, his entire body rigid. "What talk is this? I have been installed at Wyldehaven since before Felicity's death."

"News of the brawl has reached all the drawing rooms in London. I'm sorry about that, Wylde. I know how you hate gossip."

"There was no bloody brawl, Darcy. Someone made a mistake." Wylde sat back, sucking air into his lungs. Bloody rumormongers. As if he did not have enough misery on his plate without their input.

"No mistake, Wylde. Jonas Pendleton saw you there and spread the word. Of course you were utterly drunk at the time, so perhaps that explains it."

"This is madness."

"If you had taken me with you, I could have helped you avoid the whole distasteful mess." Darcy fingered the slightly worn edge of his coat. "You know I am always available for a game of cards."

"This tale is all over London?"

"I am afraid so."

"Upon my honor, Darcy, I tell you I was not even in Town at the time." He caught and held his friend's gaze. "Pendleton must be trying to blacken my name for some reason. You must believe me."

"Perhaps." Darcy frowned. "I must admit to being taken aback by the story."

"How can it be that gossip like this spreads when I am not even in the city?" Wylde curled his lip and cast a disgusted glance out the window at the buildings of London. "Father would no doubt be quite amused, were he alive."

"I suppose Pendleton could be trying to discredit you," Darcy speculated. "It makes more sense than the current version of events."

"You know me better than most people, Darcy. I do not lie, I do not gamble, and I have never in my life engaged in fisticuffs outside a friendly match at Gentleman Jackson's."

"I would have agreed wholeheartedly until two days ago, when I first heard of the incident." Darcy frowned. "Very well. If you say it never happened, then I will take that as truth."

"Thank you." Wylde tapped his fingers on his knee. "I will have a word with Pendleton and see what mischief he is about."

"Excellent notion. If you need any help, you know you can call on any of us." Darcy flashed a quick grin as the coach came to a stop outside his residence. "Or all of us, for that matter."

Wylde nodded. "I will keep that in mind."

"See that you do." The footman opened the door, and with a jaunty salute, Darcy hopped out of the carriage.

Wylde watched him go. Once, the offer of help from his friends would have meant the world. He, Darcy, Kit, and Wulf had all been young boys tormented by the bullies at school. Then Michael— bigger, braver, and more clever than all of them— had convinced them to band together to fight back against their oppressors. With the arrogance of the very young, they called themselves Sons of Grendel, named after the mythical monster from *Beowulf* whom no one could defeat. The plan worked, and their friendship, which included Michael, had lasted well into adulthood.

But when Michael had needed him, he had not been there. Michael died alone in the middle of the ocean with only strangers around him. With that on his conscience, Wylde did not dare ask any of his other friends to extend themselves on his account. He would get to the bottom of this scurrilous rumor and put a stop to it. Alone.

Since it was not yet even noon, he found Jonas Pendleton at home, still abed. The butler tried to indicate that his master was not currently receiving callers, but Wylde would have none of it and pushed past the older man into the house. Given the reality of a duke standing in the foyer, the servant had no choice but to summon his master.

Wylde awaited Pendleton in a tiny salon whose decor looked somewhat the worse for wear. When the man himself entered the room, he did not look much better, hurriedly dressed in shirt and coat without his cravat, his hair a hastily finger-combed mess. His pale blue eyes were bloodshot and his skin waxen, except for a greenish bruise on his jaw.

"Wyldehaven. What in blue blazes are you doing here at this hour?" he demanded.

Wylde glanced out the window. "The sun is well up, Pendleton, and the world is awake."

"The world did not crawl into bed with the dawn." Pendleton went to the window and yanked the drapes closed. "Now I demand to know your purpose here."

Wylde raised his brows, taken aback by the hostility. "I am here to request an explanation for rumors you have started about me."

"What rumors?" Heedless of the fact that his guest remained standing, Pendleton threw himself into an armchair. "I have not said anything that is not the truth."

"Indeed?" Wylde did not sit but instead came to stand over Pendleton's chair. "What of that nonsense about Fulton's three nights ago?"

17

Pendleton glared at him. "As I said, nothing but truth. Perhaps you do not remember the details clearly since you were so bloody drunk, Wyldehaven, but I cannot forget." He touched the bruise on his jaw. "You sent me home with a reminder."

Wylde reared back. "Are you now accusing me of striking you?"

"Too right. I tried to peel you off poor Winchell and got this for my trouble."

"Impossible. I only arrived in London last night."

"The hell you did." Pendleton stood, pushing nose-to-nose with Wylde. "I saw you myself, called you by name, played cards with you. You won my money but then lost badly to Winchell. Then you accused him of cheating and thrashed the poor sod until he was incoherent." He sneered. "Have to admit, Wyldehaven, I didn't know you were so handy with your fives."

"But it was not me," Wylde murmured, more to himself than Pendleton. "I was not even in London."

"It was you, all right, *Your Grace*. Took a bit of time, but it looks like you took more after your sire than anyone knew. You truly are the son of Madcap Matherton, aren't you?"

The words chilled him. "I tell you it is a mistake. I was at Wyldehaven until yesterday."

Pendleton jerked a finger at the bruise on his face. "This was no mistake. You were the one who chopped me in the jaw when I tried to pull you off Winchell. Luckily for me Fulton employs those big louts to break up these things. They dragged you out and probably saved poor Winchell's life."

"It did not happen," Wylde said. He stripped off his gloves. "Look at my hands. Why are they not bruised or scraped?"

Pendleton barely glanced at Wylde's bared knuckles. "Those of us who were there know what we saw, what we *felt*." He swept a scathing gaze over Wylde's impeccable clothing. "You are no gentleman."

Wylde stiffened and tugged his gloves back on. "Step carefully, Pendleton. I came here to discover what game you are playing, and I warn you, I *will* find out."

"I have no desire to rise with the sun to meet my maker. Everyone knows you are a crack shot, and I am fond of my own skin." Pendleton returned to his chair and glowered. "Your consequence may be enough to hide your true nature, Wyldehaven, but you cannot silence those of us who have seen that side of you. The world will learn the truth about the Duke of Wyldehaven."

"You are mistaken," Wylde gritted out, shaken by the intensity in Pendleton's gaze. The fellow believed every word he had spoken. With a curt nod of his head, Wylde strode out of the drawing room and out of the house.

Had the entire world gone mad?

From across the street, he watched Wyldehaven storm out of Jonas Pendleton's residence and down the stairs to the glossy black coach waiting at the curb. Footmen jumped down to open the door to the elegant equipage, making the coat of arms on the door blaze in the morning sun.

Mocking him.

His bloody Grace, the Duke of Wyldehaven, climbed into the coach without a word to his servants. Pretentious sod. He could see the duke's stony countenance through the window as he settled back into the seat. The poor fellow looked as if he wanted to take a bite out of something—or someone.

Well, well. Out of sorts, was he? A grin tugged at his lips. Apparently Pendleton had not received His Grace with a fatted calf. Too tragic, that. But what could a fellow expect after thrashing a man over a gaming dispute? He chuckled and rubbed his bruised knuckles. Some pain was worth the reward.

The coach pulled away, no doubt headed to Mayfair, where His Grace would be soothed by his army of servants at the elegant town house that had long belonged to the Matherton family.

For once he felt no envy—only a delicious anticipation. "That's right, dear boy," he murmured. "Hurry home to your darkened rooms and the spirits that haunt you. Leave the night to *me*."

Wylde arrived at his town house and sought the privacy of his study immediately upon returning from Pendleton's. Seated at his desk, he took out a crystal decanter from a nearby cabinet and poured a large portion of whisky into a matching crystal glass. As he lifted the glass to his lips, he sat back in his chair and began to sort through the post his secretary had left for him.

After a moment he carefully set down the glass.

Bills from tailors, demands of payment for gaming debts, even an invoice for a horse he had never purchased. There were dozens of them. All purchases supposedly made by the Duke of Wyldehaven. All from London. All in the last several weeks.

This was impossible. He had not been in London for nearly two years. During his self-imposed exile at Wyldehaven he had seen no one—with the exception of Michael—and had tried to lose himself in the opera he was composing. He was mourning, not mad. He *knew* he could not have possibly incurred these debts.

But someone had, using his name.

Pendleton's words came back to him. Pendleton

had seen *him*, claimed to have played cards with *him*, accused *him* of giving him the bruise that currently decorated his jawline. Except he had been in Dorset at the time.

Someone was impersonating him. Someone who looked enough like him to fool those who did not know him well.

With a frustrated sweep of his arm, he shoved the bills aside. How many years had he carefully followed the strict parameters of behavior set by Society? His father had done considerable harm to the family name with his scandalous exploits, but Wylde had been the one to set the example after Father's death. He had avoided London and its gossip mill as much as possible, choosing instead to live most of the time in quiet solitude at Wyldehaven. But despite his care, someone was destroying the good name he had fought so hard to achieve, the honorable reputation that finally made people forget about the disreputable one left by his father.

He had done everything right, walked every step with excruciating care, and *this* was his reward? To be used by some stranger?

Enough. He had tolerated years of his father's undisciplined swings from disreputable rogue to strict parent. He had suffered at the hands of bullies as a schoolboy. He had handed out thousands of pounds in gaming debts on his father's behalf as well as to any of his sire's many by-blows who presented themselves on his doorstep. But no more. This scheme was outside of enough. He did not deserve such treatment, and he *would* stop the villain behind it.

He scooped up the papers from the floor. One letter caught his eye because of its feminine handwriting and plain appearance. It did not look like a demand for payment.

Curious, he ripped it open. The few sentences in the missive first made his heart freeze in his chest, but then it began pounding again—too fast. His blood surged through his veins, red hot. He grabbed a piece of stationery and his quill and jotted a short reply. He sealed it with wax and put it on the pile of post that needed to go out tomorrow.

Bills he could manage. God knew he had enough money to pay these honest tradesmen until he could find out who was behind this mischief, and he would rather do that than add to the gossip by appearing to avoid his debts. But this last letter had nothing to do with overdue bills or rumors of fisticuffs. He knew for certain he was not responsible for this matter, and better that he tell the young lady the truth at once, so she might continue to search for the real culprit.

He got up from his desk and blew out the lamp, heading for his bed. Forty-eight hours be damned.

There was no way he could leave London now, not without discovering the identity of the villain who was impersonating him. He would have to pursue the blackguard and stop these nefarious activities . . . before Society began to believe its own rumors and determined that he was, indeed, his father's son.

Chapter 2

One month later

Miranda stood on the doorstep of Matherton House, her eyes fixed on the heavy brass knocker that decorated the door. Her heart thundered in her chest, and her hands trembled. No decent woman would be seen visiting a gentleman at his home, but here she stood, mentally summoning her courage to lift that knocker and announce her presence.

What if he refused to see her? What if he tossed her into the street?

Just the thought of it straightened her spine. She had promised Lettie, and baby James needed someone to stand up for him. This duke had sent a pithy dismissal to her letter informing him that he had a child. Perhaps he would not be able to set aside her person as easily as he had a piece of paper.

Using her righteous anger as a crutch, she rapped on the door.

Wylde strode down the hallway of his London home slightly the worse for wear, as he had not found his bed until dawn. He had spent last evening as he'd spent all others since Michael's funeral, combing the gaming hells of London in an effort to track down the blackguard posing as the Duke of Wyldehaven. He always seemed to be just a step behind the fellow, and everyone he spoke to said the same thing: that they had witnessed *him* gaming or fighting or seducing a woman or some other mischief. Gathering even that little bit of information had proven time-consuming and expensive.

This cat and mouse chase had begun to weary him, especially since he was beginning to believe he was the mouse and not the cat. Therefore, he was not inclined toward a pleasant demeanor in any shape or form, and most especially not to the young woman who had presented herself at his door this afternoon and demanded an audience with him. His head pounded from both lack of sleep and frustration, and the last thing he wanted to do was deal with unwanted company. However, every caller might have some clue to the imposter, so he was obliged to see each and every one of them. Though today he was determined to see this visitor dispatched with all haste.

The female in question awaited him in the blue parlor, and when he walked into that room, his first thought was that she did not look like a woman of questionable morals, which was his natural reaction to any unwed young miss who presented herself uninvited at a gentleman's home. She sat primly and quietly on the edge of a settee, her gray dress serviceable yet out of date. Dark hair peeked from beneath a simple straw bonnet, which was all he could see of her as she stared down at the gloved hands folded in her lap.

Impoverished gentility, he thought. Another one of Father's by-blows, no doubt.

"I am Wyldehaven," he announced as he made his entrance. "And you are . . . ?"

She gave a start and got to her feet, immediately dipping a curtsy. "My name is Miranda Fontaine."

He frowned, the name plucking a familiar chord in his mind. "What is your business here, Miss Fontaine?"

She had to tilt her head to look up at him. A lovely face, somewhat unusual with sloping cheekbones and full, pouting lips that made a man think of anything but church on Sundays. Her eyes were green and slightly slanted, like a cat's. She furrowed her lovely brow at him, no doubt in response to his curt tone.

He hoped like hell she wasn't his half sister.

"I wrote to you, Your Grace, on a matter of some urgency."

"Wrote to me." Damn and blast, where had he heard her name? He waved a hand at the settee, and she sat down again, though he remained standing. "What was this matter of urgency?"

"The matter of your son."

Recollection snapped into place. He had shoved the memory of the letter aside, assuming the matter was closed. "As I recall, Miss Fontaine, I replied to your missive. I am not the father."

Her lip curled with a cynicism that surprised him. "A common refrain."

He stiffened. "I am not in the habit of denying my own actions, Miss Fontaine. You are mistaken."

"I do not believe I am, Your Grace."

Impudent chit. He slid an admiring glance down her fine, feminine form and had the satisfaction of seeing her fingers clench in reaction. "I would certainly recall a liaison with you, dear lady."

She glared at him, all fire and indignation. For an instant he regretted that he *hadn't* been the one to get her with child. Did she bring such passion to the boudoir? Would the sheets be singed after their coupling?

Dear God, how long had it been since he had even noticed a woman?

"I am not the child's mother, as you well know," she snapped. "His mother was Lettie Dupree. Now do you recall?"

28

"I am not acquainted with Miss Dupree," he said with a shrug, still distracted by her curves. By God, this was a woman made for bedding. His wife had been gone for nearly two years, and no female had attracted his attention in all that time—until now. Then the guilt of Felicity's memory made him frown. "If you are not the mother, why is it that you are here but she is not?"

"Lettie died in childbed."

Her voice caught, just a wisp, but her defiant stare never wavered. A hint of sympathy tempered his growing lust, and he met her eyes with all sincerity. "My condolences, Miss Fontaine."

She gave a cool nod. "Thank you, Your Grace." She took a breath, as if to compose herself. "Given that he is now motherless, I have come to discuss your son's welfare with you."

He gave a harsh laugh, compassion collapsing beneath reluctant admiration. "I have twice denied that the child is mine, Miss Fontaine. Perhaps you were not paying attention."

"Lettie's dying wish was that her son would be raised as a gentleman. Educated as befitting his station as the son of a duke."

"Miss Fontaine, I admire your tenacity. However, your ruthless determination to brand me a liar is beginning to wear thin. Pay close attention." He came to stand over her, locking his gaze with hers. "I am not this child's father."

29

Slowly, she stood. He did not move, but she did not fall back on the settee as he expected. Instead she straightened her small frame, her head only reaching his shoulder, until she stood practically in his arms, mere inches separating them. "It has been my experience that most men of power do not accept the consequences of their actions. I had hoped you would be different, Your Grace."

Her words burned like salt rubbed in the wounds of his heart. Who was this mouthy chit to be ordering him about? Why did she come here, to his house, to remind him of all he had lost, all he had left to lose?

"I regret I must disappoint you. Good day, Miss Fontaine. Travers will escort you out."

He turned away from her and left the room without a backward glance.

Bloody hell, but he was going back to bed.

Miranda entered the small, comfortable house and slammed the door behind her. The crash of the portal should have satisfied her simmering temper, but it did not.

"Arrogant prig," she snapped, yanking off her gloves one at a time.

Thaddeus LeGrande came out of the parlor, a slumbering James on his shoulder. "I assume that matters did not go well."

"They did not." Some of her anger fizzled at the

sight of the baby's sleeping face. "Where is Mrs. Cooper?"

"She went to the market. I agreed to watch the young fellow until you returned." He turned his head to glance at the infant out of the corner of his eye. "I never fancied myself a grandfather, but I imagine I would do quite well in the position."

Miranda smiled as she untied her bonnet. "Considering this is Lettie's child, you practically are his grandfather."

"Poor Lettie." The aging actor's face sagged with grief. "She was so lovely. So talented. I would have seen to it that she was the toast of London."

"I know." She hung her bonnet on the peg beside the door. "That is why my mother sent her to you."

"Another beautiful actress." He smiled. "You look like her, you know."

"My mother was stunning. I am but passable." She peered at the baby. "Do you want me to take him?"

"Not quite yet." Thaddeus laid a gentle hand on the child's back. "He is no burden to me."

"I wish his father had said the same."

"Oh, dear." He took her elbow with his other hand and guided her into the parlor, where a tray of tea and biscuits awaited. "Come and tell me what happened."

Miranda sat down on the sofa and watched as he settled himself into his favorite armchair beside the cold fireplace. "You have gotten quite good at balancing our little man while accomplishing other tasks," she teased.

"I have worn costumes on the stage that weighed more than he does." He waved a hand at the tea tray. "Would you pour? I am eager to know what the duke said."

She lifted the teapot and poured the steaming, fragrant liquid into one cup. "He said it is not his child." She set down the pot and dropped two lumps of precious sugar into the cup, as Thaddeus liked it. "He showed me the door."

"My goodness." Thaddeus caught the saucer with one finger and dragged it across the table so he could reach the tea cup. "Personally?"

His wry tone drew a chuckle from her. "No, His Grace merely walked out of the room. His servant showed me the door." She finished pouring her own cup of tea and put down the pot so she could look at him. "I admit I am disappointed, Thaddeus. I had hoped the man would do the honorable thing."

He gave a bark of laughter. "You have much to learn about dukes, my dear, and Wyldehaven in particular."

She took up her own tea, plain with not even a dab of sugar. "Perhaps you can tell me more. For someone not born to it, you seem to know everyone in the upper echelons of Society."

His lips curved. "Mrs. Weatherby's salon. The polite world mixes with the art world every Thursday night at that lady's home. Even though I rarely perform any more, I still enjoy the company of my fellow thespians."

"Of course you do." She settled back on the sofa, keeping an ear alert should the child stir.

"Mrs. Weatherby's salon is a wonderful place to discover the latest *on dit*," Thaddeus said. "I have heard talk of Wyldehaven, both the father and the son."

Miranda arched her brows. "Indeed?"

"The father was a terrible scapegrace." Thaddeus's voice settled into the deep drama of an orator. "There are scandals about him to this day, though he has been with Old Nick these past five years."

"And the son?"

"He lost his wife about two years ago." He sipped his tea. "And was in deep mourning for months, of course. Then no sooner did he cast off his mourning clothes, but he went a bit wild. Became the worst sort of gamester and rakehell here in London, feeding the gossips with his many exploits."

"And was Lettie merely an exploit?" Miranda's lips twisted. "Men of his ilk consider women merely playthings."

"That I cannot answer."

She sighed and looked once more on the baby's sweet face. "He claimed he was not the father, Thaddeus," she repeated.

"He told you so in the letter he wrote."

"Yes, but I hoped that a personal encounter might make him admit that he did have an affair with Lettie. That he is James's father. But he did not, which means I can expect no aid from him."

Thaddeus sighed. "I wish I could have saved more of your inheritance, Miranda, but I selected that last investment poorly. You lost over half your dowry."

"I'm glad to have any funds at all," she said. "I cannot even fathom that Mama sent you money to put away for me."

"I wondered why she had not sent anything in so long. But that did happen on occasion. Sometimes she did not send any money for several months." He shook his head. "I did not even know she had died until you wrote to tell me about Lettie. And then when I could finally present you with your inheritance, one mediocre business decision nearly did away with it all."

"I am still grateful. And you are lending me the use of your house. That is a tremendous boon."

"Nonsense. Where else would you live? I do not mind staying at the hotel. It is more fitting for a decent woman like yourself to stay here."

"Still, I appreciate it, as it will save me money

while I am here in London." She frowned. "But now that the duke has again rejected James, I must find some way of surviving here."

"I thought you were employed in Little Depping? In the last letter your mother sent me, she mentioned that you were helping some rich old crone write her memoirs."

"That ended when James came along." Miranda glanced at the child again, her heart melting in her chest. "She did not appreciate that I needed to care for him, so I was dismissed."

"Harridan," Thaddeus sniffed.

His sneering tone made her giggle. "Now, Thaddeus."

"Let her write her memoirs in her own scribbling hand," he declared. "I shall help you find employment here in London."

"That is most kind, Thaddeus, but—"

"No." He held up a hand to silence her. "It is because of my bungling that you are in financial straits to begin with. Had I not invested in the wrong venture on your behalf, you would have a handsome dowry to attract a husband."

"I do not want a husband, as I have told you several times."

"I know you do not want the alternative—mistress to some wealthy nabob."

"No." Her stomach churned at just the thought, and she put down her tea to lay a hand against her midriff. "I saw what happened to my mama when she chose that path."

"And you do not want young James to go to an orphanage."

"No." She tried to swallow past the lump in her throat. "That above all is my worst fear."

"Then you must let me help you." He leaned forward as far as he could without disturbing the baby. "You are very beautiful. We must find a way to use that to your advantage."

She shook her head. "I do not see how that will help. I have some schooling. I can write a fine hand and I can read and cipher. In fact, I did bookkeeping for the tavern where we lived. Surely I can find a position somewhere as a companion or clerk."

"I would not recommend such a thing. I know you want to be valued for your skills, but just because you try to ignore your beauty does not mean others will. I fear you being forced against your will by one of your employers, and you would not be able to escape."

"Then what else is there?" Despair sharpened her voice as she stood and began to pace around the sofa. "I do not wish to marry or whore myself. I will not put myself in a position where I am prisoner to the whims of a man. In Little Depping, I held three positions all at the same time: bookkeeping for two businesses, serving in the tavern, and helping Mrs. Etherington with her memoirs. Here in London, I offer to do a good day's work for a day's pay, and still I take the chance of rape or something worse. Curse me for being born a woman!"

Thaddeus laughed and banged his free hand on the table. "Brava, my dear! Such passion! Such fire! If the stage were not the surest way to fall under some man's protection, I would suggest you look there."

"I am no actress." But she could not stop her lips from curving at the compliment.

"No, not an actress." Thaddeus stood, his face rapt with the expression of a man who had glimpsed paradise. "A singer."

"What?" She frowned. "How is that any different from being an actress?"

"Because a singer is an artist. A goddess. Someone who commands reverence." He came toward her, a grin stretching across his face. "You could do it."

"You have never even heard me sing."

"But I have. I listened to you one evening as you sang the little one to sleep. You have an excellent voice. And if we tell everyone you are foreign . . . "

"Foreign! Are you mad?"

"Not at all." He waved a hand in dismissal. "The English adore foreigners. Especially if they are mysterious. We can say you are . . . let me see . . . Italian."

"But I am not."

37

"Nonsense. Your dark hair, your lovely bone structure, your olive skin . . . You could be Italian."

"I see." She crossed her arms, amused. "And how am I supposed to become this goddess?"

He grinned like a young boy in the midst of mischief. "Mrs. Weatherby's salon."

"No. Out of the question." She shook her head, unwilling to even entertain such a notion.

"Now, now. I would introduce you to Mrs. Weatherby. And we would spread the story of your background. How you left Italy when your husband died—"

"My husband!"

"Of course. First of all, you do not want to advertise you are an innocent country miss, for there is no greater lure to the rakes of the world than purity. Secondly, you have a child." He spun so she could see the baby's face. "Therefore, you are a widow."

"Thaddeus . . ."

"And I believe you must have a dramatic title. Contessa, perhaps."

"You have gone mad. Hand me the child, lest your lunacy be catching."

He stepped nimbly away from her outstretched arms. "With a title, you can be haughty. Inscrutable. Demanding of respect. Do you not see? People will pay you handsomely to perform at their musicales and theatrical productions. Even if your voice was awful—which it is not—they would pay you for the prestige of having the enigmatic contessa perform at their functions."

She crossed her arms again and tapped her foot. "I think you believe your own rantings."

"Oh, such cruelty. Hard-hearted lady!" His eyes widened. "How perfect. That is what we shall name you. La Contessa della Pietra."

"And what does that mean?" She stalked over to him and scooped the child off his shoulder. "Italian madwoman?"

"The countess of stone." He rubbed both his hands together. "It is too perfect. And today is Thursday, so there is no time to waste."

Miranda carefully sat down on the sofa so as not to wake the baby. "I cannot possibly do such a thing."

"Oh, so you would rather pander hand and foot to some ancient hag who would treat you worse than she treats her oldest pair of slippers?" He propped his hands on his hips, his voice staccato and sharp. "Or perhaps you prefer the workhouse. The laundry? The backbreaking work of a seamstress? How will you care for James under those circumstances?"

She dropped her eyes. "I do not know."

"This is a good idea, Miranda." He knelt down in front of her and lifted her chin with his finger so she had to look at him. "The stage was my career for thirty years. I know what I am doing."

She bit her lip. "I cannot afford to make any mistakes. I had hoped that the duke would accept James and perhaps allow me to stay on as nursemaid. But now . . . now I am on my own."

"My dear child, you are not alone." He gave her the charming smile that had made princes and peasants alike rise to their feet in applause. "You have me."

Chapter 3

M rs. Weatherby's Thursday night salon was the only thing that kept Wylde from going utterly mad while he was trapped in London. Of all the entertainments to be found in Town, he considered Mrs. Weatherby's to be the most amusing of the respectable ones.

He came forward to greet the portly lady herself, where she sat in her favorite chair, a throne-like construction of gilt and purple pillows. Elizabeth Weatherby had begun as a mistress and married her lover just in time for him to make her a wealthy widow. She amused herself by shocking society and spending flagrant amounts of money on the arts. Her Thursday night salons were actually an opportunity to showcase painters, sculptors, poets, musicians and the like who were seeking patronage.

These days he felt like the salon was the only place he could truly call home.

"Good evening, Mrs. Weatherby." Wylde made his leg and grinned at her. "Once more you outshine every lady in the room."

"Rogue!" She laughed and tapped his arm with her fan. "You flatter me, Your Grace. Do sit down."

"I speak only the truth." He took the chair beside her and surveyed the room. "I do not see young Willingham. Did he succeed in finding a patron?"

"He did." She grinned with none of the artifice he'd seen practiced by young misses. "Lord Hemphill has offered."

"Willingham was a fine painter. I expect we will be seeing many a portrait from him—hopefully not all of Lord Hemphill."

She gave an unrestrained burst of laughter. "Wicked man."

"Truthful," he corrected.

"And you, Your Grace?" She cocked her head to the side, much like a curious bird. "Do you see no one you would care to sponsor? I know how you love the creative mind."

"Not at this time."

"I don't suppose you would care to play for us this evening? I fear the keys of the pianoforte grow stiff from disuse."

Curse him for indulging himself that first night and revealing his penchant for the pianoforte. With effort, he kept the charming smile in place. "I prefer to leave the stage to those seeking patronage."

"As you wish. Please excuse me while I introduce our first performer." She cast him a sly smile. "I look forward to your opinion of her talent."

Wylde nodded, and a servant rang a small gong. His hostess moved to the front of the room and held up her hands for quiet. Conversations died as all attention focused on Mrs. Weatherby.

"My dear guests, I would like to announce our first musical performance of the evening—the Contessa della Pietra." She looked around the crowd. "The contessa is newly arrived to London and is delighted to favor us with her lovely voice this evening."

The crowd parted and a woman came forward.

Wylde sat straight up in his chair, jerked to attention as if by invisible strings.

The contessa looked to be quite young, barely out of the schoolroom, yet she possessed a sensuality about her that grabbed a man's attention and would not let go. Her dress was mulberry tulle, lavishly embroidered and cut low to showcase the globes of her perfect breasts. Her hair was a color between dark brown and black, swept up in elegant disarray that made her appear to have just left some man's bed. Her skin glowed like pearls, her face a combination of sloping cheekbones, darkly lashed eyes, and plump, luscious lips above a piquant chin.

She was an exotic plum in a simple apple orchard.

Polite applause accompanied her as she seated herself at the pianoforte. "Thank you for your kind welcome," she said, her lips parting in a slow smile that seemed an intimate secret shared with all of them. "It is good to be back in England among my countrymen."

Then she began to play.

Her husky contralto wrapped around the verses of the sweet country song, adding nuances of flirtation to the simple lyrics. Just watching her mouth form the words had Wylde's body reacting, tensing, drawn to her as if she were Salome beckoning him to the boudoir.

She closed her eyes as she sang, caressing the notes with her voice and the keys with her fingers. The song was her lover, and she was seducing it into sin.

Seducing *him* into sin.

Her voice rose with the last note, hovering, lingering, vibrating throughout the room like a poignant climax. Then she opened her eyes and smiled with sweet innocence, as if she did not realize she had just aroused every man within hearing distance.

Silence greeted her. Then thunderous applause erupted as the spell broke. The crowd rushed forward, surrounding the pianoforte, blocking her from view.

Wylde sat frozen for long moments, the breath hesitating in his lungs. His body shook with the echoing power of her song. The only time he had experienced a response of this magnitude had been while composing his own work. How was it that a slip of a woman could appear from nowhere and shake the foundation of his soul with merely her voice?

And how was it that after feeling dead inside for so long, he found himself so strongly attracted to two women in the same day? Perhaps the malaise that had plagued him for so long was finally lifting.

"Your Grace." Mrs. Weatherby appeared before him. "Were you pleased with the performance?"

He nodded, still unable to speak.

"If you would like to meet her, I shall be happy to perform the introductions."

He nodded again, climbing to his feet. Mrs. Weatherby beckoned.

The dark-haired beauty stepped away from a conversation with a nearby dowager and came to stand beside Mrs. Weatherby. "Yes, Mrs. Weatherby?"

"Contessa, this is the Duke of Wyldehaven. His Grace is a great admirer of the arts."

"Your Grace." As she dipped into a curtsy, she glanced up and met Wylde's gaze for a split second. Her eyes were green, slightly tilted at the ends . . . and familiar.

He had looked into them only this afternoon in

his very own home. His fascination shattered as the truth became apparent.

A hint of panic entered her gaze. And well she should be worried. What game was Miranda Fontaine playing? If she was an Italian contessa, he was a three-legged pony.

Tempted to keep her guessing, he nodded an acknowledgment as she rose from her curtsy. "Contessa. You are a very talented woman."

"Thank you, Your Grace."

"How is it you are from Italy, yet you have no accent?"

"I am English. My husband was Italian."

"Was?"

She glanced down. "He died."

"My condolences."

"Thank you."

Silence weighed on the conversation. Even knowing she was not who she said he was, he could not take his eyes from her. The initial simmer of attraction he had felt for her at their first meeting had burst into an inferno after hearing her sing. It was all he could do not to drag her to some dark corner and taste those lips that so tempted him. But perhaps there was another way. He turned a persuasive smile on his hostess. "Mrs. Weatherby, I must admit that I am inspired to play this evening after all . . . but only if the contessa consents to accompany me with her beautiful voice."

"Oh, how splendid!" The portly lady flicked open her fan and waved it rapidly near her flushed face. "Contessa, you simply must agree. His Grace is a most gifted pianist."

The little songbird looked a bit green, but she managed a smile and nodded. "Of course. I would be honored to perform with His Grace."

He offered her his arm, unable to suppress the mischievous grin that curved his lips. "Come, Contessa. Let us make music together."

Miranda hesitated, uncertain if he was mocking her. He did not appear to recognize her. And why should he? The worldly contessa was so different from plain, ordinary Miranda Fontaine. But that wicked smile curving his lips as he offered his arm made her wonder. And was there an implication beneath his words? Maybe he did recognize her and was playing with her . . . or was she reading too much into the situation because she feared being denounced as a fraud?

"Come, Contessa," he coaxed again, arm still extended. "Your audience awaits."

She paused one second more, caught like a mouse in the presence of a cat. He was too big, too confident, too handsome. Those dark eyes of his hid much, but watched her with an intensity that made her insides bubble like simmering porridge. She reminded herself that she disliked him intensely, both for his treatment of Lettie and his dismissal of his child. She had no desire to attract his attention or to do anything that would stimulate his memory. But the Contessa della Pietra would never refuse the invitation of a man as wealthy and powerful as Wyldehaven. Reluctantly, she took his arm.

His flesh was warm even beneath her gloved hand, his arm appealingly firm and well-muscled. Somehow she had thought an aristocrat would be soft, sickly. Not this man. She glanced at him from the corner of her eye. He was as tall as any prince in any fairy tale, his back straight, his waist trim, his face pleasing to look upon. Dark hair, dark eyes—even she, who had never been taken in by a man's looks, was affected by his countenance. But she would not allow herself more than that, a female's admiration of a striking male physique. Men expected a woman to surrender everything to their whims, but she was a woman who could—and would—stand on her own.

He led them toward the pianoforte at the front of the room.

Murmurs followed them, and furtive glances as well. A hum of excitement rippled throughout the throng, making her uncomfortable. While performing, she'd enjoyed such attention. Now that she was not, she wanted to be just one more person amongst many. Apparently, walking on the arm of a duke was not the best way to remain unnoticed.

She tried to calm herself, to ignore the unusual attention of the crowd. She would sing and he would play. There was no dishonor in that. No scandal involved. Why, then, did it feel as though they were about to do something sinful? Even the smooth wood of the pianoforte inspired wicked fantasies as she reached it.

Wyldehaven—how easy to think of him as Wylde—sat down at the pianoforte with a grace that made her mouth water. She quickly took a position on the other side of the instrument, as if keeping the pianoforte between them would somehow negate the crackle of attraction in the air. He watched her take her place, and his mouth twitched with amusement.

Her pride shriveled, but she resolved not to show it. Regally, she nodded for him to begin. He leaned forward, fingers hovering over the keys, then his hands coaxed the opening bars of "Think Not My Love" from the instrument.

Sweet heaven, if she had thought him appealing before . . .

Arrested by his skill, she nearly missed her mark, but caught herself just in time and started singing at the appropriate juncture. She refused to look at him, to see if his mouth had quirked up in devilment at her near faux pas, and instead looked at the audience and surrendered to the song.

Music was a place where no one could reach

her. No one could touch her or hurt her or scorn her. Always before she had accompanied herself, knowing where the notes would go, confident they would be there like planks on a bridge over a vast chasm. She could walk that bridge with confidence and poise, not needing to look down.

She was surprised—and delighted—to discover that his musical prowess formed a strong barrier, like a stone wall on either side of her as she walked that bridge. With joy she lost herself in the melody, the two of them making the journey together, hand in hand.

She could not stop herself from glancing at him. His dark eyes reflected the same unspeakable joy she felt, his fingers stroking the keys, wringing from them the best they could offer. Would those hands do the same to a woman?

Her cheeks heated and she wanted to look away. But she could not, dared not, reveal such vulnerability to him. Perhaps he would think she was warm from the temperature of the room. Or that she was excited by the music. Both were true; she *was* warm and she *was* excited. But only because of him.

There was a knowledge in his eyes that unnerved her. She might as well be standing naked before him, completely defenseless. The notion struck a dissonant chord within her. It was not fair that one of them was so affected and the other was not. Between man and woman there must always be equal ground, otherwise someone got hurt—usually the woman.

So she forgot the audience, forgot her disguise. She dropped her mask and sang directly to *him*, woman to man. Showed him her feminine strength. *I will match you, note for note.*

A flare of awareness chased through his eyes. His jaw clenched, but he maintained perfect control over the instrument, his touch sure and loving on the keyboard. Were his fingers trembling? Hers certainly were.

A door closed somewhere nearby, reminding her of her surroundings. She managed to glance away from him, to smile at the audience. But she could feel his presence, like a bonfire running wild.

When she sang the final note, she could not help but look back at him. His dark eyes seared her with heat as he lifted his hands from the keys. For one mad instant she wanted to lean across the pianoforte and sink into his arms.

Then thunderous applause jerked her back to reality. Well-wishers surged forward. She stood frozen, then felt a strong hand close over her arm.

"Come with me," Wyldehaven said, and dragged her away from the crowd.

She was a liar, he thought. An imposter. Almost certainly an opportunist. But a witch as well, for there was no other explanation for his reaction to her. No other logical reason for him to want her so badly right now that he would have willingly taken her right there in the music room in front of everyone. Not when he knew she had almost certainly maneuvered him there.

Wylde pulled her through the crowd, glaring the well-wishers into submission with the mere force of his consequence, until they reached the door to the salon and escaped into the cool solitude of the hallway.

"Where are we going?" she asked, breathless.

To my bed, he wanted to say. "To find a private corner to converse."

"I cannot imagine what you might wish to discuss, Your Grace."

"Can you not?" He flashed her a sharp glance, impatient with the pretense, hungry from the seduction. "Perhaps you should consider the matter . . . Miss Fontaine."

Dear God, he knew.

Her heart nearly stopped, panic shimmering along her nerve endings. Like a docile hound, she allowed him to lead her down the hallway, amazed that she did not stumble. He moved with surety toward a room at the end of the hall, then opened the door and swept an arm in a gallant gesture for her to precede him.

She stepped into the tiny chamber, which was lit by a single candle and a low fire burning in the grate. The decor was decidedly feminine, hardly the setting for a confrontation with an angry duke.

He must have seen her puzzlement, for he said, "This is Mrs. Weatherby's private sitting room." Then he closed the door and leaned back against it, folding his arms across his chest. "Now tell me, Miss Fontaine, the reason for this pretense."

"Your Grace?" The solitude concerned her. What was his plan? Why did he watch her like a tiger scenting fresh venison? Had their performance affected him as strongly as it had her? Would he pounce?

Did she want him to?

Uncertain, she ran her hand along the back of a lovely armchair upholstered in pale blue.

"Do not be coy, young woman. You are no more an Italian contessa than I am."

She raised a haughty brow at him as if she really were displaced Italian nobility. "You know nothing about me, Your Grace, and as you so arrogantly conveyed only this morning, you have no desire to know anything about me or my affairs."

"Arrogant?" He chuckled, but it was hardly a pleasant sound. "You know nothing about my desires, my dear." He slid his gaze over, a visual caress, masculine appreciation tightening his features. "Had you worn this lovely attire to my home this morning, we might have had a more pleasant conversation."

She stiffened her spine. "This image is an illusion, a theatrical costume."

"So you *are* pretending."

"You know I am pretending!" She scowled at him. "Really, Your Grace, you are hardly the one to cast stones at me. If not for your high-handed dismissal of me *and* your son—"

He rolled his eyes. "Back to that, are we? Tell me, Miss Fontaine, how did you know I would be here tonight? Did you bribe one of my servants?"

Her mouth fell open. "I had no idea you would be in attendance tonight."

"Of course not." His lips twisted around the sarcasm, and he pushed away from the door, approaching her with an intent that both alarmed her and made her quiver. What was wrong with her, reacting like a goose girl to a handsome prince?

She backed away. "I have done nothing wrong, Your Grace."

"So that performance . . . that musical seduction. That was not aimed at me?"

"I do not even *like* you!"

"Your recital said otherwise." He narrowed his eyes. "Mrs. Weatherby is a particular friend of mine. I will not see her humiliated or her gatherings used for your conniving ends."

"But you have no compunction about humiliating *me*?" She slipped behind the safety of the armchairs, keeping the furniture between them. If he touched

54

her, she was sure she would melt in his arms, and that she could not allow. "I have done nothing to you. *You* asked *me* to sing; I did not request you accompany me. Do not assign such devious motives to innocent actions."

"You, my dear, are far from innocent. You made that perfectly clear."

She stiffened, uncomfortable with the emphasis he put on the word "innocent."

"Do you condemn me for being here?" she asked. "When you refused responsibility for your child, I had no recourse but to seek respectable employment."

He barked out a laugh, then reached across the chairs to seize her arm and haul her back from behind their shelter. "You call this respectable? Passing yourself off as a foreign siren, luring unsuspecting men with your voice? If you are looking for a protector, my dear, you could have simply told me so."

She tugged at her arm, but his greater strength won the battle. He dragged her against him. His body was big and warm and smelled of something spicy and alluring. The contact only threw fuel on the fire she tried to control. She could feel her will weakening, her knees trembling, her flesh aching to soften against him.

Stop him before he realizes the power he has over you.

"I am not looking for a protector," she snapped.

"Are you in the habit of forcing unwilling women, Your Grace?"

Her sharp tone did not dissuade him. "How can you claim to be unwilling, dressed like that, singing like that? You are an invitation to sin, my dear. I can only surmise that when your ploy to foist your brat off on me failed, you must have learned I would be here tonight and sought to capture my attention." He lowered his head, inhaled the scent of her hair. "You have caught it."

"You are quick to judge." She jerked her head back, hungry for his touch yet knowing his warm breath tantalizing the skin of her neck could destroy her. He already had little regard for her. "Release me at once or I will call out."

"Should you call out, I will simply tell whomever responds the truth about 'la contessa.'" He nuzzled her throat.

Her eyes nearly rolled back in her head when his warm lips found her flesh. For one blissful instant she reveled in the explosion of sensation. Her body warmed, softened, liquefied inside. Her knees melted like hot wax, and it was all she could do not to dissolve into his embrace and beg him to take her.

He scraped his teeth against her skin. She could not suppress a quiver of reaction.

He chuckled.

She would not surrender. Jerking her head away, she

56

shoved at his chest. "How gratifying it must be," she spat, "to be a duke, to have the entire world toadying to your every wish. To ruin lives on a whim. Lettie's. Mine."

His lips parted in surprise, his eyes creasing in annoyance. "What the devil are you going on about? 'Tis people like you who ruin lives—charlatans, opportunists."

"You got Lettie with child, then abandoned her. I came to you to make certain your son is taken care of, and you turned your back on him. Now you would force yourself on me based on misguided judgments, even though I have refused you. You are a disgrace."

"I have never forced a woman in my life."

"Probably because no one has dared refuse you!"

He released her abruptly, and she grabbed the back of the armchair to steady herself. "I do not know what game you are playing, Miss Fontaine—"

"What game *I* am playing? You are the one who acted dishonorably here, not I."

She expected him to be shamed by her declaration, but he only looked irritated. "Young woman, you came to my house dressed like a Quaker and prattled on about a child I have not fathered on a woman I never met. The very same day, I meet you here, where you are dressed like a temptress, pretending to be someone you are not. One of us is playing a game, and it is not me."

"It is not me, either. This"—she indicated her dress—"is a result of your callous disregard for your son. *Someone* has to put food in his belly. And a mysterious foreign contessa has more chance of being offered lucrative performance opportunities than plain Miranda Fontaine."

"A clever argument. I doubt this child even exists."

She straightened with pure indignation. "I resent being called a liar, Your Grace."

"As do I. One of us is mistaken, Miss Fontaine, and I do not believe it is me."

"Of course you do not. Heaven forbid His Grace the Duke of Wyldehaven be caught in his own duplicity."

"You have a sharp tongue." His lips parted in a wicked smile. "How unfortunate that you claim you are not looking for a protector. We could redirect all that passion into a more amenable direction."

A blush swept into her cheeks. "You are no gentleman."

"So the gossips are saying." He stroked a finger down her cheek. "Should you decide to be honest about what you want, do contact me. I believe we would do well together."

She swiped his hand away, denying that tantalizing touch. "I do not know why I expected a man like you to do the right thing. Your kind never does."

"This is your one chance, Miss Fontaine. Leave this place now and I will tell no one of your deception."

"So generous of you," she sneered.

He only arched an eyebrow, then quit the room, once again with no proper pleasantries.

She stood there watching the doorway where he had exited, her insides a churning, whirling tangle of rage and confusion. How could she have thought him handsome, even for a moment? He had gotten Lettie with child, then abandoned her. For that alone he deserved to be reviled. Then he had rejected little James out of hand—the baby whose very existence he doubted. She should have brought the baby with her that morning. Perhaps then he would not consider her some sort of opportunist trying to catch his eye. But she had been too afraid he might take the child from her on the spot and she would never see James again.

But perhaps that was what it would take. Maybe the overbearing man needed to see the child with his own eyes. Possibly then he would step forward and provide in some small way for the innocent result of his affair with Lettie. And if that was what it would take . . .

"My dear!" Thaddeus ducked into the room, concern creasing lines around his mouth and eyes. He reached her and took her hands in his, lowering his voice. "I have been looking everywhere for you. Imagine my shock when I heard you had been seen leaving the salon with Wyldehaven. Are you all right?"

"I am fine." She gave him a rueful smile and gently tugged her hands free. "The disguise did not fool him, Thaddeus."

"Did he threaten to reveal your true identity? Oh, that would be disastrous!"

Knowing Thaddeus would try to defend her to the duke, Miranda lied, "No, nothing like that. But he still maintains he is not James's father."

"Not his father! I myself saw him escort Lettie more than once from the theater. Aye, he is the one; no doubt of it."

"Perhaps bringing James to him will prove that. I intend to go there tomorrow with the baby."

"Do not do it," Thaddeus hissed. "What if he snatches the boy from you and sends him to an orphanage? His behavior these past few months indicates he is not above such a thing."

Since his fear echoed her own, she tried to put on a brave face. "I will not allow such a thing to happen. Trust me, Thaddeus."

"I do trust you; it is *him* I do not trust. Lettie trusted him, and look what happened to her."

"Calm yourself, Thaddeus." She summoned a reassuring smile, masking the panic she herself felt. "I do not believe I have anything to fear from the Duke of Wyldehaven."

"I pray you are right, because if he decides to take James away, we cannot fight him, Miranda. He is too powerful."

"No one will separate me from James, Thaddeus." Resolve hardened like ice in her heart. "No one."

Chapter 4

The fire burned low in the grate, infusing the dimly lit drawing room with a dull glow that suited the eyes of gentlemen a shade or two past sober. Wylde regarded his half-empty glass of whisky and considered that he might end up more shades than that if his friends had anything to say about it.

But then again, perhaps the oblivion of intoxication would do him some good. Perhaps he could forget about a pair of green eyes and the duplicity of women for at least a few hours.

With an affable if slightly intoxicated grin, Kit Penthill, Viscount Linnet, tapped his whisky glass on the table. "The meeting of the Sons of Grendel will now come to order."

"And who put you in charge?" Wulf raised neither his voice nor his eyes from his glass, but the big man's quiet growl had Kit's grin fading.

"Someone has to do it." Kit slouched down in his chair, one blue eye glaring from beneath his tousled blond locks. "You can do it if you like."

"It's Wylde's house. Let him do it." Lounging indolently on a comfortable sofa, Darcy saluted them all with his own whisky. His dark good looks and wicked smirk gave the impression of a sinful angel. "What say you, Wylde? Do we name you our leader now that poor Michael has gone to his reward?"

Silence fell. Wylde regarded Darcy as he would a flea in his bed. "No one can replace Michael."

"Not replace." Darcy swung his feet to the floor and straightened, alerted by the warning tone. His whisky splashed over the side of the glass. "But the Sons of Grendel need a leader."

"We do not, and have a care for that rug. It's Persian." Wylde sipped from his glass and wondered how long until he was drunk enough not to care about the bloody rug. The drink had already loosened his tongue too much, and somewhere between the third and fourth glass of whisky he had reluctantly confided his recent difficulties with the imposter to his friends. There was no one he trusted more than these three men—all that remained of his schoolboy mates, the Sons of Grendel. And yet knowing that, he still did not tell them about Miranda Fontaine.

He wanted to forget about her. If she were smart,

she would heed his warning and cease her chicanery. Leave London, or at least his part of it. But how ironic that the first woman he had responded to in years proved to be just one more grasping female.

"Of course we need a leader." Kit grinned like a fool and laid his head back on the chair. "Michael has been ours since Eton. We cannot expect to go on without one for much longer."

"We are grown men." Dragging his thoughts away from that maddening woman, Wylde held up his glass and pondered the flicker of firelight through the amber liquid. "I see no reason to have a leader."

"I agree," Wulf said. "All the Sons of Grendel inspire fear in the hearts of men to this day, even with Michael gone."

Wylde tipped some whisky into his mouth, then contemplated the fire again through the new level of alcohol, pretending his chest did not tighten at Michael's mere name. "Indeed. The threat that forged us is long past."

"But there are other threats now." Darcy pointed his finger at them, somehow keeping the other four wrapped around his glass. "Your recent troubles for one."

Wulf turned concerned silver eyes on Wylde. "You should have told us sooner."

"I am telling you now," Wylde said.

Kit leaned forward. "Have you called Bow Street?"

"Not yet. That seems the next logical step." He reached for the decanter on the table beside him. "Today another cardsharp approached me with another forged set of vowels."

"What did you do?" Kit asked, agog.

"Paid, of course. What else could I do?" Wylde carefully measured another finger of whisky into the glass.

"Tell him to go to the devil!" Kit exclaimed.

Wylde shook his head. "That would only worsen matters."

"I imagine the gossips are making the most of it," Wulf said, making Wylde wince. "And I know you detest that sort of titter-tatter."

"Because of your sire, God rest his soul." Kit nodded to himself. "Madcap Matherton all over again."

Wylde glared. "Thank you so much for rubbing salt in the wound, Kit."

"Aye," Darcy agreed. " 'Tis not bad enough that some villain is running about Town impersonating the Duke of Wyldehaven, but now poor Wylde must contend with the resurrection of his father's misdeeds as well."

Wylde sipped his whisky and closed his eyes, savoring the burn and wishing it could erase the events of the past couple of weeks. "I just do not know how he is doing it. Acquaintances claimed they saw me in places I never went. Gamesters have appeared with markers in their hands, supposedly signed by me. Young ladies have condemned me for trifling with their affections."

"Good God!" Wulf exclaimed. "What if he goes too far? Drags you into dun territory?"

Wylde set his jaw. "I will stop him well before then."

"At least your pockets are deep." Kit gulped back the last of his whisky. "Yours and Wulf's. 'Tis just the opposite for me. Only today m'father declared that I have bankrupted the family coffers. Claims I waste my future inheritance on fripperies."

"If you feel the need to throw your money away, Kit, throw it to me," Darcy said with a laugh. "For all that I have my title, there is naught but a moldering pile in Leicestershire to go with it."

"You are doomed to disappointment, my dear Darcy, at least for now." Kit turned to face him, a generous amount of whisky sloshing in his glass. "Father has set forth an edict that I shall cease being a drain on the finances and instead seek to augment them. He intends to wed me to some mewling heiress."

Darcy set down his drink with a clank. "Which one?"

"Miss Olivia Wherry."

"Ah, bloody hell." Darcy fished a crumpled piece

of paper from his coat pocket and stared at it with bleary eyes. "Number four."

Wulf chuckled. "Still got that list of heiresses, Rywood?"

"Of course." Darcy rose from his sofa and took up the quill from Wylde's desk, dipped it in the ink, then scribbled out a name on the paper. "Good-bye to you, number four."

"You can have her," Kit snapped, taking a huge gulp before flopping back into his chair. "God knows I do not want some hatchet-faced baggage ordering me about."

Darcy blew on the paper to dry the ink. "And I, my friend, would like nothing better. However, it seems no one wants their beloved daughter leg-shackled to the son of a murderer."

"Nothing was proven about your father," Wulf interjected loyally. "Of course, that does not stop the gossips."

"Indeed," Kit said, nodding sagely.

"If I were you, I would accept wedded bliss with a smile," Wylde said. "The alternative would be far worse."

Kit furrowed his brow in confusion. "Freedom?"

"Poverty," Wylde corrected.

Wulf and Darcy roared with laughter.

"Bollocks to that," Kit muttered, and sipped his whisky again.

"Such a pair we are." Darcy tucked his list away

as he came back to the sofa. "I would do anything to have an heiress merely acknowledge my presence, and here is Linnet whining because one is too eager to meet him at the altar."

"Would that I could give her to you, Darce," Kit said with a sarcastic twist to his mouth. "For I have no doubt that my life will be sheer misery."

"You do not have to wed her," Wylde said. "You can always say no and make your own way in the world."

Kit gave a little shudder. "No, thank you."

"Then stop your sniveling and do what must be done," Wulf said.

"Enough of this." Wylde carefully stood and raised his glass. "To Michael, who led this ragtag group of runts and weaklings in rebellion against the bullies at school, forging our friendship for life. And for the first time since his funeral, we are all gathered together to remember him." He paused, worked past the lump in his throat. "God-speed, old man."

A murmur of agreement rose, and glasses were raised. Wylde sank down in his chair, draining his glass to the dregs.

"Who's a runt?" Kit demanded.

"None of us anymore." Wulf stood and stretched, a lion of a man with silver threaded hair and a powerful build. "Though we cannot be considered boys any longer either."

68

"Speak for yourself, grandfather," Darcy hooted. "You are older than all of us!"

"By merely a year." Wulf set down his empty glass. "Still, best I take these old bones home."

"I still think we need to elect a leader," Kit mumbled.

Wulf glared at him. "There's time enough for that. We're the Sons of Grendel, aren't we? Stand up for each other and watch each other's backs. You trifle with one Grendel . . ."

"You trifle with us all!" Kit and Darcy shouted out in unison.

Wylde rose and walked with Wulf, pausing as the footman opened the door to the hallway. "Good night, Wulf. It's been good to see you."

"And you as well." Wulf clapped him on the shoulder. "Call Bow Street to go after this blackguard. Do not wait any longer."

"I will contact them tomorrow."

"Good night, my friend."

"Good night." Wylde waited until Wulf started down the hallway behind a servant, then turned back to his two other friends. "Shall I summon your horses, gentlemen, or will you stay the night?"

"Ah, such a decision." Darcy held up a hand and began counting off on his fingers. "Your chef is better than mine, your bed chambers more luxurious—"

"And I am expected to take my grandmother shopping on Bond Street tomorrow."

"Zounds!" Darcy leaped to his feet with a limberness that belied his drunken state. "Come, Linnet. Wylde needs his rest."

"I will rest when I am dead," Kit announced, his head nodding forward.

"Not you, paper skull." Darcy hauled Kit out of his chair and slung the viscount's arm around his shoulders to keep him from falling back down again. "Wylde must be well rested for the duchess."

"The duchess is coming? Now?" Kit squinted around the room.

"Bloody hell." Darcy sent a look of exasperation to Wylde. "I believe we will need a footman. Or three."

"Indeed." Smothering a grin, Wylde signaled to the footman beside the door, who nodded and left to summon assistance.

"Well, aren't you going to help?" Darcy asked.

Wylde peered at Kit's face and determined that his friend had slipped into the stupor of the truly sotted. He grabbed the viscount's other arm and helped Darcy support their unconscious comrade. "I haven't seen him this foxed in years."

"'Tis the heiress. The whole business has him addlepated. He hates that his father has forced him to this end."

70

Wylde grunted in agreement. "Understandable."

"This is the best thing that ever happened to him, if the fool would but realize it." Darcy shook his head at Kit, his face creased with exasperated affection.

"We will see this through." Two footmen entered the room, and Wylde relinquished Kit's weight to one of them. "We have always looked after each other."

Darcy stepped back, allowing the other footman to take over supporting his friend. "Against schoolyard bullies and outraged husbands." He nodded in Kit's direction as the footmen hauled him off. "And making certain our drunken comrades reach their homes safely. However, helping a fellow *to* the altar is a bit out of our territory."

"Should that stop us?"

"No." Darcy grinned and started toward the door. "I will see Kit home. I assume we are taking your carriage?"

"I will arrange it. And I will send someone along with your horses tomorrow."

"Good night, then." Darcy hesitated, emotion flickering across his face. "I would never have thought that a couple of reprobates like us would last in a friendship like this. Given our families, that is."

"We are in control of our destinies, my dear

Rywood." Wylde began steering him toward the door. "The sins of our families are in the past."

"Are they? Then why don't you marry again?" Darcy stopped in the doorway. "Do you still blame your father for choosing Felicity to be your bride?"

Wylde stiffened. "The whole matter was arranged before I was out of the nursery. She seemed perfectly normal."

"Until she—" Darcy clamped his lips shut. "I am foxed and have said too much. Good night, my friend. Pleasant dreams."

"Good night." Wylde watched as the footmen escorted Kit and Darcy out of the room. He managed to keep his emotions under control until he was alone again. He glanced around the dimly lit drawing room, at the empty glasses, at the low fire burning in the grate.

"It's not the same without you, Michael. Damn you for dying. And damn me for not saving you."

He turned away and slammed the door as he quit the room, sealing the ghosts of the past inside. Michael. Felicity. Then he took the stairs two at a time to the next floor, where some modicum of peace awaited him in the small room at the end of the hall.

The music room, where solace summoned him with open arms.

He sat down at his treasured Broadwood grand

pianoforte and lifted the cover to reveal the keys. He should go to bed, half soused as he was. But he knew he would not sleep. The camaraderie of this meeting of the Grendels, the first without Michael, had made his soul weep with the promise of what would never be again. And Darcy's casual mention of Felicity had sliced open the barely healed wounds of his scarred heart.

She had fooled him indeed, his beautiful wife. Made him believe she cared for him, that she wanted the same things he did. That she was eager to bear his child. But it had all been a careful masquerade. The potion she had swallowed to rid herself of his child had also taken her own life. All she'd ever wanted was the prestige of being a duchess.

He had never suspected, never saw a glimmer of the truth.

Two years now, and still he wondered if he could have done something to save her. She had been his wife, his responsibility. Why had he not seen her true self? He never noticed her obsession with being beautiful, being a duchess. He never knew anything was wrong—not until she died.

And then, if he had not been so shocked with grief and guilt over Felicity's death, would he have let Michael go off to India in that cork-brained manner? Michael had died far away from the shores of home. And alone.

Now there was this imposter, running about town ruining his sterling reputation. The blackguard gambled in gaming hells and seduced women in Wylde's name, resurrecting the memories of the old duke—Wylde's father, Madcap Matherton.

And as if that were not enough, there was Miranda Fontaine.

A beautiful woman, so striking in her exotic looks that she had reawakened his sleeping libido with a vengeance. But she had proven to be a lying jade just like the rest of them. He was certain he had been clear in his warning to her. No doubt she'd already moved on to a more susceptible dupe, and he would never see her again.

Damn her.

All he had ever wanted was a family, good friends, and to be known as an honorable man. Fate taunted him, taking first his bride and his child, then his best friend, and now his good name, the only thing he had left.

But it could not take his music.

Emotion raged within him, so fierce it nearly tore out through his skin. He needed to purge himself of it, to regain some control over his life. There was only one way he had ever been able to do that.

He lifted his hands to the keys and began to play.

Chapter 5

━━━━∽◯◯∽━━━━

Mr. Everton Wallace did not have the look of a lawman about him. He was not very tall and somewhat thin of frame. His brown eyes appeared good-natured behind his spectacles, and he had left his hat with Travers, revealing his balding pate. He shuffled his feet and hummed to himself as he made notes in a small book. Yet Bow Street claimed he was their best.

He had been scribbling for so long that Wylde was beginning to think he might have to send for refreshments when the runner finally looked up. "I believe I have nearly everything I need to begin the investigation, Your Grace."

"Excellent." Wylde glanced at the clock. A quarter before noon. Grandmother would be arriving shortly for their trip to Bond Street.

"One more question. When did the incidents begin?"

Wylde brought his attention back to the runner. "I estimate at least three months ago."

"Very good, then. Is there anything else?"

He hesitated, then finally gave in to the demon that had been plaguing him. "I want you to investigate a young lady. Her name is Miss Miranda Fontaine, and she is new to London. I want you to find out everything you can about her background."

"Yes, Your Grace." Mr. Wallace dipped his head in deference. "Is she related to this case or is this a separate matter?"

"No, an entirely separate matter." He tapped his fingers on his desk, already regretting the impulse. "She sang at Mrs. Weatherby's last night under the stage name the Contessa della Pietra. I do not want you to trouble Mrs. Weatherby with your inquiries— I will speak to her to see if she has the young lady's direction—but please do question the Weatherby servants to see if Miss Fontaine arrived or left with anyone."

"I will, Your Grace. If there is aught to know of this Miranda Fontaine, I will find out about it."

"You reassure me," Wylde drawled.

"Bow Street has earned its reputation," the little man said with a proud huff.

Wylde raised his brows. "My grandmother is expected at noon, Mr. Wallace. Perhaps it would be best if you took your leave."

"Of course. Good day, Your Grace."

"Good day." Wylde watched as the odd fellow scrambled out of the room. He was trying desperately not to judge by appearances, but Mr. Wallace did not look all that competent. Of course, that could be a ruse and the reason for his reputed success.

He glanced at the clock again. Ten minutes before noon . . . which meant he could expect Grandmother sometime in the next hour. His grandmother's clock often ran more slowly than the rest of the world's, rendering her fashionably—though constantly—late.

Wylde stood and stretched a bit, moving his neck from side to side to get rid of the kinks. It had been a long day, starting with an irate tailor with an unpaid bill for a coat he had never ordered and a horse trader who demanded payment for a nag he had never purchased. The imposter continued to rack up the debts, leaving him to pay them. And pay he did, for he did not want to further besmirch his reputation by adding debt dodger to the list. Hopefully, the runner would succeed where he had failed, and the matter would soon be resolved.

But what had possessed him to ask the man to investigate Miranda Fontaine? He had no desire for that sort of complication. If she were as smart a woman as she appeared, she would probably be long gone already, moving on to the next man who might fall for her wiles.

Perhaps when the investigator proved her duplicity, he would be able to forget her and shift his focus to more important matters.

A discreet knock came at the door, and then Travers opened it. "Miss Fontaine to see you, Your Grace. I have put her in the blue parlor."

"The cheeky baggage!"

The servant hesitated. "Shall I escort her out, Your Grace?"

Wylde's lip curled as anticipation simmered. "No, Travers. Allow me."

When he entered the blue parlor, he experienced a moment of déjà vu, for there sat his little Quaker of the day before in her prim gray dress with her straw bonnet. Only this time she did not bow her head and fiddle her fingers like a nervous miss. No, she might be dressed like the Quaker, but the green eyes that challenged him reflected the fire of the contessa. He noticed, too, a basket that sat on the floor, next to her chair.

"Good afternoon, Miss Fontaine. I am astonished at your boldness."

"I do what must be done," she said, then rose to her feet long enough to bob a curtsy. Its brevity punctuated without words that she wished him to the devil.

He could not help the grin that tugged at his mouth. She was like a hedgehog, all prickly and cautious but ready to bite should the situation call for it. Like any impish boy, he could not resist the opportunity for a bit of mischief. He lounged across from her in a comfortable armchair, itching to put a dent in that cool demeanor. "I am all but ready to boot you to the curb, young woman, but never let it be said I am not a gracious host. Such a tragedy that you chose not to wear that burgundy creation from last night."

She narrowed her eyes at him, nearly skewering him with her sharp gaze. "I have not come here to allow you to poke fun at me."

"No, you have come here to irritate me to blazes. I see you have a basket there. What have you brought? A picnic lunch for the two of us to share in private?"

Her gloved fingers clenched in her lap. "You are a vile man. I can hardly credit that you are this sweet baby's father."

He jerked into a sitting position. "You mean there really is a child?"

She lifted her chin. "Of course there is. *Your* child."

He wanted to stand up and quit the room, to get as far away from the infant as possible. But that would be cowardice, and he refused to show weakness when those perceptive green eyes were upon him. He tried to ignore the basket. "Very well, I will concede that I did not believe the babe existed. However, nothing has changed. I have already told you I am not his father."

"If you can look at this angel-faced baby and still reject him, then you truly cannot call yourself an honorable man."

"You think me soft-hearted?" He smiled with black humor, ignoring the sting of her very clever jab. Something about this woman awoke his fighting spirit, making him feel more alive than he had in years. Enough that he would force himself past aching grief to demonstrate his resolve. "Very well, then. Let us have a look at the mite, and then you may leave me in peace."

"He is asleep." She glanced down at the basket by her feet, and her face softened like a madonna's. "I expect he will wake soon enough."

"Come now. I will not wake him." He rose and came over to her chair, squatting in front of her to peer into the basket. From the corner of his eye he was aware of her stiffening at his nearness, of the subtle shifting of her feet.

Of the delicate aroma of rose water.

"His name is James, after Lettie's father."

"Indeed?" He cast a quick, cautious glance at the baby, all he could stand without dredging up agonizing memories. Then he focused on her, allowing himself to be distracted by the scent of her, the warmth of her. Her skin was soft and radiant as only youthful skin can be. He wondered if it looked that way all over.

"You are staring."

He jolted. Bloody hell if he wasn't gawking like some green lad, but every time he saw her, he noticed some small detail that he had not seen before. This time it was the gentle dent in her chin, just a shallow little dip, but enough that he knew she would not be easily swayed from any path she chose.

Could it be he had only met her for the first time yesterday?

"Excuse me, Your Grace." She gritted out the courtesy through clenched teeth. "You are supposed to be looking at the child, not at me."

"Make you nervous, do I?" Grinning at this small crack in her prickly armor, he summoned enough bravado to look again at the child, but all he saw was dark hair and a tiny face scrunched in slumber. He glanced away, feigning disinterest, hiding his pain. "He looks like any other infant. I am afraid there is nothing to be learned from his countenance."

He stood and retreated back to his chair.

Her luscious pink lips thinned. "So you still dismiss him?"

He gave a dark chuckle. "Young woman, I have been dismissing him from the beginning. You, however, are persistent. Very well, let us determine why I could not possibly be this child's father. Do you happen to know what month he was born?"

"I know the exact day, Your Grace." She rose to

her feet, shoulders stiff and jaw clenched. "Lettie died giving him life on the third of March of this year."

"The third of March. Which means he would have had to have been conceived . . . hmm . . . last spring. Late May or early June, perhaps."

She gave a stiff nod. "I will defer to your greater knowledge of such things."

He met her gaze now, suddenly chafed by her righteous attitude. "Indeed, I do know something about it. For you see, my wife died carrying my unborn child. That was two years ago this past February." He sent her his coldest stare. She did not flinch or look away or in any manner concede a single inch. But he could see the way her expression softened, the sympathy that lit her eyes. And he hated her for that soft heart, curse her. He did not want to feel anything of the tender emotions. Not ever again. "This past year, Miss Fontaine . . . this past May and June, when I supposedly got your friend with child . . . I was still in deep mourning for my wife in solitude at my country estate."

Her lips parted and he could see he had startled her. Good. Perhaps now she would cease challenging him. She glanced down at the baby, then back at him, and then her eyes narrowed. "Lettie swore on her deathbed that you were the father. She named you specifically. I doubt she would lie under such circumstances. And other people saw you together. How can you explain that?"

"Explain?" His voice rose as the anger of ill-use flooded him. "Young woman, I am the Duke of Wyldehaven, and I owe *no one* any explanations for my actions—with the exception of my king."

Her lips thinned. "Wrong, Your Grace. You owe this child."

"The hell I do!" he roared.

The baby jolted awake with a soft cry. Miranda cast Wylde a chastising look, then bent to lift the child from his basket. Despite her attempts to soothe him, the infant's piercing wail sliced through the silence and slowly rose in volume.

Travers chose that moment to present himself in the doorway. "The Dowager Duchess of Wyldehaven," he announced, then moved aside as Wylde's grandmother hobbled into the room.

"What ever is going on here?" she demanded.

Miranda rocked the baby with her eyes averted, hesitant to look at the highborn lady directly. A man might hesitate to toss a young woman out on the street, especially if he found her attractive. Indeed, she had been counting on Wyldehaven's evident masculine interest to buy her enough time to convince him to help James. A woman of power, however, was a different story. A woman would be *more* likely to eject another female, especially if she considered a man in her circle to be threatened.

"Answer me, Thornton," the duchess demanded of the duke, and then an odd thumping noise made Miranda glance over.

The Dowager Duchess of Wyldehaven was a tiny lady who looked as if the slamming of a door might blow her down. The duchess's head of silver curls would probably only reach her own shoulder, and her delicate frame was swathed in yards of pale blue silk. In her bejeweled fingers, the duchess clutched an elaborate cane that had been painted with colorful violets against a white background, and it was this that created the odd noise. Her slow, shuffling steps indicated that the cane was a necessity rather than an affectation of fashion.

"Grandmother, I did not realize the time." The duke hurried forward to kiss her cheek, towering over the spritelike duchess as he offered his arm. She rested her hand on his sleeve as delicately as a butterfly alighting on an oak branch, and accepted his assistance to the sofa. "Come and sit, and I will have Travers fetch you some tea," he said.

"There is a baby in your parlor, Thornton," the duchess announced, gingerly perching on the edge of the sofa. "And a young woman with no chaperone."

"Miss Fontaine was just leaving."

Miranda glared at him, even as she bounced James in her arms to pacify him. The child was quieting, and with any luck he would fall back to sleep. "I do not believe we have concluded our business, Your Grace."

If looks were weapons, his flinty gaze would have felled her. "I disagree. Have you a carriage? If not, I will have the servants summon a hack."

Clearly the duke did not want her in the same vicinity as his grandmother. She swallowed back the bitter taste of disappointment, then straightened her spine. What had she expected? She should be used to such behavior from the rich and titled. She was less than nothing to him.

"Thornton," the duchess chided, smoothing her skirts against the cushions. "How can you be so rude? At least let this young woman finish calming her child before you cast her into the street."

Startled by the older lady's dry tone, Miranda ducked her head and fussed with James's blanket. Any other female of noble birth would have been appalled to find her paying a call on the duke, unaccompanied by a maid or other servant. That the Duchess of Wyldehaven paused long enough to consider the baby rather than have her and James tossed from the house said much about the dowager's character.

"I am not casting her into the street." Wylde's irritable tone made Miranda's lips curve. "We simply have nothing more to discuss."

The duchess peered at Miranda, her gaze alighting on the bundle in her arms. "What is your child's name, Miss . . . Fontaine, was it?"

"Yes, Your Grace." Miranda managed to get up and bob a quick half curtsy while balancing the babe. "Miranda Fontaine. And this is James."

"A good strong name." She waved a hand in summons. "Come, let me see him."

Miranda glanced at Wyldehaven, but he only cast her a sour look and stalked to the other side of the room. She approached the elderly lady and bent down so the duchess could see James's face. The baby had squeezed his eyes shut and was sucking furiously on one fist.

"Oh, how precious." The duchess beamed, first at the child, then at Miranda. "You must be so proud."

"I am," Miranda said, straightening. She tucked the blanket more securely around the baby's face. "Though I am not his mother."

The duchess chuckled. "Oh, I believe you are, at least in the way that matters." Then she looked at her grandson. "Is this child yours, Thornton?"

The duke stiffened and sent a killing glare at Miranda. "No, Grandmother, he is not."

Miranda pressed her lips together to keep her fierce rebuttal contained. As much as she was willing to debate with Wyldehaven until the end of time, she did not wish to upset the Dowager Duchess. How typical of him, though, to deny what was clearly evident. Closeted in the country, indeed!

The duchess looked at Miranda. "I take it you disagree, my dear."

Miranda nodded.

"Well, then." The duchess raised her brows at her grandson. "Let us find out, shall we?" She held out her arms. "Give the child here, and we shall determine if he is a Matherton or not."

Miranda hesitated at the strange request. First the duchess had not had them ejected from her presence, and now she actually wanted to hold the babe? She glanced at Wyldehaven, but he looked just as puzzled.

"Come, come, young woman." The authority in the old lady's voice had Miranda complying before she thought. Gently, she placed James in the duchess's arms.

He fussed just a little, but the duchess had clearly handled infants before. She cooed to him and jiggled him until he calmed again and settled to sleep, slurping on the fist jammed in his mouth. Then she slowly unwrapped his blanket and, to Miranda's surprise, pushed aside the baby's gown so his feet were exposed. She peeled off one bootie and then peered at the tiny foot in her hand.

"Well," she announced, "he is indeed a Matherton."

"What the devil . . . ?" The duke jerked to attention and crossed the room in three long strides. "Grandmother, what are you saying?"

The duchess glanced up at him. "I realize you are overset, Thornton, but you *will* have a care for your language when ladies are present."

"My apologies, Grandmother. And I am not overset."

"You are," she corrected. "Look here. See the child's toes? The second and third cluster together, as if growing from the same base. A Matherton trait."

Miranda leaned in for a closer look and nearly bumped her head with the duke's as he did the same. She caught a whiff of sandalwood from his nearness before they both jerked back. Heat crept into her face as he raised a brow at her.

"Thornton," the duchess said. "You look first."

The duke leaned in, observed the baby's toes, then jolted back as if shot. "How can this be?" he demanded.

"Miss Fontaine," the duchess invited.

Miranda leaned down to study James's toes. The large toe and two smallest toes both grew directly from the babe's foot, but the second and third ones appeared to come from one base, splitting into two toes halfway along. It was not a grotesque oddity or deformation of any kind, not anything that would draw attention if one were not looking for it. But based on what she knew about her own feet, her own five toes all grew separately, unlike James's.

"This child is a Matherton," the duchess announced. She handed the baby back to Miranda, who set to wrapping his blanket around him again. "What say you, Thornton?"

"I am not the father." Miranda snorted, and he glared at her before looking back to the duchess. "Grandmother, you know as well as I do that nine or ten months ago, when this child was conceived, I was not even in London."

"It is a puzzle," the duchess agreed, then turned to Miranda. "When was the child born?"

"The third of March, Your Grace."

"And if you are not his mother, who is?"

"Her name was Lettie Dupree. She died in childbirth."

"A pity." The duchess cast an eye at her grandson. "You never left Wyldehaven, Thornton?"

"Never. You know why."

"I do. And if you tell me you are not this babe's father, I will believe you."

"I have never even met this Lettie Dupree, so I can hardly be the father."

"You were seen with her several times," Miranda said.

"By whom? You?"

"No. I am only recently arrived in London. But there are others who knew of your . . . acquaintance . . . with her."

"I would bloody well like to meet these 'others.' "

"Thornton, your language," the duchess rebuked him.

His face tight with frustration, he gave the older lady a respectful nod. "I apologize, Grandmother."

"As I said, you are overset."

"Too right I am overset. I did not do this thing."

"Yet the evidence seems to be to the contrary," Miranda said. For the first time, she felt some optimism, at least for James's future. Yet she was also disappointed. She had begun to hope that Wyldehaven was different from other men of his class, other men like her own father, who rejected their unwanted children like a wrinkled neck cloth.

"This child appears to be a Matherton," the duchess said. "Please understand that I do believe you, Thornton, if you say you never met the babe's mother. However, the evidence indicates that this child *is* a member of our family, which makes him your responsibility, even if you are not his father."

"Accepting responsibility is akin to admitting guilt," he protested. "And I am innocent in this."

"You are also the head of the family, Thornton."

"Very well. Since you wish it, Grandmother, I will provide funds for the raising of the child. On a *temporary* basis," he emphasized. "Only until we discover the identity of the babe's true father."

Miranda wanted to protest for James's sake. Money was a cold substitute for a parent's acceptance, but in her current circumstances, she realized, she had no choice but to settle for what was offered. "I am willing to continue to care for James, Your Grace, until you decide on a permanent situation."

"I am certain you are, Miss Fontaine." His words carried a scorn that she could not mistake. "Do leave your direction with Travers, and I will send word to you tomorrow about what that new arrangement will be." He signaled to a footman to show her out.

"Very well." She placed James in his basket, picked it up, and headed toward the door, then hesitated on the threshold.

"Have no fear," the duchess said, obviously sensing her uncertainty. "My grandson keeps his word."

"Yes, Your Grace." With one last look at the duke's stern visage, Miranda bobbed a curtsy to the duchess and followed the footman from the room.

"That young woman reminds me of someone." Alone with her grandson, the duchess pursed her lips in thought. "I cannot think of whom, but it will come to me."

"I do not see how you could ever have met her before," Wylde said, still frowning after the persistent Miss Fontaine. "She is hardly in your circle."

"Botheration, Thornton! You have no idea who is in my circle." The duchess gave an annoyed sniff. "Or who might have been in the past. I could tell you stories of my youth that would curl your hair."

"Please, do not." He held up a hand and tried to

smile. "Let us forget all this unpleasantness and continue on to Bond Street."

"Ha!" The duchess stood, balancing on her cane and not waiting for Wylde's helping hand. "If you can forget about that lovely young lady, Thornton, you are not half the Matherton I think you are!"

"I consider that a compliment."

The duchess snorted and began to walk from the room, but Wylde noticed her lips curving when she thought he was not looking. Pushing aside thoughts of Miranda Fontaine, he increased his pace to keep up with his grandmother. Better to stay at her side lest she get another mad notion into her head—like trying to drive the carriage!

Chapter 6

M iranda climbed down from the hired hack, still simmering about her encounter with the duke. Clutching James's basket, she marched up the pathway to Thaddeus's small house, grateful the duke had at least paid her fare beforehand—the very least he could do.

Though the duchess had shamed him into providing monetary support for James for the moment, it disturbed Miranda greatly that he still maintained he was not the father. She had only his word that he had been deep in mourning for his wife for the past year, and yet Thaddeus had told her other stories of Wild Wyldehaven, a man driven by hard gambling and soft women since the death of his wife. Unfortunately, Lettie had apparently been one of those women. Hardly the actions of a grieving widower. Someone was lying, and all indications pointed to Wyldehaven.

She could not believe she had thought him the

least bit attractive, even for a moment. People lied all the time, but she wanted to believe his protestations of innocence. And why? Because he was handsome and his smile made her insides tumble around like kittens in a basket. Because their music together had made her believe for one crazy instant that there was something more at work, some destiny that drew them together.

But she knew better than that. How often had she witnessed it firsthand, with both her mother and the other women who worked at the tavern? Women were so gullible when it came to men, so willing to believe every word that fell from male lips. They all wanted to fall in love, to be rescued by a handsome knight on a white charger.

Well, more often than not that shining knight turned out to be no more than a sweet-talking charlatan on a stolen mule . . . and usually one with no compunction about trampling a woman's heart or stealing her hard-earned wages.

No, the Duke of Wyldehaven could take his charming smile and wicked dark eyes to the devil. She herself might have been abandoned by her own blue-blooded father, but she would not accept such a future for James. The duchess had already confirmed that James was related to their family. She only needed the duke to admit the truth, for even a reluctant father was better than none at all.

Miranda reached out to open the front door. As she turned the knob, a hand shoved hard at her back, propelling her inside. She cried out and clutched the basket, terrified she would fall and take the baby with her. Rough hands grabbed her upper arms and steadied her as the door slammed behind her.

"We're looking for Thaddeus LeGrande."

She was spun around and found herself facing two men she had never seen before. Both of them were dressed in the serviceable, plain clothing that marked them as laborers and not gentlemen. One of the men leaned against the front door, watching out of the tiny window beside it. The other still had her in his grip, his large nose slightly crooked, as if it had been broken once upon a time. One of his mud-brown eyes focused on her, but the other had a tendency to slide to the right of its own accord.

She had seen men of this ilk before, in the tavern and at the docks near where she'd lived. Dangerous. Unpredictable. She clutched the handle of the basket more tightly.

"Where's LeGrande?"

The man's breath smelled of ale and onions, and it was all she could do not to turn her head and retch. "He is not here."

"When will he be back?"

"He is not living here at the moment." She straightened her spine and looked them in the eye as she fibbed, "My husband and I are renting the house."

"Husband, eh? I don't think so." He tightened his grip on her and dragged her up on her toes. "You LeGrande's woman?"

"Certainly not!"

Her outrage must have amused him, for he gave a brief chuckle. "You tell him that Mint and Barney were here."

She held onto her composure with all her might. "If you care to leave your direction . . ."

"He knows where to find us." The ruffian finally let her go, then cast a quick glance at the basket. "Nice baby. If you like him so much, make sure LeGrande gets the message."

"I will." She forced herself to meet his gaze without wavering. "Good day."

His mouth quirked in amusement. "Good day to you, yer ladyship." He turned away, gave a nod at his companion, and the two men slipped out the front door, leaving it ajar.

Putting down the basket, Miranda rushed forward, slammed the door, then threw the bolt and leaned back against the solid wood. Dear God. What did such riffraff want with Thaddeus? They had clearly been ready to resort to physical violence at any moment. Her heart pounded, and she sucked in breaths through dry lips. Anything could have happened, to her or to James.

She had become adept at avoiding unwanted male attention after years of living first with her mother, then on her own above the tavern. Now and again one of her mother's gentlemen callers had taken a fancy to a younger face and form and tried to convince her to yield herself to him. She had always managed to escape, except for the last time, when Jack Hinton came looking for her late mother and had instead nearly taken Miranda's innocence by force when he discovered that his paramour had died. Lettie had stopped him with a well-aimed chamber pot to the head.

How she wished Lettie were there now.

The baby stirred, making those breathy grunts that indicated he was waking. She shook off the ghosts of the past. James was her present and possibly her future. He needed her now.

"Miss Fontaine, is that you?" Mrs. Cooper, the wet nurse Thaddeus had hired for the baby, came down the stairs, a cheerful smile on her apple-cheeked face. "Oh good, you're back. I was folding the baby's linens and did not hear you until you closed the door."

A wail rose from the basket, starting low but escalating in volume with each passing second.

"I believe James is hungry," Miranda said, untying her bonnet with shaking fingers. She turned away to hang it up on the peg beside the door, taking a moment to regain her composure. She could not resist glancing out the tiny window, but there was no one outside.

"For certain, he is." Smiling, the nurse scooped the baby out of the basket. "I'll just take him upstairs and see to that before I leave for the afternoon. My young ones will be looking for their supper."

"Thank you, Mrs. Cooper." Miranda picked up the basket from the floor and set it on a nearby table as the wet nurse climbed the stairs, cooing to James. Again her gaze settled on the window. Still no one out there.

She stripped off her gloves, pushing back the fear with the mere strength of her will. She intended to have a few choice words with Thaddeus when she saw him. She had risked everything to come here to London, to make a better life for James. Ruffians barging into the house hardly made London any different than Little Depping. When she turned to put her gloves on the table, she noticed the letter sitting there, addressed to the Contessa della Pietra. Curious, she picked it up and opened it.

She scanned the lines within and slowly smiled.

"Haven't had this much fun since my salad days," Kit said with a grin as he and Wylde exited the coach in front of Ball's gaming establishment. Wylde had instructed the servants to conceal his coat of arms on the equipage; he did not want to add to the gossip about the Duke of Wyldehaven patronizing gaming hells. Kit, on the other hand, practically vibrated with enthusiasm, more excited than a stripling with his first woman.

"If this villain maintains his current pattern, I would expect him to arrive here at some point." Wylde regarded the nondescript town home with distaste.

"Or perhaps we have anticipated him."

"Perhaps. We might be able to warn the owners of this establishment and ask them to alert us if he does appear."

Kit laughed. "You truly do not understand the mentality of the underworld, do you, Wylde?"

Wylde cast him a grim glance. "I understand that these people want to make a profit. I expect to make it worth their while to help us."

Kit shook his head, amusement still curving his lips. "Lead on, Your Grace. I will watch your back, in the event someone tries to put a knife in it."

"I would appreciate that."

Wylde marched up the steps of the gaming hell and paused on the landing, eyeing the brute of a man blocking the door. The doorman stared right back, his glower a silent challenge. "We would like to enter," Wylde said.

The doorman pointed at Kit, then flipped a thumb at the door behind him. Kit flashed a grin, then darted around the fellow and opened the door. Wylde made to follow, but a ham-sized palm slapped into his chest, halting him.

"Him," the doorman said. "Not you."

Wylde grabbed the man's wrist and shoved his hand away. "Do you know who I am?"

"Wyldehaven."

"Oh." Nonplussed, he considered his options. Clearly the imposter had been here already . . . and left a less than flattering impression. "You let him in, but I am richer than he is."

The doorman folded his arms across his massive chest and regarded him as if he were a cow pie on the drawing room carpet. The hard glint in his eyes dared Wylde to try something physical.

Wylde glanced at the closed door, wondering why Kit did not come back to find him. No doubt his friend, ever searching for the quickest way to increase his wealth, had deserted him for the tables. He made a mental note to bring Wulf with him the next time he sought to infiltrate a gaming hell.

He looked the guard in the eye. "You will not let me in?"

The brute simply stared.

Wylde produced a guinea. "Will this change your mind?"

Outrage rippled across the doorman's homely face. Baring his teeth in a growl, he slapped Wylde's hand, sending the coin flying. "Annie is worth more than gold."

"Annie?"

The doorman grabbed two fistfuls of Wylde's perfectly tailored coat and lifted him easily to his toes. "You know what you did to her."

The genuine offense in the guard's tone made Wylde's senses go on alert. Something terrible had happened here, and the imposter had something to do with it.

"I want to speak to the owner of this establishment," he said, keeping his tone reasonable with effort when faced with a giant who looked like he might send him flying after the guinea. "I want to make things right."

The doorman's grip loosened, surprise and suspicion warring on his face. "You want to see Ball?"

"Yes. Is that possible?"

The doorman hesitated, and then an unholy grin split his face. "We'll go see Ball." He turned and opened the door with one hand, hauling Wylde along with the other still clenched on his coat. Faced with the possibilities of either falling or being dragged, Wylde managed to keep up with the doorman's pace.

The noise of the place assaulted his ears—voices striving to be heard over others, shrill laughter, the clinking of bottles to glass, the quiet slap of cards against table. Once inside, the doorman nodded at a fellow nearly as big as he was, and that behemoth slipped outside to take the guardsman's place at the front door.

Wylde's nostrils flared at the odors of tobacco and excessive cologne, and as they passed the common room, he glanced over in search of Kit. He thought he caught a glimpse of familiar blond hair, but then he was yanked down a hallway.

They finally stopped outside a door guarded by yet another huge man, who nodded at the doorman and thumped a meaty fist on the door. A voice replied from within, and the guardian to this doorway pushed open the door, then nodded to them.

"The Duke of Wyldehaven to see you, Ball," the doorman said, then shoved Wylde into the room. As Wylde stumbled on the plush red carpet, the door shut with ominous finality behind him.

He registered a fire burning in the grate, several bookcases stuffed with books, and behind the enormous desk piled with ledgers and papers, the woman.

He judged her to be somewhat past her prime, but the generous, smooth breasts barely covered by her form-fitting jade silk evening dress would have attracted attention at any age. A spectacular necklace of diamonds and emeralds lay across that impressive bosom and sparkled with every breath she took. She might have been a stunning beauty once, but her wide mouth, colored a dramatic scarlet, was surrounded by lines carved by hard living. Her brilliant blue eyes glittered with the well-learned lessons of survival.

"You've got some nerve showing that pretty face of yours around here," the striking redhead said. "I don't want to hang for killing a duke, but some of the boys aren't as picky."

"You are Ball?"

She laughed. "Don't play games, Wyldehaven. Have you come to compensate me for Annie?"

"There has been a misunderstanding—"

"You beat my girl and she can't work. I say you owe me for the money she would have been making me."

Wylde drew himself up and gave her his coldest stare. "Madam, as I said, there has been a misunderstanding. This is my first visit to your establishment."

She barked with laughter. "You cold-hearted bastard. You were here just last night, drunk as a lord. You took Annie for your pleasure and then used your fists on her. The girl can barely walk today."

"I did not. Unfortunately, Mrs. Ball—"

"Just Ball. It's a nickname."

"As I was saying, someone who resembles me is going about town pretending to be the Duke of Wyldehaven. He has been causing me no little trouble."

She gave a cackling laugh. "That's a new story to avoid a scandal. You nobs are a queer lot for certain."

"I assure you, madam, this is no joke." He pulled out his purse and counted out a number of coins and bills, then slapped the money on her desk with a clank of coin. Ball pounced on it like a cat on a mouse.

"There is more than fifty pounds there," he continued. "I believe that should compensate you and Annie for the lost income?"

She cast him a long look of blue-eyed suspicion. "It will do."

"I am quite serious," he continued. "This villain resembles me so closely, I am told, that those who do not know me well might be fooled."

"Is that so?" She scooped the money back into the bag, then squirreled it away in a drawer. "I don't care if you are queer in the attic," she said. "You paid for Annie, so we're square."

"If you see him again, would you please send a note around to Matherton House in Mayfair?"

She sat back in her chair. "If I see you, I'm supposed to send a note to your house that I saw you?"

He could not fault her skepticism and accepted it calmly. "Yes."

"All right, if that's what you want me to do."

"It is. I will make it worth your while."

She shrugged, nearly dislodging one precariously tucked breast. "Fine."

"Might I also ask your assistance in locating my companion?" he asked. "Your guard let him through the door and I have not seen him since."

"Of course." She stood, her green dress shimmering around her spectacular figure as she stepped out from behind the desk. "Come with me."

She took his arm, curling her fingers possessively around his coat sleeve, and led him to the door. They stepped out into the hall just as a disruption flared at the end of the corridor. The guard from the door was holding back a skinny blond woman who clung to him with one hand and slapped at his massive arm with the other.

"Let me go, Moss! I want to see Ball throw him out into the street!"

"Calm yerself, Annie. You're going to hurt yerself."

"You saw what he did to me, Moss. He'll never pay for it; no one will ever make him pay. All I got is watching Ball toss his highborn arse into the gutter!"

"Annie." Ball's quiet voice froze them cold. "Come into my office. You too, Moss." She glanced at Wylde. "My apologies, Your Grace, for detaining you. I can have one of the men help you locate your friend."

"Not necessary." Wylde watched the slender

blond girl as she approached, the way she shrank into the hulk of the doorman, her one eye—the one that was not swollen shut, that is—wide with wariness. The girl was passing pretty, but she walked slowly and carefully, as if every step were agony. Moss, the doorman, eyed Wylde as if he wanted to tear him apart with his bare hands.

Wylde turned to Ball. "Perhaps we should all step into your office, madam, that we might clear up this matter."

Ball shrugged. "Fine, but if you go for Annie again, I'll have Moss toss you out."

He clenched his jaw. "I understand."

They all filed back into Ball's office, and the way Annie tried her best to curl away from his gaze made Wylde's gut clench with anger. This imposter, when he was found, had much to answer for.

"The duke has paid for your lost earnings, Annie, so you can stay in your room tonight," Ball said. "But if you're not able to take customers in a day or so, I'll have to give it to another girl."

"I know," Annie murmured.

Moss glanced at his boss as if he wanted to say something but did not dare.

Wylde frowned at Ball. "You are expecting her to go back to work as if nothing has happened? She is injured!"

"You're the one who done it!" Moss snarled.

Ball held up her hand to silence her employee and turned her attention to Wylde. "This is a business, Your Grace, not a charity house. If Annie can't work, she can't stay. She knows that."

"There must be something else that can be done."

"I don't know why you're acting all nice all of a sudden," Annie muttered.

"Because I did not do this to you, Annie."

The girl sneered. "It was you."

"No, it was not." Wylde kept his voice calm and gentle. "There is a man going about London who looks like me and is pretending to be me."

"What? Like your brother?" Annie scoffed.

The careless remark gave him pause with the denial still on his lips. His brother? One of Father's by-blows, perhaps?

And if the same man causing all this trouble was also the fellow who had fathered the baby Miranda had brought to him . . . Well, that would account for the Matherton toes, wouldn't it? And it would mean that the blackguard had been causing trouble for much longer than they suspected.

He kept his expression calm, though his blood surged with the certainty that he had stumbled onto the truth. "Look carefully at me, Annie. Do I look different than you remember?"

"What's he talking about?" Annie wailed, looking at Ball.

"Do as the duke says," Ball told her. "Take a good look and tell him what he wants to know."

Moss glared at Wylde as Annie turned her attention to scrutinizing him. "You look thinner," she said finally. "But that could just be your clothes. And your hair is longer. But there's ways around that, too."

"Is he tall like me? Tell me anything you can."

"About the same size." She stared into Wylde's face, finally looking closely, then gasped. "Blimey, your eyes are different!"

"Different how?" Wylde ignored Ball's sudden stillness and Moss's narrow-eyed stare.

"His eyes were green, real green. I remember thinking they looked like the devil's own eyes when he hit me. Your eyes are brown." She let out a slow breath. "It wasn't you that hurt me."

"That is correct."

"Then who did?"

"That," Wylde said with a glance at Ball, "is what I am trying to discover."

Annie shifted, and Moss took a step back from his protective stance. "But Ball said you paid for me. Why did you do that if you weren't the one?"

"Because it is the right thing to do." Wylde looked at Ball. "As a man can hardly change his eye color, I believe we have established that the person who did this horrible thing was not the Duke of

Wyldehaven. Madam, I would like to negotiate for this girl's release from your employment."

"Anything can be negotiated, Your Grace," Ball purred.

"What do you want her for?" Moss demanded, suspicion coloring his tone.

"I will give her a position in one of my houses." Wylde looked at Annie. "Would you like that, Annie? I assure you that I will pay you a fine wage."

"Like a maid?"

"Exactly."

"I can do that. But I got my own bed here."

"You will have your own bed in my home, as well as hot meals every day."

"Every day?" Annie grinned as much as her swollen face would allow. "Blimey. But no one puts a hand on me 'less I say so."

"Agreed." Wylde raised his brows at Ball. "Shall we begin the negotiations, madam? And while we are discussing terms, perhaps your man here would locate my friend for me."

"Of course." Ball dismissed her employees with a jerk of her head toward the door. "Moss, find His Grace's companion. Annie, pack your things. I have a feeling you will be leaving us tonight."

"Yes, Ball."

Ball swept over to her desk and sat down. "Come, Your Grace. Let us discuss terms."

* * *

The Contessa della Pietra accepted the gushing compliments of Lord Arenson, keeping her smile in place with effort. Sir Alec Bennett and his wife had secured her services for their soiree, and she'd already received two more invitations to sing, one from the aging earl. Unfortunately, the earl appeared to believe that hiring a performer entitled him to lay his hands on whatever part of her person he cared to.

"You sing like a nightingale," Arenson said, stroking her arm. "I know you will be a lovely addition to our card party." His watery gaze locked with almost pitiful obsession on her bosom.

"Thank you, my lord." She leaned away an inch or so, forcing him to drop his hand, though his eyes remained fixed where they were. "How unfortunate your lady wife could not join you tonight. I do hope her health improves."

"Bah." He waved a dismissive hand. "Megrims, as always. She will be right as rain come the morning."

"I am glad to hear it." She fixed a polite smile and looked beyond him. "Oh, here is our hostess. I hope you will excuse me—"

"You remind me of someone." He caught her arm again before she could walk away, and this time his hold did not allow her to escape.

"Contessa." Lady Margaret Bennett stopped beside them, her expression a perfect balance of polite authority. "The Marchioness of Welsfield would like an introduction."

"Of course." Miranda tugged at her arm. "Lord Arenson, if you will excuse me, I must attend the marchioness."

The baron did not appear to hear. "She reminds me of someone, Margaret," he said. "I should remember in a moment."

"Now, Uncle." Lady Margaret cast Miranda an apologetic glance. "Let go of the contessa. Her ladyship is waiting."

"I am flattered by your admiration, my lord," Miranda said. "Every performer seeks to touch her audience."

"Touch her audience. Aha! I have remembered." He held up a finger. "You remind me of an actress who was all the rage about twenty years ago. My friend Rothgard and I were mad for her. Sent her roses every performance." He chuckled, clearly lost in his memories. "Fannie Fontaine. A beautiful woman. You could be her image."

Miranda's heart seemed to stop in her chest. "Thank you, my lord."

"Of course you are too young to remember her." Arenson finally released her arm. "Wait until I tell Rothgard."

"Lady Welsfield awaits, Uncle." Lady Margaret managed to steer Miranda out of range of Lord Arenson's roving hands.

"Yes, yes, go on." He smiled wistfully, clearly lost in the past.

Lady Margaret led Miranda away. "Please forgive my uncle, Contessa. He is getting on in years. Sometimes his mind wanders."

"There was no harm done," Miranda said, still shaken by mention of her mother's name. "I find it flattering that I reminded him of someone he once admired so much."

"You are very kind. Come, the marchioness awaits."

Chapter 7

Mrs. Cooper had arrived and left again after feeding James his morning meal. The cheerful woman was clearly fond of the baby, but she had her own family to attend to in the meanwhile.

Miranda sat in the parlor at a small table near the window, her head bent over her accounting. If she continued to receive invitations to perform, as she had last night, she and James might live comfortably indeed—with or without the Duke of Wyldehaven. James kicked and squealed in the basket on the floor, delight in every sound. She looked up from her numbers and smiled at his joyful innocence as he amused himself with his flaying hands. But her smile faded as she considered that while she could certainly feed and clothe the babe on her earnings, she could never provide a father's love.

A rap came at the door. With a sigh, she set down

her quill and, with a glance at the baby to make certain he was secure, went into the foyer just as another authoritative knock echoed. She glanced out the window beside the door, then gasped and hurried to throw it open.

Wyldehaven regarded her with disapproval from his lofty height. "Miss Fontaine, are there no servants to attend the door?"

His mild chastisement was just enough to stiffen her spine. "This is a humble household, Your Grace, not a Mayfair manor. Do come in." She swung the door wide. As he strode into the house, she glanced out at the two gleaming carriages standing at the curb.

"Miss Fontaine!"

"Yes?" She closed the door and turned to face him. "You need not bark my name like a general, Your Grace. I was merely curious." She crossed her arms and asked with feigned sweetness, "Is your consequence so great that you need more than one carriage to accompany you on your calls?"

"You are a cheeky baggage, considering you are the one who came to me for aid."

"And you are rather high in the instep."

"I am the Duke of Wyldehaven, young woman. There is no instep higher than mine."

He said the words with such solemnity that it took her several seconds to realize that his eyes were glinting with humor.

114

A chuckle burst from her as her defensiveness waned. "You are a man of peculiar amusements, Your Grace."

"I trust you will keep such knowledge to yourself." He took off his hat, then looked around. "You truly have no servants?"

"Cook is cleaning up the kitchen from the morning meal, and Mrs. Cooper, the wet nurse, will be back by luncheon." She took his high-crowned hat from his hands and turned to set it on the table beside the door. A whiff of sandalwood from the costly beaver teased her senses, and she quickly turned back to face him. "To what do I owe this honor, Your Grace?"

"For pity's sake, you may refer to me as Wyldehaven, or Wylde if you prefer."

"As you wish." A tiny mewl from the parlor grabbed her attention. "Do come into the parlor, Your . . . I mean, Wyldehaven. I must attend to James."

She hurried forward into the parlor, heedless of the lack of courtesy in leaving him to follow. James was working himself into a fit. As his cries grew louder, she scooped him out of the basket and jiggled him in her arms. "There, there. Miranda's come."

The duke entered the room more slowly. "Is there something wrong with him?"

She glanced up, amused by the hesitant tone in

his voice. "No, he is just tired. I expect he will drift off to sleep soon."

"I see."

She cuddled James close to her body and began swaying, turning so she might see the duke. "Babies do little else but eat and sleep when they are so young."

"How do you know he is tired?"

"By his cry." She smothered a smile at the awkward way he remained standing before the chair. "Do sit down, Your Grace."

"Wyldehaven," he corrected mildly. "And I cannot sit while a lady stands."

"I cannot sit and rock him at the same time," she said. "Really, you will not offend, and you make me uneasy standing there so grimly."

"You have no reason to feel uneasy. I have agreed to support the child until his true father is found."

As quickly as that, their easy rapport dissolved.

"How good of you to offer shelter to an innocent babe." Conscious of the bite in her voice, she turned her back on him, ostensibly to return James to his basket, but in fact to hide the disappointment she was certain showed on her face. Why did she keep relaxing her guard around him only to be reminded of who and what he was?

A man, and a rich man at that. A duke. Someone who could never care for others as much as he cared for his own boot blacking.

She glanced down at the baby, reminding herself again of what was important. What mattered. James had his eyes scrunched tightly shut, and he sucked furiously on one fist, well on his way to sleep. Her heart ached with love.

She would do her best by him.

Gently, she adjusted his clothing so he slept comfortably. Then she gathered her defenses around her and turned back to face the Duke of Wyldehaven.

To her surprise, he was watching the baby with a mixture of pain and something that looked for a moment like longing. "It is amazing," he mused, "how we all start so small and helpless and yet somehow grow into who we are meant to be."

Her heart slowly turned over in her chest.

No. She would not soften toward him. She could not trust him.

"Yes, well, that is the way of things, isn't it?" She sat down in her chair by the window again, and he finally seated himself in the armchair. "Why have you granted me the honor of your presence, Your Grace?"

The hint of sarcasm rolled off Wylde without inflicting any damage, but he was certainly aware of it. He paused before responding, searching for some modicum of warmth in her eyes. But her expression remained polite and distant—not his objective at all.

Curse it, what had he said to put her on her guard? When he had first arrived, she had been laughing and joking with him. Now she watched him as if he were a thief in a jewel shop. He wanted her to be comfortable with him, and not just because he suspected that she had information he would need to solve his most current difficulty. He just wanted her to like him—for reasons he dared not explore too closely. And thus far he had not given her much incentive to regard him as friend rather than foe.

But neither would he lie to her.

"I am here because I said I would provide for the child on a temporary basis, at least until his paternity is determined. I have come to take you to your new home."

"My new home! What is wrong with this house?"

He glanced around, his shrug dismissing the welcoming surroundings as substandard. "I have rented a fine town house for you, Miss Fontaine. You will be quite comfortable there—especially since there is a staff."

She had stiffened up like a billiards poker as soon as he began speaking. "I do not like living at the behest of another."

"Is this not what you wanted?"

"Not really." She stood and began pacing, her arms folded protectively over her bosom. "I had

118

hoped you would accept your son and raise him yourself."

"And so I would—if he were mine."

She whirled to face him, outrage widening her eyes and coloring her cheeks. "How can you deny him? Your own grandmother has declared him a member of your family."

"I have told you that I cannot be the boy's father."

"Yes, because you were cloistered at your country estate, grieving for your wife." She waved a dismissive hand. "I hardly see how that precludes you from being capable of fathering a child, Wyldehaven. It is not as if you were out of the country or felled by disease."

He clenched his hands on the arms of the chair. "I might as well have been," he replied softly. "I was not at all inclined to be in the company of anyone during that time, not my friends and not my family. Certainly not a mistress."

"How terrible." The glance she sent him held compassion, but resolve as well. "But I have seen men carousing with tavern maids while their wives lay abed birthing children. A duke seeking the comfort of a woman after the death of his wife is hardly a stretch of the imagination."

He pushed out of the chair. "And where did you see such sights, Miss Fontaine? You profess to be a woman of sound moral character. How could a

119

female with such delicate sensibilities be in a position to witness such things?"

"My beginnings were humble."

"I sense a mystery." He came closer, scrutinizing her face. Just when he thought he understood her, another layer of secrecy unfurled. "Who is your family, Miranda Fontaine? Where did you come from?"

"We were talking about James."

"Yes, and now we are talking about you." He came close enough to disturb the dangling tendrils of her hair as he exhaled. "You are a fierce champion, Miss Fontaine. James is very lucky to have you. But why would an unmarried woman of your exquisite looks burden herself with another woman's child?"

"There was no one else." She glanced at the sleeping baby, then back at him. "Lettie died, abandoned by the man who fathered her child. She asked only that I look after James and fight for him to take his rightful place in society."

"You certainly have fought," he acknowledged. "A veritable Boadicea."

"You mock me."

"I do not. I simply want to understand you." The delicate scent of rose water lingered on her skin, in her attractively coiled tresses, and he filled his lungs with it. Wanted to fill his hands with *her*. How could so innocent an aroma incite such hunger? "So brave you are, battling with me sword-to-sword for a child who is not even yours."

"He feels like mine," she whispered.

Her valiant heart intrigued him. Was she the self-less young woman she appeared to be, or a clever opportunist set on bettering her own lifestyle? "Do you want children?" he asked, tracing a finger down the back of her arm.

"Most women do." She edged aside, putting inches between them.

"Some women do," he corrected. He swept his gaze over her simple muslin dress, admiring the graceful form beneath the pale green folds. The modestly scooped neckline only hinted at the magnificent breasts he knew were there. "It seems a natural thing, something a female would crave. Yet for some reason there are those who cringe from it."

"I do not know anything of that. I can only speak for myself."

"We are only speaking of you. Where do you come from? Who are your parents?"

"My parents are dead. I am alone in the world, Your Grace, so you will see why I am cautious."

"You would be foolish not to be. An unscrupulous man might try to take advantage of a woman of your beauty."

Yes." She met his gaze boldly. "He might."

Rather than be offended, he found himself

amused. "Very well, little hedgehog. I suggest you collect your charge and come with me to your new home. The servants will bring your belongings in the other coach."

"You are very certain of yourself."

"I am providing for the child—and for you as well. Is this not what you wanted?"

"There was never any discussion about providing for me, Your Grace. I wanted you to take *James* into your care." Her tone was defiant, but he did not miss the longing glance she flicked toward the baby.

"You wanted me to simply take the child from you and raise him? You are able to part from him so easily?"

"It would be best for him." She raised her chin, green eyes defiant, but for the first time he caught a flash of vulnerability.

He took her chin in his hand. "No, Boadicea, *you* are what is best for him. He needs his fierce warrior queen for a while longer."

Her eyes misted with tears, and her lush lower lip quivered. He knew what he did was unwise even as he leaned in and pressed his mouth to hers.

For one dulcet moment, she responded. Her mouth slackened beneath his and she leaned closer to him as he slid his arms around her. It had been so long since he had held a woman against him, and passion flared to life within him almost instantly. Her soft curves pressed against his chest, female to male. He wanted to lose himself in her, to ease the hunger and soothe the loneliness. Her sweetness ensnared him, lured him like honey. But she could not disguise the innocence of her kiss.

She was untried. Probably a virgin.

He knew he should stop. He should act the gentleman and step away. But from the moment she barged into his life, she captured his attention, made him notice a woman for the first time in more than a year. And he found he was not ready to let her go so easily.

Then she pushed him away, her small hands fisting against his chest. She looked at him with those exotic eyes, her mouth moist from his kiss. "Stop. I am not part of the household belongings to be packed up and carted away to your house, to your protection."

The words stung and shook him from the nearly romantic spell he had been under. But he would not let her see that her protest had pricked him.

He took a step back, adjusted his coat sleeves. "What is wrong with protection? As a woman alone in London, you should be glad to have me watching over you."

"I will not share your bed, Wyldehaven."

He raised his brows and gave her a cool smile. "Who asked you to?"

She was not cowed and crossed her arms over her chest, hedgehog prickles rippling. He should have been irritated; instead he was charmed.

"If that kiss was an invitation," she said, "consider it declined."

"It was a kiss, Miss Fontaine, not a proposition."

"Better if it is said, Your Grace. I will have no misconceptions between us."

"As you wish."

"I am here for James, nothing more."

"Understood."

"Not to be a companion for your convenience."

"You have made your point."

"And—"

"Miss Fontaine, I believe you protest too much."

Outrage flickered across her face, and though she did not rise to his bait, the battle was there in her eyes. He almost wished she would let go of that control of hers, let her passion lead her back into his arms.

"Indeed," she said finally. "Please watch James while I fetch my things."

And without waiting for a reply, she marched from the room, leaving him alone with his unquenched desires and a slumbering infant.

She must be mad to even consider such a situation.

Miranda tucked her meager belongings into her

satchel, annoyance causing her to take less care than she might otherwise have. She had never once asked the duke to provide any sort of living for her; it was *James* she'd wanted him to shelter. *James* she wanted him to support. She had known there was a slim chance she would be able to stay with the baby, but hoped to do so in the capacity of nursemaid—valid employment for which she would earn a wage. She had never expected the duke to scoop her up like so much furniture and remove her to a residence for which he paid the rent. The fact that he had not discussed the details of this arrangement did not escape her—nor did the memory of his kiss.

By God, had she learned nothing from watching her mother? From watching Lettie? She knew how men could so easily take advantage of women, especially women without prospects, like herself. Thaddeus had managed to save some money for her, but half of it was already gone for a wardrobe for the contessa. If she was going to somehow manage on her own, she would need to continue performing and save up enough so she could retire to a quiet cottage somewhere. The only way to do that was to stay in London, at least for a while.

To stay with James.

She could not deny that the idea of spending more time with that precious child filled her with joy. However, the only way to accomplish that was to accept the offer of the duke to live in a house he paid for, on his terms. But what did that make her?

Beholden.

She longed to stay with James, to make certain he received the loving care he deserved. But what if the duke pressed the matter, tried to coax her into his bed? Would he be so heartless as to toss them both into the street if she refused him? He had already abandoned Lettie, and for that she should already hate him.

But she didn't. And that scared her more than anything else.

The situation was intolerable. If she went with him and lived in a house that he paid for, she was implying he had rights that she had no intention of granting him. But if she refused to move, he might well take James—despite his bold words about the baby needing her—and she would never see the child again. Never know what happened to him or if her promise to Lettie had come to pass.

She closed up the satchel. She would have to be strong. Yes, the duke was attractive. Yes, for some reason her traitorous body flared to life when he was near. But in the end it was James who held her heart. James who needed her. And she would stay with him until his future was decided, the Duke of Wyldehaven be damned.

* * *

Waiting in the parlor, Wyldehaven cast a wary glance at the dozing babe. "You are quite lucky to be sleeping through all of this," he said. "Miss Fontaine is more prickly than usual."

The child did not so much as twitch. Relieved, Wylde seated himself. When a woman went to pack her things, a man could expect to wait indefinitely.

He supposed he hadn't needed to go through all this trouble. He could probably have simply provided money for the babe, but something inside him wanted to assure that they had a decent place to live—and he didn't want Miranda to continue to think he was an ogre. Naturally, he had every intention of leaving her to her own business and not lurking around, watching over her like an obsessed bedlamite.

She had made a valid point when she informed him that while he was indeed paying her rent, her person was off limits to any advances. They were entering into this agreement to find the best solution for James and for no other reason.

But he could not deny to himself that he had come along today mostly to be certain she accepted his offer of assistance, and not just because his grandmother insisted that he help her. Miranda was apparently telling the truth about the baby as she understood it, so he was willing to entertain the thought that she might not be the opportunist he had originally thought her. She truly believed that he had fathered James. But there was more to his interest than just handling a potential scandal. She stirred something in him he had not felt in a long time, and he wanted to investigate these feelings. He wanted to know if she felt the same connection he did.

Until today, he knew he had not conducted himself well with her. He had never given the least indication that he would take the baby from her, but still she apparently feared it. So he had decided to show her he was not a monster; he was just a man seeking the same answers as she.

And if they ended up lovers, so be it.

One of his servants came to the door of the parlor. "Thaddeus LeGrande is at the door, Your Grace. Shall I allow him entrance?"

"Yes, send him in."

Moments later LeGrande stormed into the parlor. "Your Grace, might I inquire why I was stopped at the door of my own home by one of your servants? What the devil are you are doing here?"

"I am waiting for Miss Fontaine."

"For what purpose? And why is there an army of servants loading the carriages outside?"

"Miss Fontaine has asked for my assistance regarding young James. I am therefore providing a house and servants for her and the baby until we can sort out this matter." Wylde waved a hand at the armchair. "Do sit, Mr. LeGrande."

"Fine thing, being invited to sit down in my own parlor!" LeGrande flopped into the chair with a huff. "You take much upon yourself, Wyldehaven, duke or no."

"I find it is often most expedient to take the reins to make certain things are done correctly."

"You apparently did not consider that when you abandoned Lettie, did you?"

Wylde stiffened. "Is that what you think?"

"That is what I *know.*" LeGrande held Wylde's gaze. "Unlike Miranda, I was a witness to your affair with Lettie. I saw you come for her at the theatre at least three times that spring. I tried to tell her to be careful, that a man of your status would never consider her more than a plaything. But she would never listen to me. She believed that you loved her."

Wylde came to attention. "You *saw* this fellow yourself?"

"I saw *you.*"

He shook his head. "Never me, LeGrande. I was cloistered at my country estate until two weeks ago. For some time now some blackguard has been going about town using my name to wreak havoc."

"I *saw* you," LeGrande repeated.

"Apparently this fellow resembles me quite closely."

LeGrande snorted. "A likely tale. Just so you are aware, Your Grace, Society may bow down to you, but Miranda and I do not. In our eyes, you are the worst kind of cad who sent our beloved Lettie to her death."

Wylde clenched his jaw. "I have been tracing this fellow's movements, LeGrande, since I was made aware of him, and I have engaged Bow Street to assist with the matter. Would I do that if I were the guilty party?"

"Since money means nothing to you, I would not put it past you to engage in such subterfuge just to draw attention away from yourself."

"You really do dislike me, don't you?"

LeGrande glared with the certainty of the righteous. "I dislike any man who abandons a woman he has gotten with child."

"In that, we are in complete agreement."

LeGrande gave a disbelieving hoot. "You are a bold one, Your Grace."

Wylde steepled his fingers. "Since we are speaking of blackguards, personally, I truly dislike those who cannot control their tendencies for gaming. Especially if they borrow money and then lose it at the tables. Don't you agree?"

The triumph faded from LeGrande's expression. "Of course. A most inexcusable transgression."

"Indeed. But if that is your belief, why did two ruffians—known to work for a certain businessman who loans funds to gamesters—come here yesterday and force their way into the house?"

"What?" LeGrande jerked straight up in his chair. "They were here?"

"Yes." Wylde gave him a grim look of censure. "And so was Miss Fontaine."

"Dear God." LeGrande swiped a hand over his face and sagged back in his seat. "Why did she not tell me? And how the devil do you know about it?"

"I had a man watching the house. Miss Fontaine appears unharmed, but I believe you will agree that if such incidents continue to occur, the safety of both her and the baby may be at risk."

"Yes, yes." LeGrande withdrew a handkerchief and mopped his brow. "Dear God, they were here. Anything could have happened. I cannot believe my own foolishness!"

"You will see now why I believe Miss Fontaine and the child will be safer under my protection."

"Yes, yes, of course."

"She is somewhat uncooperative regarding the matter, so I expect your support, LeGrande. If you can convince her to move to the house I have procured for her, then she will be safe from any further unsavory encounters."

"I understand." LeGrande shoved his handkerchief back into his sleeve, then met Wylde's gaze, his own firm with resolve. "I will concede that I have made a muddle of things regarding my own affairs, and in doing so have endangered Miranda's safety, but I still contend that you are only the lesser of two evils, Wyldehaven. As far as I am concerned, you murdered Lettie with your abandonment of her. Do not think to seduce Miranda as well. One dead woman on your conscience should be enough."

Wylde gave a stiff nod, though it chafed that even this reprobate would question his innocence. "Her honor is safe with me."

"It had better be, Your Grace, or not even your towering consequence will be enough to save you."

Chapter 8

⌒⌒◯◯⌒⌒

When Miranda came downstairs, Wyldehaven's servants bustled through the floors of the house like ants at a picnic. One of them relieved her of her satchel, leaving her no choice but to return to the parlor. There, she found Thaddeus sitting on the settee across from the duke, the baby slumbering away in the basket between them.

"Miranda, good morning!" Thaddeus called out, standing. The duke also rose from his chair. Though he said nothing, his dark eyes gleamed with a certain male satisfaction that immediately got her hackles up.

Ignoring Wyldehaven, she turned her attention to the aging actor. She had not forgotten the unpleasant visitors who shoved their way into the house the day before, but she had yet to mention the incident to Thaddeus. "Good morning, Thaddeus. I have been wondering when you would come to call."

Something in her tone must have alerted him

because his smile dimmed somewhat as he rose to his feet. "Is everything all right?"

"Quite," she answered, conscious of the very astute gaze of Wyldehaven upon them. She took a seat on the settee, and Thaddeus sat back down a few feet away, as did the duke, across from them. "Some friends of yours paid a call yesterday, but we will not bore the duke with such trivialities. Has he told you that he has come to remove me and James to a house of his choosing?"

"He has."

"I have informed His Grace that we are quite comfortable here, but he insists." She arched her brows at the duke.

"And I have informed Miss Fontaine that she will have no worries as long as she is under my care," Wylde said.

"I have made it a moral standard that I will never be beholden to another person," Miranda replied. "I do wish you would respect my wishes."

The duke gave her a charming smile that affected her more than she liked. "As admirable as that may be, Miss Fontaine, it is also somewhat unrealistic. You requested my help, and this is the aid I have chosen to give."

"And you make me sound quite churlish for attempting to refuse your offer."

"If you will recall, we have already set the parameters of our arrangement, have we not?"

She did not miss the hint of insinuation in his voice, which brought back with vivid clarity the stolen kiss they had shared. Warmth crept into her cheeks, and she hoped Thaddeus did not take note of it. "So we have, Your Grace."

"I think it is a good idea," Thaddeus said. "You have not been long in London, Miranda, and with the duke looking after you, you will continue to be safe."

She sent him a baleful look. When had his opinion of Wyldehaven changed? "I seem to recall you thinking differently only two days ago, Thaddeus."

"Yes, well . . ." He sent a quick glance at the duke. "His Grace and I have been talking, Miranda. It seems that we may have wronged him."

"I beg your pardon?" Aware of Wyldehaven's confident smile, she leaned forward. "In what way have we wronged him?"

Thaddeus shifted in his chair. "Apparently there is someone impersonating the duke and causing all this mischief."

"Oh?" Her brittle tone made Thaddeus flinch. "What proof is there of this, Thaddeus? Who is this mysterious twin who is out to destroy the reputation of the kind and virtuous duke?"

"Miss Fontaine, I believe that is enough."

Miranda abruptly turned at Wyldehaven. "I cannot believe that you are so craven as to assign your own misdeeds to a mysterious stranger who happens to be your twin. How gullible do you think I am?"

"Mr. LeGrande has no problem accepting my explanation. One wonders why you are so intent on believing the worst."

"Because it is too fantastical to be true."

"You are a cynic," Wylde murmured, understanding lighting his eyes. "Who would have believed a fierce warrior like yourself would have no faith in others?"

"I know what life has taught me," she said. "I know I can depend on myself. Others are not so reliable."

"You are too young for such hard beliefs," Thaddeus said. "You should trust the duke to do what is right for you and James."

"What is it that he has said to you, Thaddeus, that makes you believe he did not do all the things we have heard about?" Miranda demanded. "He still will not admit to fathering James."

"Perhaps he didn't," Thaddeus said.

"Lettie declared that he did. She would have no reason to lie. And you yourself said that you witnessed him with Lettie several times. How do you explain that?"

"Apparently this imposter looks very much like the duke."

"How very convenient!"

Thaddeus scowled. "Miranda, I was the one who

actually saw the man, and I am telling you it was not the Duke of Wyldehaven."

"Is that so? What is different about him?"

"His . . . uh . . ."

"I am told this fellow has green eyes," Wylde said. "As you can see, my eyes are brown."

The last thing she wanted to do was look into those velvety dark eyes of his. Instead, she gave a dismissive sniff. "Quite a fanciful notion."

Thaddeus took her hands in his. "Miranda, you must listen to me. This is what you wanted. Wyldehaven is willing to care for James. Why are you hesitating?"

"Because he still does not admit he is James's father. Material trappings are all well and good, but this boy needs a father. He did not ask to be born, to be an inconvenience." Miranda slashed a look at Wylde, taking small comfort in the way he frowned at their clasped hands. "It seems to me that if a man was so careless as to create a child, he should take some responsibility in the raising of that child."

"He is taking responsibility. He is providing a home, food." Thaddeus squeezed her hands. "Accept what he can give, Miranda. Maybe the rest will come."

"Thaddeus . . ."

"Miranda." Thaddeus gave her hands another squeeze, then released her. "People have their limitations. Take the duke's offer."

"Fine." She stood, still frustrated that Thaddeus sided with the duke. "In that case, I am ready to leave."

"At last." Wylde stood as well. "I believe you will be pleased with your new home."

"I am certain it is quite fashionable, Wyldehaven, but it is not my home. It is yours."

He gave her a gentle smile, and she hated that he could make her belly flutter so easily. "No," he said, indicating the baby. "It is his."

The house Wyldehaven had procured for them impressed her the moment she set eyes on it, but she would never encourage this scandalous situation by granting the duke any compliments about it.

Small but elegant and set on a quiet street in an old but still fashionable neighborhood, the graceful residence appealed to every part of her that longed to be accepted by Society. This was how she had always imagined the home of her dreams. The fact that Wyldehaven provided it both chafed and thrilled her.

She was not his wife or his mistress. This was a business arrangement, and she would see to it that things remained that way, no matter what ulterior motives His Grace might have. But she could not deny, at least to herself, that deep in her heart she wished all of this were permanent. Real.

"Do you like it?" Wyldehaven asked, watching

her closely. They still sat in his coach, the duke having relegated Thaddeus and the baby to the second vehicle. She had noticed that he seemed uncomfortable in the baby's presence, but assumed it was a man's natural awkwardness around an infant.

She glanced out the window again at the house. Her heart opened in welcome, but she managed to keep her face impassive and her tone disinterested. "It is quite nice."

His jaw clenched, and she took a moment's victory in that, but then the footmen were opening the door to the coach. "Let us see what you think about the inside," he said. Rather than waiting for the footmen, he climbed out of the coach, then turned and held out a hand to her.

Her heart skipped a beat. He looked all the world like a bridegroom welcoming his new wife to their home, but she cut off the thought before it could fully form. She could not afford to entertain any fanciful notions about this man. He denied his own actions in fathering James. And even if she could make herself look beyond his attitude and take his recent actions into account, he was a duke, far above the touch of the daughter of an actress who could not even name her own father. He would never offer anything honorable to a woman like her.

"Come, come, Miss Fontaine."

The impatience in his voice snapped her out of her thoughts. She pulled herself out of the seat but hesitated in the doorway of the coach. His hand remained extended. Slowly, she took it.

The warmth of his skin penetrated even through their gloves. His casual strength guided her easily down the steps until her feet touched the ground. He held her hand a moment longer than necessary, his gaze locking with hers.

She sucked in a breath, trying to get her pulse back to normal. She had never been so affected by a man, and he'd already voiced his interest in her. Such a dangerous situation, especially for a woman who had sworn never to fall beneath any man's spell. The sooner they resolved the situation about James, she thought, the better.

Thaddeus emerged from the other coach, along with Mrs. Cooper carrying James in his basket. The actor glanced at their hands, still touching, and raised his eyebrows. She snatched her fingers from the duke's clasp and marched toward the house.

The next hour was full of introductions to the staff—one housekeeper, three footmen, three maids, and the cook—and Miranda did her best not to be overwhelmed. The house was beautiful, the servants well-trained. She had never imagined that she would ever enjoy such comfort. Wyldehaven watched her the entire time, so she struggled to keep her expression cool. She did not want him to believe he had turned her head by providing this lovely home for her and the baby—even if he had.

It was not permanent. He was not some handsome hero in a fairy tale, sweeping her off to his castle to live in peace and happiness forever. This was a temporary situation while he decided what to do about James. She had to remember that.

When the day came that she had to leave this wonderful home, she would do so knowing that James was well cared for and her promise to Lettie fulfilled.

Miranda went up to the third floor to look at the nursery. Wylde remained downstairs, the look on his face when she had asked if he was coming reminiscent of a man who had recently eaten bad meat. She, Thaddeus, Mrs. Cooper, and James went instead, guided by the upstairs maid. That young lady was called away within minutes and invited them to tour the area on their own.

James began to fuss, and Mrs. Cooper excused herself to see to the baby in the tiny bedroom, leaving Thaddeus and Miranda in the schoolroom area of the nursery.

"Well," he said. "Have you changed your mind?"

"About what?"

"About being a man's mistress." He looked around. "This is a fine house Wyldehaven has provided for you, Miranda. I cannot help but wonder what price you will pay for it."

"*You* encouraged me to take his offer!"

Thaddeus shrugged. "I thought you were simply being smart, letting a nob like the duke pay the bills until he found the courage to do what was right. But then I saw that little scene by the coach just now."

"I have no intention of sharing the duke's bed, Thaddeus. How can you think that? You know me better than that!"

He shrugged. "I can only go by what I see."

Anger sharpened her tone. "Speaking of what is seen, perhaps you might like to explain your dealings with the two ruffians who forced their way into the house the other day? Mint and Barney?"

"I must apologize for that. I never thought those two would take a joke so far." He gave her a placating smile.

She would not be pacified. "Thaddeus LeGrande, tell me you do not consider me that much of a simpleton."

His smile faded and he sighed. "Very well. They were not friends. I owe money to a fellow from a card game. He is not always patient."

"How much money?"

He drew himself up, clearly affronted. "Young woman, that is my affair."

She propped her hands on her hips. "My affair as well if these men think they can burst into your house and threaten us!"

"Now, now. Do not even think about it."

"How can I not, Thaddeus?"

"Because it is no longer your concern." He swept his hand to indicate their surroundings. "You live here now. You are out of danger."

"So there is danger."

He looked away from her direct gaze. "Wyldehaven will look after you now, Miranda. He will keep you safe."

"I am not Wyldehaven's responsibility. I am here for James and for no other reason."

Thaddeus gave a laugh. "Indeed. But does he know that? Have a care, Miranda, or you may yet lose your heart to him."

She jabbed a finger at him. "You stop hiding things from me that may put James in danger. *I* will see to my heart."

"Ah, dear Miranda, you forget I saw you out by the coach." He gave her a sad smile and patted her arm. "I believe it may already be too late."

Shadows skulked in the taproom of the tavern, though sunlight streamed down from the heavens outside the filthy windows. A cloaked figure lingered at the table in the corner, the hood of the garment concealing any hint of a face or figure. Only the hand clutching the handle of a tankard betrayed his sex as male.

Footsteps approached, then stopped beside the table. "Is this a joke?"

The hooded figure glanced up. "Sit down. You are attracting attention."

The newcomer gave a quick laugh and seated himself at the table. He glanced around and caught the attention of the barmaid. "Ale," he called out. She gave a quick nod and hurried to fetch him a tankard.

The hooded one glared at his companion. "You are supposed to be discreet."

"Is this what you call discreet?" With a hoot of amusement, the newcomer reached across and yanked back the other man's hood. "No one knows you here, my lord. And even if they did, they are all so sotted they would believe you an apparition. For what would the elegant and refined Viscount Linnet be doing in a tavern at the docks?"

Kit glared. "You never know who may talk to whom."

"You worry overmuch." The ale arrived, and Kit's companion gave the barmaid a lecherous grin and a fond swat on the backside as she turned away. "Life is for living, Linnet. And lately, I have been living well."

"You certainly have." Kit watched with distaste as the other man gulped back some of the ale and

144

swiped the back of his hand across his mouth. "But I believe it is time to stop the charade. Surely you have made enough money by now."

"So spoken by a man who has always had money at his fingertips." The newcomer sat back in his chair and gave Kit a smile that was familiar and chilling at the same time. "There is never enough."

Kit looked down at his ale to escape the penetrating stare. He must have been mad to accept this man's proposition so many months ago. How could he have been so foolish? Why had he allowed pride and jealousy to drive him into betraying one of his best friends?

"Never tell me you are suffering the weight of a conscience, Linnet?"

Kit glanced up again. "Of course not," he lied. "It is just—well, it was easy when Wylde was sequestered at his estate. Now that he is here in London, it might be dangerous to continue. What if he discovers who you are?"

The other man leaned forward, green eyes as hard as jade. "Are you implying that my dear brother the duke might actually look away from his bloody pianoforte long enough to unravel a plan that has been years in the making?"

"He has heard the stories. He has been receiving the bills—"

"And paying them!" The other man threw back

his head and roared with laughter. For an instant he looked so much like Wylde that Kit nearly forgot who he was talking to. But when the other man reached for the ale, still grinning with malicious glee, reality came home with the force of a bullet. This was Daniel Byrne, Wylde's bastard brother. He could have been Wylde's twin, except for those distinct green eyes.

And the fact that the man was a lunatic.

Dear God, what had he done?

"I just thought it might be prudent to stop for a while," Kit said. "At least until he has returned to Wyldehaven."

"Are you mad, Linnet? Having him here only adds to the challenge!" Byrne leaned across the table. "Unless you are afraid of what he will do when he finds out you have betrayed him."

Kit hoped he appeared nonchalant as he reached for his ale. "Of course not. My concern is for my own hide—and yours."

"That is something I can drink to!" Byrne lifted his tankard again.

Kit smiled and tapped his tankard against Byrne's, but inside he cringed from what he had become. He'd always seen Wyldehaven as a man who had everything, and could never understand why Wylde considered himself tortured by Fate. To his way of thinking, it was damned churlish of Wylde to bemoan the imperfection of his life when

146

he had so much wealth at his fingertips with which to soothe his ills.

Byrne had approached Kit at just the right moment, at a time when his father's financial strictures were strangling him, when he was eaten up with jealousy upon discovering that Michael had invited Wylde to go with him to India and did not include him. And when he asked Wylde if he could go along on the excursion, his old friend's refusal had been blunt.

His rage and hurt at being excluded overshadowed his common sense. Damn, but he had been an easy mark for a rogue like Daniel Byrne. What started as a way to get a little revenge—a share of the wealth and influence that Wylde enjoyed so casually—had turned into something completely different . . . and more dangerous.

And what did he have left? Michael was dead, and he was riddled with guilt as he watched Wylde deal with the mischief Byrne had wrought. And now Byrne's stunts were getting more daring. How long would it be before he went too far?

He should go to Wylde, confess, tell him where to find Daniel Byrne. But it would mean implicating himself—which would cost him Wylde's friendship forever. And that was a price he could not bear to pay.

He signaled to the barmaid. "More ale here!"

"Two," Byrne said, setting down his empty tankard.

Kit nodded and held up two fingers to the bar-maid. Then he turned back to Byrne—the devil he knew. "What is next in your plan?"

Byrne's lips parted in a slow, diabolical smile that made Kit's gut knot. "You are going to truly appreciate this . . ."

Chapter 9

~~~~~~~~~~~~~~~~~~~~~~~~

Why the devil were women so contrary?

Wylde stared out the window at the London gloom. Pages of his opera lay spread across the pianoforte, but his fingers did not itch for the keys as usual. Instead his thoughts were consumed by Miranda Fontaine.

What in Hades was wrong with him? She was just a woman—one with no prospects, at that. So she was comely. Many women were. So she had the voice of a seductress. The same could be said for many females treading the boards at Drury Lane. How was it that she caught his attention so completely, in a way no woman had since before his wife had died?

Was it the baby, the mere fact that she cared what happened to him? Or was it the fierce way she protected the child, not even backing down when he challenged her?

For some reason he had trouble staying vexed

with her, even when she tried him to the end of his patience.

She had come to his door begging for support for the baby she claimed was his. But perhaps begging was not the right word. Demanding was closer. She had arrived on his doorstep and demanded that he embrace this child as his own. Even in the face of outright rejection, she had not given up, passing herself off as an Italian countess, so she might perform for the upper ten thousand and provide for the child. Thank goodness he had nipped that in the bud! Such a vocation was in league with an opera dancer or an actress. Despite her humble circumstances, Miranda Fontaine was better than that.

But was she good enough for a duke?

Bloody hell, where had that come from? Was he going mad, imagining some romantic, star-crossed pairing with a female of unknown origins? She had not even had the good grace to thank him for providing a home and servants for her and the babe. He had expected some sort of gratitude yesterday— especially after that moment by the coach—when he had proudly opened the door of the townhouse. But she had marched into the building as if he had introduced her into a barnyard, her spine stiff and lips pursed with staunch disapproval.

It was all he could do not to kiss those lips into the sweet submission he had tasted earlier.

Instead he left her to her displeasure, satisfied that he had won that round. Miranda was living in a home he provided with servants to see to her needs. The wet nurse Mrs. Cooper had been hired to care for the child on a more permanent basis. He had done his duty to the babe. Once the authorities captured the imposter, he could arrange a more suitable arrangement, perhaps a cottage in the country.

Of course if he did that, he would never be able to see her with any regularity.

Damn and blast. He did not want her gone from his life.

A knock sounded at the door. He scowled, as his servants knew not to disturb him while he was in the music room. But then again, he had not been working on his music anyway.

"Come!" he called, well aware that his annoyance carried in his voice.

The door opened and Travers looked in. "My apologies, Your Grace, but Mr. Wallace is here."

"Has he found the blackguard already? That was fast work." He gathered his composition pages into a neat stack and set them on the desk. "Put him in my study, Travers. I shall be there directly."

"Very good, Your Grace."

When Wylde entered the study several minutes later, Wallace stood in front of his desk, fussing with his glasses, as was his habit. He looked up with some eagerness, quickly replacing his spectacles. "Good afternoon, Your Grace."

"Mr. Wallace, I trust you have news for me?"

"Indeed I do, indeed I do."

Wylde moved to sit behind his desk. "Very efficient of you, Wallace. So who is he?"

"He, sir? I have come today to talk about Miss Fontaine."

"Indeed?" His curiosity rose, which annoyed him greatly. She was just a woman, and a difficult one at that. She should not command so much of his attention.

"You did ask me to look into her background."

"I did."

Wallace pulled out a small journal. "She arrived in London almost a week ago. Before that she lived in a small sea town called Little Depping. Since arriving in London, she has been living in the home of Thaddeus LeGrande, an actor of some renown on the London stage."

"I am acquainted with Mr. LeGrande. And you might want to note that Miss Fontaine is no longer staying in his home. I moved her to one of my properties."

Wallace made a scribble in his notebook. "So noted, Your Grace. Shall I continue investigating Miss Fontaine, then?"

"Why would you not?"

Mr. Wallace cleared his throat but held Wylde's gaze squarely when he replied, "I was not certain if the lady's relationship with you was one of a private nature."

Wylde suppressed the glimmer of irritation with effort. "If you are inferring that she is my mistress, she is not. I am looking after her at the behest of my grandmother."

"Ah. Very well, then." Wallace pushed up his spectacles. "I just . . . one assumes . . . well, given that the young lady's mother was known to be a woman who gave her favors easily—"

Wylde leaned forward. "What are you implying, Wallace? That Miss Fontaine's mother was a lightskirt?"

Wallace's face reddened. "Ah . . . she was, Your Grace, at least in the last years before she died."

"The devil you say!" Utterly shocked, Wylde sat back. Never would he have imagined such a thing. He'd known she had some mystery in her past, but assumed it was a romance gone sour or just simple poverty. Could she be an opportunist after all?

Wallace shifted his feet. "Actually, it is quite a common tale, Your Grace. Miranda Fontaine's mother was the actress Fannie Fontaine. She caused quite a stir on Drury Lane before she disappeared from London some twenty years ago."

"Who is Miss Fontaine's father? I am assuming

Fannie Fontaine left London because she was with child."

"I believe that is the case, Your Grace, but no one I spoke to can name the father. It was all quite secretive."

"Who did you speak to, Wallace? I admit you have stunned me with your quick response to my query."

"The servants who work for Mrs. Weatherby," Wallace said. "However, that lady herself proved quite knowledgeable on the matter."

"Mrs. Weatherby! Did I not specifically tell you not to interrogate her?"

"You did, Your Grace, but she came to me while I was questioning her staff. She offered the information of her own volition."

"Indeed?" Wylde tapped his fingers on the desk. "A very interesting situation. Perhaps she recalls Fannie Fontaine."

"A possibility, sir. I will continue to investigate if you require it."

"Perhaps." He pondered the matter. When he had believed Miranda to be an opportunist after some quick money, it seemed ethical to have her investigated. However, now that he knew her a bit, he had to admit that he felt a bit guilty for looking into her past.

Still, according to Wallace's findings she was the daughter of an actress turned prostitute, one whose father had not chosen to acknowledge her. This would imply a life lacking in comfort. Had she seized an opportunity to better her lot by claiming Lettie Dupree's child at birth?

Blast it all. Just when he believed that he had uncovered the woman's true character, facts arose to throw doubt into the mix.

Did he continue the investigation or did he order Wallace to cease?

"Is that all you have learned?" he asked.

"There is more, Your Grace, though not about Miss Fontaine."

"About the imposter, then?"

"No, sir. During my investigation of Miss Fontaine, I naturally looked into the background of Mr. Thaddeus LeGrande."

"I am acquainted with Mr. LeGrande."

"I have discovered that he has been the trustee for an investment account in Miss Fontaine's name. Recently the account was closed, but I am told substantial withdrawals were taken from it over the past few years."

"And yet Miss Fontaine only arrived in London recently." Wylde scowled as he realized the implication. "LeGrande is indebted to one of the most ruthless moneylenders in London."

"He is a gamester, Your Grace."

"Indeed he is. And his luck has not been good lately."

"Would you like me to observe his movements?"

Wylde pondered the idea for a moment. "No, I will speak to him myself. I would like you to continue to follow the imposter."

"Very good, Your Grace."

A knock came at the door. Wylde frowned as Travers poked his head in. "My apologies, Your Grace, but there are some callers who demand to see you."

"Tell them—"

"We shall speak to His Grace immediately!" Two women pushed past the servant and into the room. "How dare you attempt to avoid us, Wyldehaven! After what you did!"

Wylde slowly got to his feet. "Lady Nantwick, Mrs. Colley. How may I be of assistance?"

"Assistance!" Lady Nantwick, an overly plump bear of a woman, strode forward, her oversized bosom heaving with outrage and her face red with temper. "You may account for the damage you have done to Clarise's new curricle, you scoundrel!"

"Your new curricle?" Aware of Wallace quietly retreating to a spot out of the ladies' way, Wylde looked at Lady Nantwick's bony, horse-faced companion and noted she was paler than usual. "Madam, I am afraid you have me at a disadvantage."

"Mr. Colley has finally received his inheritance

from his distant cousin," Lady Nantwick said before Mrs. Colley could open her mouth. "He has bought her a fine new curricle that was delivered just this morning."

"Congratulations, Mrs. Colley," Wylde said. "However, I cannot understand how your new curricle pertains to me."

"Because you caused the accident!" Lady Nantwick declared, stabbing a finger at him.

Wylde cast a glance at Wallace, awful suspicion creeping through him, then returned his attention to Mrs. Colley. "What accident?"

"The one in Hyde Park just this afternoon," Lady Nantwick said. "You and that devil's stallion of yours ran us off the trail while you were racing with that young pup Westermann. The wheel broke, and Clarise and I were almost killed!"

"I was not in Hyde Park today," Wylde said.

"Do not even attempt to deny it," Lady Nantwick warned, shaking her finger at him. "I have known you since you were in the nursery, Wyldehaven, and I cannot condone such behavior. What will your grandmother say?"

"I am certain I cannot imagine. What time did this occur?"

"I do not understand the need for foolish questions," Lady Nantwick said with a huff. "Clearly it is obvious that Clarise and I were touring the park at the very fashionable hour of four o'clock so that all of the ton could observe her new curricle."

"Of course you were." Wylde caught Wallace's eye and inclined his head toward the door. The runner gave an imperceptible nod and quietly left the room.

"I cannot fathom what you were about, racing through the park at such speed. And at such an hour! Why, we could have been killed!"

Wylde looked past Lady Nantwick. "Mrs. Colley, was the carriage badly damaged?"

"It was," Lady Nantwick said.

Wylde pinned her with an impatient glance. "Lady Nantwick, I was speaking to Mrs. Colley."

"Dear Clarise is overset." Lady Nantwick went to her comrade and placed an arm around her shoulders. "She needs her friends around her."

"How lucky that you were with her." Wylde took a step forward that edged Lady Nantwick aside and left him facing Clarise Colley. "Mrs. Colley, what happened?"

"Well, I never!" Lady Nantwick gasped.

Wylde cast her a hard look that had her clamping her lips closed.

"The carriage," Mrs. Colley whispered. Her pale blue eyes looked huge in her face, and the look of accusation she gave him sent guilt curling through his gut, though he had done nothing wrong. "My husband told me to wait for him."

"There, there, Clarise." Lady Nantwick shoved her way between the two of them, patting Clarise's arm. "His Grace will take responsibility for his actions, of that I am certain. He will make things right with Mr. Colley." Her glare dared Wylde to contradict her. "You should be ashamed of yourself, Wyldehaven. If her coachman had not acted quickly, the curricle would have overturned and someone would have been injured."

"I hurt my arm," Mrs. Colley whispered, lowering her shawl to show him a nasty scrape along her forearm.

His anger ebbed. However trying the situation, these ladies were innocent victims of the imposter.

"Clarise, why did you not tell me?" Lady Nantwick marched to the door and opened it, but Wylde took two strides and blocked her before she could summon a servant. Lady Nantwick opened her mouth to protest, eyes sparking with fury.

"See to Mrs. Colley," he said quietly, then looked at the footman standing in the hallway. "Please send Mrs. Bentley with some water and bandages."

"Yes, Your Grace." The footman scurried away. Wylde met Lady Nantwick's gaze.

"And what about the curricle?" she demanded.

"I will take care of the matter. Please, allow my staff to see you to the parlor while we wait for my housekeeper to bring the bandages. And Lady

Nantwick, if you would kindly refresh my memory of what happened?"

She sniffed. "At least you are willing to do what is right."

He merely nodded, resigned to once again be judged guilty without trial. "I try."

"Mrs. Langston is one of the richest widows in London," Thaddeus whispered as he and Miranda made their way across the crowded salon toward the lady in question. "She has specifically requested an introduction."

"I try not to anticipate anything," Miranda said, but inside she was quivering with excitement. Every new performance brought her one step closer to total freedom, to a time where she could be financially independent without compromising any of her principles or succumbing to the whims of a man.

The memory of Wyldehaven's kiss crept into her thoughts, and she ruthlessly pushed it aside. The fact that he had moved her into a home he paid for still chafed. If not for James, she would never have tolerated such boldness. But until she accumulated enough funds to live comfortably and support a child, she had no choice but to bide her time.

Dear God, she hated waking every day wondering if today was the day Wyldehaven would either tire of James and send him away or decide that she should show her gratitude for his generosity with other, more personal, favors. And she feared her answer if pressed.

The contessa would provide enough income so she could make her own decisions about her life, but the illusion could not protect her heart should Wylde turn his full power of seduction on her.

"Mrs. Langston," Thaddeus said, coming to a halt beside the handsome woman who stood talking with Mrs. Weatherby. "May I present the Contessa della Pietra?"

"Contessa!" Mrs. Langston clapped her hands together. "I am so pleased to meet you. I simply must have you perform at my dinner party on Tuesday. Do tell me you are not already engaged."

Miranda glanced at Thaddeus, who gave an imperceptible nod, indicating her schedule was free. "I would be most delighted, Mrs. Langston."

"Splendid! And you, Mr. LeGrande." She gave him a playful tap on his arm with her fan. "Do escort me to the refreshment table."

"It will be my honor." Gallantly offering his arm, Thaddeus escorted the woman away, leaving Miranda blinking at the mercurial temperament of her new patron.

"You have become all the rage, Contessa," Mrs. Weatherby said.

"Thanks to you," Miranda replied. "It was you who provided the opportunity."

Mrs. Weatherby smiled, her famous blue eyes sparkling with humor. "I remember what it felt like to crave that chance to make something of myself." She lowered her voice. "I don't know if you are aware, but I was born a fisherman's daughter. I spent most of my life outside the doors of Society—at least the acceptable part. The gentlemen enjoyed my company quite well, while their wives crossed the street when they saw me. And then Mr. Weatherby decided to spurn convention and make me his wife."

"And everything changed for you."

Mrs. Weatherby gave a bark of laughter. "Hardly, my dear! I was quite horribly ostracized . . . but then dear Allen passed away and left me a wealthy widow. And suddenly I had more 'friends' than I could count." She glanced around the room. "I decided to use my newfound position to help others in my position. Others like you."

It had been so long since anyone had expressed concern for her welfare that Miranda blinked back the sudden sting of tears. She glanced around at the crowd to compose herself. "I wish there were more people in the world like you."

"Now, dear." Mrs. Weatherby took a handkerchief from her reticule and handed it to her. "You must not have red eyes when you perform."

Miranda laughed and surreptitiously dabbed at her eyes. "Heaven forbid."

"Use your beauty and your talent, dear girl. It will

162

take you far in this world. I predict you will have a great career on the stage."

"No." Miranda shook her head and twisted the handkerchief in her fingers. "I have no desire to join the theater. I am content to sing at private functions, nothing more."

Mrs. Weatherby gaped. "Are you mad? You could easily become the most sought-after performer in London. It is a great opportunity."

"I have no desire for fame, Mrs. Weatherby."

"I admit I am astonished. Your mother certainly had the highest of aspirations."

Miranda froze. "I beg your pardon?"

"Your mother. We were friends, you know, at least until she disappeared from London so suddenly." Mrs. Weatherby lowered her voice. "Dear Thaddeus told me who you were that first night—as if I could not figure it out for myself! You are the very image of Fannie, my girl."

Miranda could only stare, fear nearly suffocating her. Would Mrs. Weatherby reveal her deception? If the world discovered she was not who she claimed to be, her chance to make enough money to keep James would be gone. All she would have left would be the whims of Wyldehaven.

Her face must have revealed her panic, for Mrs. Weatherby reached out to pat her hand. "Have no fear, my dear. Your secret is safe with me."

"Thank you," Miranda managed.

"Now come along, Contessa. Mrs. Langston is eager to see you perform."

"Mrs. Weatherby, my name is Miranda."

The older woman smiled. "And you may call me Lizzie."

"Lizzie, then."

They began to make their way through the crowded salon. Miranda smiled at those they passed, but as they neared the piano, one woman stared at her with an intensity that nearly made her falter. The elegantly dressed blonde looked to be past her prime, but clearly had once been a great beauty. Her eyes were a stunning green, her poise perfect, and her figure looked to be that of a much younger woman. A beauty mark near the corner of her mouth drew attention to her classic bone structure. She did not smile.

A younger version of the woman stood nearby, her youth evident in her glowing skin and the excited sparkle in her eyes. She was dressed completely in white, as befitted a debutante.

Mother and daughter, Miranda thought. But why did the mother stare so intensely?

Deciding to ignore the odd behavior, she made her way past the group to the pianoforte. Then someone from behind her gasped. Miranda glanced back to see the older woman sink to the floor in a swoon, the young girl frantically attending her. She paused.

"No, no." Mrs. Weatherby urged her along even as Miranda tried to gauge the situation. "The servants are tending to Lady Rothgard. The heat in here, you know. Do not let this interrupt the entertainment."

"Very well." Feeling odd about continuing on as if nothing had happened, she followed Mrs. Weatherby to the pianoforte, more than aware of the disturbance she left behind.

"Why did I let you talk me into coming here?" Wyldehaven strode up the stairs to Mrs. Weatherby's house.

"Because you are still in a foul mood over Mrs. Colley's curricle, and I thought it would amuse you," Kit said, keeping pace with him. "You must have the deepest pockets in Christendom to keep paying for things you did not purchase. Why did you simply not deny that you were in the park this afternoon?"

"Because I do have deep pockets, and because it is not Mrs. Colley's fault that some madman ruined her new carriage. Someone must make restitution."

"But why you? This is what I cannot comprehend."

Wyldehaven lifted the door knocker and rapped, then looked back at Kit. "Because he does it in my name. I do not want to make matters worse."

"But—"

"Understand me, Kit. When I find this blackguard, he will sorely regret crossing me." The door opened and Wylde stepped through, with Kit right behind.

"But you are making it easy for him to take advantage of you." Kit grabbed his arm and pulled him to a stop in the middle of Mrs. Weatherby's hallway. "By simply paying the bill whenever he commits one of these mad acts, you might as well be admitting guilt to the ton."

"In the end I will triumph."

"What if he does something worse than crash a curricle or run up tailoring bills?" Kit demanded. "What if he hurts someone?"

Thinking of Annie, Wylde said, "I will take care of that, too." He continued down the hallway, forcing Kit to hurry to keep up with him.

"Blast it, Wylde, but you are a cool one. If this were happening to me, I would be halfway to Bedlam by now. Just . . ." Kit hesitated, appearing to wrestle with his words. "Have a care, will you?"

Noting the genuine distress in his friend's eyes, Wylde forced a smile. "I am on my guard, Kit."

"Good. See that you are. I fear the worst is yet to come from this trickster."

"You are not alone in that." They reached the door to the salon, which was ceremoniously thrown open by a footman just as a gong rang from within the room.

Kit and Wylde stepped through the doorway and paused. Mrs. Weatherby stood next to the pianoforte by the window, a broad smile on her face. "Ladies and gentlemen, kind guests, it is my pleasure to once more welcome to the Thursday night salon the Contessa della Pietra!"

Applause rang out, and Miranda, dressed in exquisite sapphire, stepped over to the instrument.

Wylde stared, disbelieving. What was the impetuous wench up to now? He had only yesterday presented her with an elegant London town house in which to live, with servants to see to her every need. Why was she here, then, singing for her supper as if she had no other prospects?

Damn him for a fool. Was Miranda Fontaine using him?

"What is your game?" he murmured. "Whatever it is, I will put an end to it."

As if she had heard him, Miranda turned her head to look at Wylde. One moment of quivering emotion stretched between them. Then she turned her head away and launched into song.

What in heaven's name was he doing here?

Her fingers trembled on the keys, but she managed to keep her composure throughout the piece, pretending for all she was worth that the Duke of Wyldehaven was not watching her every breath with those dark, angry eyes. She had done nothing wrong. He knew about the contessa; there was no reason to feel guilty.

But he looked at her as if he wanted to tear her away from the pianoforte and drag her from the room, whether for violence or passion, she could not tell.

She remembered his animosity when he had thought her disguise was a ruse designed to defraud his friends. He had demanded that she cease at once. Surely, now that they had come to an agreement about James, he did not still believe that?

Another glance at him. His gaze had not wavered, his entire body rigid.

Dear God, he had *not* realized that she would continue as the contessa. And she had not realized that he would still disapprove.

Without a word to anyone, Wylde turned and left, passing Mrs. Weatherby and her servants as they discreetly assisted the still pale Lady Rothgard from the salon.

Mrs. Weatherby looked up as he passed, poised to offer a greeting, but puzzlement flickered across her features as he strode out without a word. His friend Kit loped after him.

Miranda managed to finish her performance, motivated by the approving smile on Mrs. Langston's face. But the night had lost its magic for her. She did not want any more complications with Wyldehaven, and she certainly did not want his enmity.

But as she took her leave of the salon that night, his displeasure still haunted her. And later, when she was alone in her rooms, she found reason to wonder if she had pushed him too far.

A note had been delivered to the kitchen door and left for her by one of the servants. A chill shimmered through her as she read it.

LEAVE LONDON OR DIE

Chapter 10

After breakfast, Wylde summoned his gleaming black coach with the ducal coat of arms emblazoned on the doors and gave the direction of Miss Miranda Fontaine to his coachman.

He sat back against the luxurious seat, staring blindly as London sped by him, the gray morning matching the gloom inside him.

Damn her. How foolish could he be, believing that she would put herself into his hands, allow her to care for her? No, she had to use pretense to assuage her greed, singing for gold like a common opera dancer. He hated that she'd played on his emotions. That she'd made him want her.

Everything about her shouted that she was not the right type of woman for a duke. Liar or innocent, virgin or siren, he could not decide. Every time he saw her, she appeared to wear a different face. Which one was the real Miranda Fontaine?

If she wanted to play games with him, so be it.

She was an opportunist, just waiting for chances to make money from other people's desires. But he was the Duke of Wyldehaven, more than a match for a young woman of uncertain birth, no matter how clever she was.

He had decided he wanted her in his bed. He had heard her protests, understood her reasoning to keep distance between them. However, she was the first woman in years to make him take notice of the world beyond his piano keys. When he was with Miranda, he felt alive in a way he had not felt since he was an untried youth, eager to make his mark on the world.

She was a mystery that begged to be solved, and he could not resist her lure. But he would not be toyed with. They would take their pleasure of each other, but he would guard both his heart and his fortune. When their liaison was over, he would send her on her way with no regrets.

Miranda was in the middle of breakfast when Wyldehaven arrived. The maid showed him into the breakfast room and escaped as quickly as possible, leaving him in the doorway, facing Miranda. With one look, he dismissed the footman standing nearby.

"I had expected you to be finished with breakfast by now," he said as the servant scurried from the room and closed the door behind him.

"I stayed abed this morning." She looked away first, shrugged. "Late evening."

He stiffened. "A liaison?"

"Do not be ridiculous." She curled her lip and focused on her breakfast. "Who are you to ask me such a question?"

"I am Wyldehaven." He strolled into the room and claimed a chair at the head of the table. He noticed the annoyance flash across her face, and found it most gratifying.

"All well and good, but you are not my master. I thought we had discussed this already."

"*You* discussed. I do not remember my opinion being sought." He took his ease in the chair, stretching his feet out beneath the table and folding his hands over his midriff. "Tell me why you were at the salon last night when I specifically warned you about pretending to be someone you are not."

"It is not your concern."

"It is when you are living in a house I provide."

Her chin lifted. "I told you I protested this situation. It is bad enough I am living in your house, Wyldehaven; I cannot depend on you for everything. I must earn my own way."

"I have money. It makes sense to use it."

"Not when you could cut me off at any moment. I will be dependent on no man."

"You already rely on my good will to allow you

to stay with the baby." He slowly straightened in his chair, part of him taking perverse pleasure in the wary way she watched him. "What if I were to pay you to be a governess for James?"

She remained silent for a moment, then said, "Until now, I had hoped for that very thing. But I have recently come to realize that I must have income outside of your influence."

"And this is the path you have chosen." He managed not to smile. Apparently she was vulnerable to him, else she would take his offer without a qualm. "What is to stop me from taking James away forever? Sending him to an orphanage? Where would that leave you?"

If looks could burn, he would have been charred to a crisp. "I am more than aware of such a possibility, which is why I *must* have my own income."

"As long as the source of that income does not include fleecing my friends."

"I do not 'fleece' anyone. I perform under another name, just like many others on the stage today."

"I do not like it." He stood and came to her side of the table, then leaned over, jerked her chair around to face him, and caged her with one hand on each chair arm. "I am the one with the power here, Miranda. If I wished it, you would never see the boy again."

He caught the flicker of fear that crossed her face and found himself impressed by how quickly she suppressed it.

She glared at the hands that imprisoned her. "You have spoken much about being different, Your Grace, and yet now I see you are like every other man, wanting only your own way, no matter who is hurt in the process."

"If that were true I would have cast you into the street the first time I saw you. Instead I am providing for you. Is that the act of a selfish man?"

"If you expect me to pay for your largesse by sharing your bed, then yes, it is."

"I have not noticed a woman since the death of my wife." The words burst forth before he could stop them, but the glimpse of pleased surprise on her face outweighed any regrets. He slid a finger down her cheek. "We are an explosive combination, Miranda. Why do you resist what is so natural? Are you not curious?"

"I will not turn my back on what is right just for a moment's pleasure." She leaned away from his touch.

He dropped his hand and closed his fingers into a fist. "And seducing men with your voice is right? How is that different from the women who display their charms more obviously?"

She reared up and slapped his face. The sharp crack stunned them both.

He rubbed his cheek as he straightened. "I am sorry. That was rude."

"You do not know me." Her response was so low,

he had to strain to hear it. Her hands fisted in her lap, twisting the simple muslin of her morning dress. "I have done what I must to survive in this world, despite the immoral actions of those around me. I have sworn a promise to Lettie to see her son cared for." Her eyes burned with determination, and a glimmer of tears, as she held his gaze. "And I will see it through."

"And your way of seeing it through is singing for coin."

"What else can I do?" she demanded. "I cannot accept money from you, not while I live in your house. It comes too close to a boundary I do not intend to cross."

"I would be pleased if you did cross it—with me."

Her sharp glare conveyed her opinion of that suggestion. "I can become a laundress and work for pennies. I can read and cipher, but what man would hire me to be his clerk? If you will not be a father to James, then I am all he has, and I must find a way to provide for us without imperiling my life or my virtue."

He stepped back. "Can you not see that this path is no better than any other for a woman alone?"

"I am not alone. Thaddeus is helping me."

"Thaddeus?" He barked a laugh. "Dear girl, Thaddeus LeGrande has his own problems. The man is completely done in."

She surged to her feet. "Thaddeus has helped me from the beginning. The contessa was his idea, and I thank him for it."

"How is it you have so much faith in a man you barely know?"

She put her hands on her hips. "He is an old family friend."

"Your mother's friend?" he asked with soft menace. "Fannie's friend?"

She stilled. "What do you know of my mother?"

"I know she was beautiful." Secure that the power had swung back to him, Wylde clasped his hands behind his back. "Fannie Fontaine, the sensation of the London stage. Then she disappeared from London, never to return."

"Who told you?" she whispered. "Thaddeus?"

"I make it my business to know these things."

Angry color rose in her cheeks. "You had me investigated?"

Rather than engage in another battle of tempers, he replied, "A woman comes to my door with a claim that I fathered a child with a female I never met. Then that very night, the same woman is introduced to me with a completely different name. I am a rich man. What would you do?"

She was quiet for a long moment. "I can see where that might look suspicious," she conceded.

"Indeed." He continued, "I assume when Fannie left London, it was because she was with child?"

Miranda nodded.

"And you do not know who your father is?"

"No. She never spoke of him. I know only that he was a peer."

"Now I understand why you defend James so vehemently," he said.

"What else is there to do?" she demanded. "At least I had my mother. James had no one, except me, and I promised Lettie that I would see to it that his father took responsibility for him."

"A noble undertaking for certain." He leaned forward. "I am not his father."

"Lettie said you were."

He sighed. "There is a man who looks like me, who was been pretending to *be* me. He has caused no end of trouble."

Rather than scoff as he expected, she just tilted her head and said, "Forgive me, Wyldehaven, but as I said before, that seems somewhat fantastical."

"I know it is. I have spent the past few weeks shouting my innocence into the wind, only to be ignored. This fellow looks like me and knows my habits. And he is clever enough to stay clear of anyone who knows me well."

"And he is James's father."

"It is the only explanation. I *know* I was cloistered at Wyldehaven during the time the boy was conceived. Forgive me for my indelicacy, but there is no other way to say it. This blackguard had started off with small mischief, so I never caught wind of it until I returned to London just recently." He paused as an idea occurred to him. "Did Lettie ever say anything about James's father? I assume you never met him yourself."

"I did not. Lettie was already several months along with child when she returned to Little Depping." Her cheeks pinkened as she said it, and she could not meet his eyes.

He found her modesty both charming and erotic at the same time. Would she blush that way the first time she disrobed for a man?

For him?

"She used to talk about you sometimes," Miranda continued, drawing him back from his imaginings. "How you would arrive after the performance in a plain hack and meet her at the stage door of the theater."

"A hack?"

Miranda shrugged. "Lettie assumed you wanted to avoid the gossips."

"Or *he* did not have his own coach."

"*You* are a private man, Wyldehaven, and you hate gossip. It does not seem such a strange explanation."

"I have more than enough carriages, should I choose to be discreet about something," he said. "Did this fellow provide a house for her? A carriage?

178

Jewels? These are typical of a man taking a mistress under his protection."

"No."

"Where did they go when they were together? Her rooms? His?"

Her brow furrowed with dawning realization. "She never went to his home, and she could not bring anyone to hers, as she shared rooms with another actress."

"Then where were they alone together?"

"I am certain I do not know." Blushing furiously now, she waved a hand as if to ward off the question. "You more than I would know where you and Lettie went to be alone."

"It was not me, Miss Fontaine." He leaned forward and captured her gaze. "A man like me has more than one home should I want seclusion. I have a yacht. I also have enough money to procure a house for my mistress in short order. So there are more than enough private places for me to take a woman, places that are not manned by strangers who would sell my privacy for a couple of shillings. My servants are well paid for their discretion. And I would never take a *hack*, especially to entertain a lady."

"You did secure this residence very quickly," she conceded. "And I imagine you could have set up Lettie in style had you chosen to do so. But you must admit that your story sounds like something out of a novel."

"I know." Keeping a tight rein on his frustration, he said, "Perhaps it would help you to know that my father was known to be miserly in discretion and liberal with his seed. I have half siblings arriving on my doorstep every week. It is my belief that this imposter is one of them."

"A brother who looks like you?"

"Yes. It would explain a lot of things."

"Including the Matherton toes."

"Exactly." He gave her a lopsided grin. "I am not the villain you think me."

Miranda looked into his dark eyes, and her insides slowly melted. He appeared so earnest, so genuine. Dared she believe this madness?

"For the sake of argument, let us say you are right, and you are not James's father. Why did you do all this?" She gestured to the house. "For your grandmother?"

He stepped to the window, looked down at the street. "As I said, James's father might well be my brother, however illegitimate. That makes James my nephew—my family. It is my duty to take care of my family."

His voice caught, just a hint. He continued to stare at the street, but his hands, still clasped behind his back, revealed white knuckles for just a moment.

She could feel the distress coming off him like strong perfume. "Do you always protect the Mathertons, even if they are not trueborn?"

He nodded. Then cleared his throat and turned to face her. "As I said, my father's indiscretions find their way to my doorstep on a regular basis. I have always provided my half siblings with a settlement to begin a life. After all, it was not their choice to be born. It was my father's carelessness."

She drifted closer to him, fascinated by the riot of sentiment she could see in his eyes. His voice was calm, his posture straight and correct, but she could sense the hot cauldron of emotion just waiting to boil over. "If you are determined to do right by James, why not just accept him into your household?"

"I cannot."

She stopped an arm's length away. She could not completely stifle the accusation in her tone. "Because he is not a trueborn Matherton?"

"No." He clenched his jaw. "Because I could not bear it."

The few curt words conveyed his pain as if he had shouted it.

"Many men are uncomfortable around children," she said.

"That is not the reason." He tried to smile, but his torment showed through. "I lost my own son, and I do not believe I could love another."

"Of course you could. The heart is capable of all different kinds of love."

He shook his head. "I am not like you. I cannot

181

just reach out—" He extended his hand and cupped her cheek. "—and pull someone into my heart."

She licked her dry lips, utterly conscious of his warm flesh against her face. Her instincts urged her to nuzzle his hand, to step closer, to curl into his embrace. But she resisted—barely. "You are afraid."

"Leave it to a woman to say that." He laughed and dropped his hand. "I failed to protect my unborn child. I will not take the chance of that happening again."

"I am certain you will marry again, have more children."

"No." He shook his head. "I have been lonely for nearly two years, locked at my estate, lost in my music. Mourning the death of a dream I can never have."

"Oh, Wyldehaven." She could not stop herself and closed the distance between them, laying a hand on his arm. "Perhaps the dream is not dead—just delayed."

He gave a reluctant chuckle and patted her hand. "Perhaps. Or perhaps I am meant to be alone."

"A person can be quite comfortable alone. No obligations, no one to act as judge. Quite freeing, actually." She smiled at him. "But you do not want that, do you? You want a family. You should have what you want."

"I know what I want." He scooped up her fingers and entwined them with his. Their palms pressed against each other. No gloves, just warm flesh. His hand nearly swallowed hers.

"Wyldehaven—"

"I was not lying to you when I told you that you are the only woman I have noticed since the death of my wife," he murmured, circling her waist with his other arm and tugging her against him. He pressed their clasped hands to his heart. "Everything about you captures my attention and will not let go."

"Oh," was all she could manage. She had fought off the drunken attentions of men in the past, utterly repulsed by their groping hands, but Wylde's embrace was something entirely new. She could feel his heart pounding beneath their joined hands, the scent of him luring her closer instead of repelling her. He was so much bigger than she was, his body so dissimilar to hers. But not dangerous. Not threatening. Oh, no. The differences between them fascinated as much as it thrilled. Instincts she did not recognize flared to life within her, demanding she get closer to him.

"You are so beautiful," he murmured. "And spirited. You do not hesitate to tell me to go to the devil."

"I am certain I never said that," she managed.

"You have, just not with words. You say 'Yes, Your

183

Grace' with your lips, and 'To the devil with you' with your eyes. It distracts me to no end." His hand slid up her back and splayed between her shoulder blades.

"I shall endeavor to be more discreet."

"Oh, no, do not do that." He bent his head, nuzzled her neck beneath her ear. "I like knowing I have such an effect on you."

The sweep of his lips along her neck sent sensations rioting throughout her body from head to toes and back again, like a ricocheting bullet. She gasped, her eyes closing as the delicious vibrations made her head spin. He kissed her neck—oh, scandal!—and then came the subtle scrape of his teeth against the sensitive flesh.

"Dear God," she whispered.

"You are so soft," he murmured. "So warm. You do not hide your emotions."

He made his way down and around, licking her— *licking her*—at the base of her throat. So close to her bosom. What was wrong with her breasts? They swelled above the laces of her corset, as if pouting for him to touch them. Good heavens—she really did long for such a thing! She had seen men groping women's bosoms at the tavern, but never had she imagined that the women enjoyed it!

He untangled their fingers and flattened her hand against his chest, then encircled her with both arms, pulling her fully against him.

Her body sang with joy, hunger surging up like a beast and demanding to be fed. She clung to his neck as he dipped his head down and strung kisses along the edge of her bodice. She heard a strange sound, like whimpering, then realized it was coming from her own throat. She clutched his neck with both hands, clinging to him as sensations stormed her body.

"Beautiful woman," he murmured, cupping her breast in one hand. He rubbed his thumb against the hardened nipple through the thin cloth, and her hips jerked against him of their own accord, a keening cry coming from between her lips. He shifted and swallowed the sound into his own mouth.

His kiss blasted through any lingering rational thought. He cupped her breast, massaged it, even squeezed it as he coaxed her lips to open to him, teased her with his tongue. Her brain nearly exploded when he nipped her lower lip, then sucked on it.

Dear God . . . why had no one told her such pleasure was possible?

Coherence quickly faded as he touched her in places no one had ever touched her before. Her modest lace fichu fluttered helplessly to the floor as he slipped his hand into her bodice, past her chemise, tugging the material down to release her naked breasts to the morning sunshine. He backed her against the breakfast table, the edge pressing against her bottom and thighs. She opened her mouth to protest . . . to question . . . maybe to beg for more. Then his mouth closed over her aching nipple, and words fell away with the burst of bliss that rattled through her.

He lifted her to sit on the table, nudging aside a chair that nearly fell over in his enthusiasm. He switched his suckling to the other breast, kneading the first in his strong hand, thumb teasing her hard, peaking nipple. She could barely breathe, barely keep up with the jumble of sensations that scrambled her wits and enflamed her loins. Dear sweet God in heaven, she wanted . . . needed . . . . God help her, if this man did not do *something* to end this wicked torment . . .

He tugged at her skirts, easing them up. His hand slipped beneath, gliding along her stockings, then finding the vulnerable flesh of her thighs. Her breath caught. She opened her eyes, glanced down at him. His mouth worked first one nipple, then the other. Then he glanced up, met her gaze, held it as he eased his hand between her thighs.

The breath caught in her lungs. Surely her heart stopped. Then it pounded like thunder as he slid his finger along the most private part of her.

She shook like a newly born foal, arching toward him, parting her trembling legs to help him. All the while he watched her, teasing the sensitive folds with superb skill that melted her will like butter.

"There you are," he murmured, gently stroking her. "Ah, Miranda. You are exquisite." He brushed a kiss against her lips just as he flicked his thumb across her sensitive folds. She moaned, the sound caught in his mouth as he softly slid his finger inside her.

Her hips arched off the table; her eyes closed. He held her securely, teasing her with shallow dips of his finger between her legs. All the while his thumb danced, then rubbed against that one spot that made her see stars behind her closed lids. Sometimes he kissed her mouth. Sometimes he licked her breasts. She was lost now, so lost to the clamoring demands of this unfamiliar body that did not feel like her own and yet was.

Pressure, such incredible pressure. Everything throbbed, swelled. She was racing toward something, desperate. "Please," she whispered. And again, "Please." And again.

"Yes, sweet Miranda. Yes, this is what you want."

Then he did something, a twist of his hand or a flick of a finger, and her body shattered into a million pieces right there in the breakfast room amid the teacups and china.

"Good girl," he murmured. "Good, good girl."

For long moments she was lost, drifting, floating in the sea or the sky or somewhere. Eventually—

minutes, hours?—the steady throbbing of her heartbeat brought her back to herself. She opened her eyes, blinking against the sunlight streaming through the breakfast room windows.

"You are so beautiful, Miranda." He touched her hair, her cheek, trailed his fingers down her throat to her breasts, still bared to him. "You are truly magnificent in your passion, my sweet Amazon queen."

"No one told me." Her voice sounded hoarse, unused. She raised a trembling hand to touch his thick dark hair, as she had always wanted to. "No one told me it could be like that."

"That and more." He pressed a gentle kiss to her lips. "That was but a taste, my sweet. Just a brief glimpse into the passion that awaits you."

"Did you . . . did we?" She struggled to lift up onto her elbows and glanced down, almost afraid of what she would see. But he was still fully dressed, though her own clothing was tugged and pulled and in total disarray. "You did not . . . ?"

"Your virtue is intact." He gave her that lopsided grin again, his dark eyes glinting with humor and still simmering with lust. "The breakfast room is no place for a lady to surrender her virtue. I endeavor toward a more romantic setting."

"Oh, my God." Surrender her virtue? What had she done? She struggled into a sitting position, and he, gentleman that he was, assisted her.

"This is only the beginning, my sweet. Now that you are here, we can have this and so much more, any time we want."

His words sent dismay creeping through her. What had come over her? What had she been thinking? Had she been thinking *at all*?

She shoved her skirt down over her limbs, and he helped, spreading the creased muslin so it covered her completely. Leaving him to that, she urgently tugged up the edge of her chemise to the point of decency, then the bodice of her dress. Without the fichu, the garment exposed far too much of her bosom for the morning hours, but there was nothing to be done about it. He had already seen all she attempted to conceal.

Oh, God, dear sweet God in heaven. Thaddeus had been right. She *was* in danger of losing her heart—and more—to Wyldehaven.

She made to climb down from her perch, and he was there to help her, hooking her around the waist and lifting her off the table. The instant her feet touched the floor, he would have swept her into his arms, but she held out both hands, stopping him with her palms flat against his chest.

He grinned down at her, resting his hands on her waist. "Dizzy, are you?"

"Incensed," she corrected, then gave a hard shove.

He stumbled a step backward, releasing her. "What madness is this?"

"*This* was the madness," she corrected, sweeping a hand toward the table. "I told you I will not share your bed, Wyldehaven, and I meant it."

His eyes narrowed. "More games from you, Miranda?"

"No games." She crossed her arms over her partially exposed bosom, feeling naked in the bright light of the morning sun despite being fully dressed. "I told you there is a boundary I will not cross. I came very close to crossing it this morning. Thank goodness I regained my wits."

"Is that how you see it?" She had expected anger, but instead he smiled, a dark, predatory, *male* smile that both thrilled and threatened at the same time. "I could have taken your maidenhead right here, Miranda darling. And you would have welcomed it."

Her face heated, but she did not relax her stance. "I would have fought you."

He gave a rich chuckle. "You would have welcomed me. Face the truth, Miranda. You would have given yourself to me right there on the breakfast table."

He was right, curse him, but she had nothing left but her stubborn nature with which to protect herself. "You are entitled to your opinion, but rest assured that such an opportunity will not come again. I will see to it."

"Believe that if it helps you to sleep at night, my

sweet girl, but we both know the truth of what happened here."

She swallowed hard. "Please leave."

"As you wish." He executed an elegant bow, not a hair out of place, not a wrinkle in his cravat. His unmussed elegance only added fuel to her ire.

She jabbed a finger at him. "And I will have you know that I will continue to perform as the contessa, Wyldehaven. You will not interfere."

He arched his brows at her as he straightened. "So fierce, Boadicea. Very well, continue to sing if you wish it. But do not think you can find a rich protector that way. Be warned I will send James to an orphanage the instant I discover such a liaison."

"I want no rich protector," she snapped. "And you are vile to threaten me."

"Like it or not, you have a protector now." He took her by the chin and pressed a hard kiss to her lips. "See that you remember what happened here, my sweet, for we are far from finished."

He turned on his heel and quit the room, leaving her disheveled and confused and still wanting him, curse his highborn hide.

She caught a glimpse of her fichu on the floor beneath the table and bent to retrieve it, tucking the lace back into place to preserve her modesty—late as it was for that. Casting a long look over the breakfast table—the dishes had been shoved aside but not broken, thank heavens—she pondered what had happened here . . . and what had almost happened.

She would summon Thaddeus. She needed more work, more money to free herself from this precarious situation. She had sworn she would not be Wyldehaven's mistress, and so she would *not*. Thaddeus could invest her money for her, as well as help her find more opportunities to perform. Then she would be free of Wyldehaven and his arrogant demands. She would still need to find a way to keep her promise to Lettie, but it would be on her terms.

But as she left the breakfast room and headed up to her bedchamber to restore her appearance, every muscle and nerve ending in her body still sang from his touch. She couldn't help wondering—in a strictly educational sense, of course—what other possible pleasures might lie beyond what he had shown her.

Just the thought sent another shiver through her, and she shoved the scandalous thought aside. It mattered not what other delights he might plan to share with her; she had no intention of surrendering to his will. But when she caught sight of her flushed cheeks and tousled hair in her looking glass, she experienced a moment of panic.

Did she truly have the fortitude to resist him? Or would she end up just one more woman discarded from a rich man's bed?

Chapter 11

By afternoon Miranda had decided two things. First, she would never let things get so out of hand with Wyldehaven ever again. She would be strong and resist his advances. Now that she knew what sensual dangers lay in his repertoire, she believed herself less likely to fall under his spell. Never mind that just the memory of that mad interlude in the breakfast room tempted her to cast aside what meager respectability she had managed to attain in favor of a whirlwind affair of romance and danger. She was forewarned now. Forearmed.

And more curious than ever.

But still, she had escaped the encounter with her virtue intact; therefore it was time to fortify her defenses and prepare for siege. And she *would* emerge victorious.

Second, she decided that Wyldehaven had probably not sent the threatening note she received. He was not the type to creep about in shadows scaring women with pieces of paper. If he wanted to, he could cast her out of London with little effort, but he was the sort of man who confronted a body face-to-face with little pretense. With Wyldehaven, you always knew who took issue with you and why.

Which meant there was someone else in London who wanted her dead.

Struggling to ignore the panic skittering along her nerves, she forced herself to ponder the matter rationally that afternoon over a cup of tea in the parlor. Being an intelligent woman, she was naturally concerned for her own safety. Having a mysterious enemy who might pop out of the shadows at any moment wreaked havoc with one's nerves. She briefly considered going to Thaddeus about the matter, but then reconsidered when it occurred to her that he might somehow be connected to the threat. The fact that he numbered among his acquaintances a ruthless moneylender and those menacing collection agents made her hesitate to look to him as a protector.

And Wyldehaven? She would sooner become a beggar in the streets before she placed herself in a position of vulnerability with him. No doubt he would seize the opportunity to "protect" her by making her stop performing—and that she could not afford to do. Not when it meant the difference between surviving and starvation for her and the baby, should Wyldehaven decide he had tired of them.

Her meager inheritance was nearly gone, having been spent to pay Mrs. Cooper's wages and to purchase the evening dresses she needed in order to perform. The duke had now assumed the cost for Mrs. Cooper, numbering her among the servants in the house he also maintained; however, Miranda knew she could not allow him to absorb the bills for her clothing as well. As soon as a man started paying the bills for a woman's dressmaker, it was only one more shaky step before she fell into his bed and surrendered her body and her independence.

Naturally, Wyldehaven edged her in that direction with calm determination. It would be so easy to just give in and let him take care of her. Let him pay for her housing and provide luxuries such as beautiful clothing and her own carriage. All she had to do was yield to his touch, allow him to use her body however he wanted. But what would happen when his infatuation faded? No, she would not take that chance. Not for her, and not for James.

How could he not understand her need to have security? He continued to refuse to accept responsibility for fathering James and persisted in the Banbury tale that someone who looked just like him was the real culprit. Really, how feather-witted did he think she was? And now he had decided that he wanted her in his bed, and apparently expected her to blindly put herself into his hands and trust that he would take care of both her and the baby.

But for how long?

She had seen it before, numerous times with her mother over the years. Some fellow with a bit of wealth would take a fancy to her mother and talk her into being his exclusive mistress.

"This one is going to last," Fannie would say, hugging her and smiling. "This will be the one to take care of us forever."

And then months later, sometimes just weeks, she and Fannie would find themselves once more on the streets because the fellow who swore to cherish Fannie forever had moved on to greener pastures and a new mistress. The pattern never wavered.

She doubted it would be much different with Wyldehaven. It was better to remain in their separate corners, never crossing that line into temptation. To do so would spell disaster, both for her and for James, for she knew that Wyldehaven would never offer marriage. Not to her.

She pushed away the appealing scenario, alarmed by her own yearning. Things were the way they were, and no amount of dreaming was going to change that. To even entertain a glimmer of such a notion spelled heartbreak for certain.

Mrs. Potts, the housekeeper, came to the door of the parlor. "Pardon me, miss. His Grace has sent over a lady's maid to tend you. He requests that you meet her and give your personal approval before I allow her to settle belowstairs with the rest of the staff."

"Oh." Surprised, Miranda set down her tea. A lady's maid? Was this another cunning way for him to slip past her defenses? "Very well, then."

Mrs. Potts glanced behind her into the hallway. "Come along."

A young blond girl about the same age as Miranda slipped into the room, her hands clutched around a worn satchel.

"Annie, this is Miss Fontaine."

Annie gave a little bob. Her voice, when she spoke, carried the distinct flavor of London's less fortunate. "Pleased to meet you, Miss Fontaine."

Miranda nodded her head. "Welcome, Annie. His Grace has sent you to be my lady's maid?"

"Yes, miss."

"I see." Miranda studied the girl's appearance, already noting the signs of poverty and abuse. "Have you ever been a lady's maid before?"

Annie raised her chin and said, "No, miss."

The hint of spirit made Miranda smile. Lack of experience would not deter this girl from attempt-

197

ing to better her lot in life. "I have never had a lady's maid before, so this will be an adventure for both of us. Mrs. Potts, do give us a few moments alone, please."

The housekeeper looked startled but obediently stepped out of the room, leaving them alone to converse.

Miranda had been tempted to send Wylde-haven's newest enticement packing with little hesitation. With only six dresses in her wardrobe, she hardly had need of a lady's maid! But when she got a look at the girl—the greenish-yellow tinge of fading bruises, the much mended clothing, the hard glint of survival in her eyes—she knew she could not turn Annie away. She had seen that same tired, jaded look in the eyes of too many of the girls who had followed her mother's path. Though it was unorthodox for a gentleman to send a woman of questionable virtue to be maid to someone pretending to be a lady, clearly Wylde had known that she would not be able to reject the girl's need of employment.

Curse his hide. She did not want to accept favors from him! But she could not doubt his cleverness in this.

"I am certain we will do very well together," she said.

The girl visibly relaxed. "That's what he said you'd say."

"The duke?"

"Yes, ma'am. He said you were a kind lady and wouldn't care none that I used to be—" She clamped her mouth shut.

Miranda pretended she had not heard the gaffe. "Sit down, won't you, Annie, and let us get acquainted."

Annie looked around at the fine furniture. "I don't want to get anything dirty."

"You won't. Sit in that chair and tell me how you came to be here."

Annie walked over to the lovely armchair and eyed it for a moment before gingerly sitting on its edge. "I told you, His Grace sent me."

"Have you always worked for the duke?"

"Not till now." She ran a curious finger along the sculpted edge of the small table beside her.

"Where did you work before?"

"Fulton's." She leaned closer to peer at the carvings. "Are those angels?"

"Cherubs, I think. What is Fulton's?"

Annie jerked her head up, her eyes wide with alarm. "Uh . . . the place where I worked."

"What sort of business is it?"

Annie remained silent.

Miranda leaned forward. "You can tell me, Annie. I will not judge."

"His Grace might be cross with me if I tell you," she replied. "And I owe him."

Miranda tensed. What did Wyldehaven hold over this sweet child? "What do you mean? Has the duke forced you to do this?"

"No, miss."

"It is all right for you to tell me, Annie. I will not pressure you to do anything against your will."

"No, he's not making me do anything I don't want to." She crossed her arms.

Miranda held her gaze. "If you are certain. I do not want the duke to make you feel obligated—"

"No!" Annie surged to her feet. "He saved me, that's what he did. Saved me from getting stuck by strangers every night and acting like I liked it. And from getting knocked about just because some drunk felt like it!" She yanked her satchel from the floor and clenched both hands around the handles. "I was a whore, Miss Fontaine, plain and simple. And I'll understand if you want me to go."

Beneath the bravado of her tone lurked a despair Miranda knew well. Her heart cracked, and she knew Wyldehaven had won.

"Of course I don't want you to go." Miranda stood as well. "I dare say being a lady's maid is better than taking five or six clients a night and only getting a small cut of the asking price. Unless the fellow leaves a bit extra for you on the bureau."

Annie narrowed her eyes. "You know a lot for a fine lady."

"My mother was in the trade," Miranda said shortly. "We are not all that different, you and I."

After a moment, Annie conceded, "Maybe."

"How did you come to leave Fulton's?" Miranda sat again and gestured for Annie to do so as well.

"I got pummeled by the bloke who looks like the duke." Annie reclaimed her perch in the armchair.

"By the . . ." The breath left her lungs. Good God, was this girl saying that Wylde's outrageous stories about an imposter were *true*? "What do you mean by that?"

"You mean you don't know? Some fellow who looks like the duke has been going about town saying he's the duke. This cove causes trouble and the duke gets blamed, you see? When His Grace came looking for the blighter at Fulton's, we all thought he'd come back—the one who'd thrashed me. But it wasn't him. They have different eyes, you know."

"No, I did not know." She took a breath, trying to calm her racing heart. If Annie was to be believed, then she had gravely misjudged Wyldehaven. And if he had been telling the truth about the imposter, was he also telling the truth about everything else? That he was *not* James's father?

Had she been condemning an innocent man?

She leaned forward, holding Annie's gaze. "So you saw this man yourself? The one who looks like the duke? And he hurt you?"

Annie nodded, her expression unguarded. "Thrashed me good. The bad one has green eyes, wild green like the devil's own. But the duke has those brown eyes that can look at you kind as can be. That's how you can tell the difference. The duke paid Ball for my contract."

"And now you work for him."

Annie nodded. "Like you said, being a maid is better."

"Indeed." She sat back, barely able to breathe, stunned by the girl's revelations. Everything she had ever thought about Wyldehaven now needed to be reconsidered. If he was not the selfish villain who had abandoned Lettie, what did that make him? A grieving widower who was being wronged by a look-alike? A man who tried to correct the damages done in his name, even though he himself was innocent of the crimes?

Oh, God, a man of honor?

Annie relaxed a bit in her chair, no doubt relieved that she would not be shown the door. "If you're not a lady then how'd you learn to talk so fancy?"

"When I was young, my mother paid for me to be educated." Miranda tried to push aside her rioting emotions and focus on the current conversation.

"Wish mine had done that. But she ran off with a bloke when I was eleven. Been taking care of myself ever since." She fingered the table's cherubic carving again. "Being a maid, what do I have to do?"

"I believe you help me dress and style my hair."

Annie grinned. "I know about hair. I used to help the girls at Fulton's."

Miranda nodded in approval, though she wanted to wince at this girl's hard life. She herself had not lived her years in luxury, but for a while at least she was educated in speech and refinement, reading and ciphering. Those skills had proven handy in the more recent, leaner years. "Then you already have some experience."

"I can help you with hair and dresses and such. What else?"

"Oh, come with me places, I suppose. The lending library or shopping."

"Shopping? When are we doing that?"

"Why, this afternoon," Miranda improvised. "I need some new ribbons for a dress I am mending. You must come with me."

"I love shopping!" Eyes bright, for a moment Annie looked just like any young woman at the prospect of a shopping trip. "When do we go?"

"Perhaps you should settle your things in your chamber, and I will summon you when it is time to leave."

"All right." Annie jumped to her feet. "Where is my room?"

"Mrs. Potts will show you."

Before she could call for the servant, however, a tap came at the parlor door; then it cracked open and Mrs. Cooper peered in. "Miss, your little man is awake," she announced.

"Come in, Mrs. Cooper." Miranda waved her in, then extended her arms for James. The baby was all pink-cheeked and drowsy-eyed, with that confused pout infants often wore upon waking from a nap. The nursemaid put the baby into her arms.

"Is that your baby?" Annie asked.

"No. It is my friend's baby."

"Where's your friend?"

"She died."

Annie contemplated that for a moment. "I once knew a girl of Ball's who got herself caught, and when the babe was born she kept telling everyone it was her friend's baby."

Miranda rolled her eyes. "It truly is *not* my baby. I just take care of him."

"Is it the duke's baby, then?"

"You are quite rude, young woman," Mrs. Cooper snapped.

Annie opened her mouth as if to retort, but Miranda caught her eye and nodded toward the chair. Pressing her lips together, Annie sat down again.

Miranda turned to the nursemaid. "Mrs. Cooper, please find Mrs. Potts and tell her that Annie is ready to see her quarters now."

"I shall return momentarily to feed the babe."
Mrs. Cooper gave one last sniff of disapproval at
Annie, then marched from the room.

"She doesn't like me," Annie said.

Flicking a glance after the departing nursemaid,
Miranda replied, "You must be more discreet in
voicing your thoughts, Annie. If there is something
you want to know, please wait until we are alone
and then ask me."

"I can do that. So have you and the duke—"

"No."

"Never?"

"*No.*"

Annie looked around at the fine furnishings. "But
you live in his house, don't you?"

"Only temporarily."

"But you're here." An expression settled on
Annie's face that looked too world-weary for her
tender years. "That's the first step, miss."

"Please call me Miranda. What is the first step?"

"When a man wants you in his bed. First he
corners you, then he seduces you." She fixed her
with that straightforward, blue-eyed stare. "Do
you feel cornered?"

"No." Miranda managed the lie without a flinch.
"Not in the least."

"Maybe you should. Because you're in a position here, sure enough. Much as I like the duke,
he's still a man. If you don't want to end up in his

bed, Miss Miranda, you should be real careful."

"Do not fret, Annie. I know what I am doing."

"That's good. More than one girl I know found herself with her skirts tossed before she could blink, even when she was swearing to God in heaven that she wasn't going to give over to a fellow. It's real easy to forget all that once a bloke has your fires stoked."

Miranda's mind flashed back to the breakfast room. "Have no fear, Annie. I am in full control of the situation."

But no matter how much she tried to believe it, something inside her mocked her for a liar.

Kit slammed into his rooms, still fuming from the meeting with his father. How was it the man could make him feel like a stripling again with just a few well-placed words?

His valet appeared from elsewhere in the flat. "Good afternoon, my lord. The—"

"I must cancel my plans at the club this evening, Smithers. My father demands my presence at a dinner party to dance attendance on Miss Wherry."

"Very good, sir. If—"

"What sort of living is it for a man to be sold like chattel at auction?" Kit stripped off his gloves, then removed his hat, threw the gloves into it and handed both to the valet. "This chit would have no chance at attaining such an elevated station if her father were not so plump in the pocket."

"Indeed, sir. Perhaps now is a good time to tell you—"

"She is a plain thing—brown eyes, brown hair. Very dull. She is buying her way into the upper echelons, Smithers, I tell you. At least once I wed the chit, the money is mine. But damned if I like being led to the altar like a lamb to the slaughter."

"You could always refuse to wed the wench."

Kit whipped his head around at the amused male voice. "What are you doing here?"

"The Duke of Wyldehaven is here to see you, my lord," Smithers blurted out. "He is waiting in the parlor."

"Rather, I am waiting in the hallway." Leaning in the doorway of the parlor, a grinning Daniel Byrne held up a glass. "I have helped myself to your whisky, Linnet."

"So I see." Kit turned to his manservant. "Thank you, Smithers. We shall be in the parlor and are not to be disturbed."

"Very good, my lord." Smithers scurried off.

Kit sent Byrne a look of annoyance. "You. In the parlor."

"I sense hostility from you, Linnet." Byrne pushed off the doorjamb and preceded Kit into the room. "Have I done something to displease you?"

Kit followed and closed the parlor doors with a snap, then turned to face him. "I have been trying to reach you. Why have you not responded to my summons?"

Byrne leaned down, his greater height lending menace to his posture. "Because I am not your lackey, Linnet."

For once Kit did not back down. Instead, he met Byrne's gaze with a hard one of his own. "You may be playing the duke, Byrne, but do not forget that you have no real consequence to recommend you."

Byrne's eyes narrowed. "I am a Matherton."

"By blood, but not by law,"

"A pox on the law!"

"I appreciate your feelings, but you must accept the truth as it is."

"What would you know of it?" Byrne stalked over to an armchair, where he seated himself without invitation. "You were born into privilege with servants wiping your soft white arse from the moment you emerged from the womb. When have you ever had to work for anything in your life?"

Kit curled his lip. "Apparently I must sell myself into marriage simply to have my own fortune. How bloody fair is that?"

"You make me laugh, Linnet. Poor little viscount has to marry a rich wench to continue his luxurious lifestyle. Such a tragedy."

"I would like to see you do it." Kit approached the sideboard, suddenly craving a whisky himself.

"In a second, laddie. Wed and bed some young virgin in exchange for a cartload of gold? I'm your man."

"Allow me to give you Miss Wherry's direction, then."

Byrne barked a laugh. "Cheer up and toe the line like a good boy, Linnet. You've only to swive the filly once and then comfort yourself with her papa's fat purse."

Armed with his whisky, Kit turned to face his nemesis. "I think . . . Good God, you have cut your hair just like Wyldehaven's."

"The better to fool the masses, my boy."

Kit tightened his grip on his glass. "This madness needs to stop."

"Fine with me. Don't marry the chit."

"You misunderstand. I meant this business with Wylde. Your dealings with Rothgard's heir were reprehensible. It is a miracle the gossips have not yet gotten hold of the story. You are taking matters too far now."

Byrne smirked. "Young Alonso knew what he was doing when he sat down at that card table. Perhaps he even learned a lesson from the incident. I, however, acquired a prime bit of horseflesh in the bargain."

"And nearly bankrupted the boy! I thought you were focusing your efforts on Wylde."

"Alonso is a grown man. And this *is* connected to our darling duke. Rothgard has had a man watching the duke's house for a couple of weeks now, though I have been unable to discover why. There must be a connection of some sort, so setting up the card game with Rothgard's son seemed the best way to ingratiate myself." He chuckled. "Of course once I discovered the fellow was a completely inept card player, I could not resist the opportunity to line the coffers a bit more."

Kit narrowed his eyes. "This ends now. This whole business with Wylde, all of it."

Byrne's face darkened. "Who the bloody hell are you to decide when it ends?"

"I will not help you anymore. Surely you will agree that Wylde has paid the price for his insult to me."

"To hell with your blasted honor! What about me? Do you think I have been planning all these years just to crawl away and hide under a rock on your word? Don't I get what I want?"

"Not if it means hurting people. That stunt in the park could have killed someone."

"You exaggerate, Linnet." Byrne's mouth curved in fiendish glee. "But you should have seen those dainty ladies lifting their skirts and screaming and scattering like geese when we came racing down the path."

"I am glad you were amused, but nonetheless, Mrs. Colley was injured when your mount scared her cattle into bolting. Her curricle was completely destroyed."

"A pity. I assume the harridan lives, as her demise has not yet become common knowledge to Society."

"Damn it!" Kit snapped. "Do you care for no one but yourself?"

"That is a fair summation."

"This is why I will no longer help you. You are losing all control."

"I am in perfect control of myself, Linnet. I believe it is you who feels the lack of control—over me."

"Yes, damn it, you are right. You have lost all direction. This game has gone on long enough, and I will not help you anymore. I cannot have this madness on my conscience." Kit slapped his glass down on the table.

"To hell with your conscience." Byrne finished off his whisky. "You have gone too far to stop now."

"Are you mad? Just take the money you have earned and disappear back to where you came from." Kit waved a dismissive hand. "No one will be any the wiser."

"You are gravely naive if you believe that can ever happen." Byrne rose, raking his gaze over the viscount with obvious contempt. "If we stop now, Wyldehaven will discover what you have done, and then where will you be?"

Kit tensed. "He will forgive me."

"Will he? Is he so saintly a person that he would forgive his best friend for helping a scoundrel like me ruin his good name?" Byrne leaned closer. "Did he forgive his own father? No, he didn't. Wyldehaven does not tolerate betrayal."

"That was different," Kit said, but even he heard the lack of conviction in his own voice.

"No, it was not. Wyldehaven does not forgive easily, and he will consider you the ultimate traitor for helping me ruin him."

Kit could not respond to that. He knew that Byrne was right. Wyldehaven would never forgive him. "I do not want anyone else hurt. No more races through the park. And no more fleecing striplings of their inheritances."

"Yes, my lord." Byrne executed an elegant bow. "As you wish."

"Do not mock me, damn it. This is serious business. It should never have gotten this far."

"How did you think it would go, Linnet old boy? Ever since I learned that *I* was the eldest son of the Duke of Wyldehaven, I have wanted to get what was mine from that usurper. It is only right. Firstborn always inherits all."

"You are illegitimate," Kit pointed out. "Bastards cannot inherit the title, no matter what you choose to believe. It can never be yours."

Byrne gave him a terrible smile. "We shall see

about that, Linnet. Now I shall thank you not to use the word 'illegitimate' going forward. It casts a tawdry image over my consequence."

"You have no consequence!"

"Indeed, I do. It belongs to the Duke of Wyldehaven. And with your help, Linnet, that will be *me*."

With a mocking salute, Daniel Byrne turned and left the flat.

Kit stood where Byrne had left him, sick with regret over the game he'd started. When had he lost control? It seemed a lark in the beginning, a trick to get a bit of covert revenge—and a bit of coin—without Wylde ever knowing he was involved.

But now . . . now Byrne was talking madness. What did he mean that he intended to become the Duke of Wyldehaven? That was impossible. A bastard could not inherit. But unless he wanted to confess all to Wyldehaven, there was nothing he could do about Byrne and his madcap actions. He could not risk the scandal, especially with the engagement to Miss Wherry dangling before him as his only hope for financial independence.

So he would hold his tongue and keep a close eye on Byrne. If he were vigilant, he should be able to stop the imposter before anything irrevocable happened. Before anyone else got hurt.

Chapter 12

Wylde arrived at the dower house precisely at eleven o'clock that morning. His grandmother's summons had been written in short, succinct sentences, and brooked no argument. He was to present himself at her home at that hour, and no excuses would be tolerated.

At his knock, the butler opened the door and greeted him, bowing as he stood aside to let Wylde enter the house. A footman came to relieve him of his hat and gloves, and Wylde said, "Winters, where is my grandmother?"

"In the Chinese drawing room," the butler replied. "Allow me to announce you, Your Grace."

"No need, Winters. She is expecting me."

Wylde took the stairs to the second floor and headed with unerring accuracy to the Chinese drawing room. A footman scurried to throw open the door, as Wylde did not slow his pace but simply walked straight into the room. He stopped short just inside the doorway.

"Good morning, Grandmother. My apologies. I did not know you had a caller."

The duchess gave him the same stern look he used to get as a child when he had tracked mud across the Aubusson carpets. "Thornton, I believe you know Lady Crisdale. And this is her companion, Miss Tenet."

The crone sitting across from his grandmother gave him a glare that should have incinerated him on the spot. Dressed from head to toe in black bombazine and crepe, the elderly Lady Crisdale had been mourning her husband for some thirteen years now. Wylde rather believed she would be buried in her mourning attire.

Her companion, a mousy-looking thing with spectacles, watched him with palpable apprehension, as if he might pounce and devour either of them at any moment.

Despite their evident hostility, Wylde nonetheless bowed and said, "A pleasure to see you both again, Lady Crisdale, Miss Tenet."

"You have nerve, Wyldehaven." With a sniff, Lady Crisdale stiffly got to her feet. Her companion leaped up from her seat and took the widow's arm, steadying her. "I cannot fathom you would dare speak to me, you scapegrace."

Wylde's polite smile froze on his face. "Have I offended you, Lady Crisdale?"

"Never mind me, young man. What about your poor grandmother? Have you no consideration for what your exploits do to her good name? You should be ashamed of yourself!"

Before Wylde could speak, Grandmother stood. "Shall I have Winters summon your carriage, Aurelia?"

"Excellent notion. I certainly will not remain in this house as long as your ne'er-do-well grandson is about."

"I understand your feelings, Aurelia. However, please keep in mind that he *is* my grandson, and I will ask you not to speak ill of him in my presence."

"He should be horse-whipped for the scandals he has caused!" Lady Crisdale pressed her lips together, then reached out to the duchess. "I am outraged on your behalf, Maria."

The duchess took her friend's hand and patted it. "I know, dear. But he is my grandson."

"An unfortunate circumstance."

"Come, let us summon Winters." The duchess accompanied Lady Crisdale and her companion out of the drawing room, sending a hard look at Wylde that warned him not to interfere.

Well, then. What in blazes had that been about? he wondered.

The mantel clock ticked steadily as he sat down

216

in a chair to await his grandmother's return. She had demanded that he present himself, then seemed annoyed that he'd done so. He watched the hands on the ornate clock move, listening to the idle conversation of the servants as they walked the halls. Twenty minutes passed before he heard the duchess's footsteps approaching.

He sprang to his feet as she entered the room, but she cast him a stern look and waved a hand at the armchair. "Sit down, Thornton. I want to speak to you."

"I am at your service, Grandmother."

She gave a little snort—an odd sound for a duchess, especially one of her advanced years—and sat down on the comfortable sofa across from him. Only when she was seated did he seat himself. "I would like to know what has gotten into you, Thornton. I have heard the most remarkable stories about your conduct, and I cannot credit that these people were speaking of my grandson. I had heard better of your father, even at his worst."

Wylde winced. "What have you heard?"

"All manner of talk, some of which should not even be whispered in a lady's presence. But my friends are loyal and most are too old to give a fig what Society thinks, so they have brought the stories to me that I might judge for myself if you have become a miscreant like your father, God rest his soul."

"There is indeed much talk about me," he said, "but most of it can be dismissed. Perhaps you should tell me what you have heard."

She narrowed her eyes at him, tilting her head as if trying to determine if he spoke the truth. "There was talk of fisticuffs at a gaming hell known as Fulton's. I am certain you have never been there."

He nodded, grateful to acknowledge the truth. "I was not involved in any such altercation."

"And a scandal about a race through Hyde Park where a lady's curricle was damaged."

"I have heard this as well."

"Is it true?"

"The incident occurred, but I was not present."

"Hmm. And also some shameful rumors about you trifling with women like the worst sort of rake and even starting an affair with some Italian countess."

"Ah." He could not help but smile. "That Italian countess is Miss Fontaine."

Grandmother gasped, blue eyes flashing with temper. "Thornton, please tell me you did not take advantage of that poor girl!"

"Calm yourself, Grandmama. We are not having an affair; I simply rented a house for Miss Fontaine and the baby to live in until we get matters sorted out about the child's paternity."

"Indeed? Then why does Aurelia assume she is

Italian? I met the girl, and she is as English as you or I."

"True." He paused, searching for words. "Miss Fontaine maintains a livelihood where she sings at fashionable events professionally. She calls herself a contessa to make herself seem exotic."

"What rubbish. The polite world will believe anything." His grandmother snapped open her fan and began to wave it. "I cannot fathom that a decent young woman like Miss Fontaine would be performing like a common Gypsy for the entertainment of the upper ten thousand. Does she have talent?"

"She does," he admitted. "Now that I have ensconced her in a decent house and provided her with servants, I do not expect that she will continue such madness."

"Excellent. I can respect her need to provide for the child, but since you will see to that, she should apply herself to pursuits more suited to a female of good breeding."

"My sentiments exactly."

The duchess closed her fan. "I take it you are treating her with respect? I do not wish to hear that you have compromised the girl's reputation."

He resisted the urge to look away from those unwavering blue eyes. "Of course not, Grandmother. You have declared the child a Matherton, and both he and Miss Fontaine will stay under my protection until we discover the identity of the father."

"No doubt one of your father's by-blows," she muttered. "It is the only thing that makes sense."

"Agreed," he said. "I have secured a Bow Street runner to investigate."

"A pity that you are not the babe's sire. I find Miss Fontaine and her child most agreeable."

He raised his brows. "I wouldn't have expected to hear such a statement from you, Grandmother. Miss Fontaine's mother was an actress, her father unknown. She appeared on my doorstep with a child she insists is mine. Most ladies of your caliber would consider her beneath them."

"Most ladies of my caliber are foolish ninnies," the duchess snapped. "This girl conducts herself well and has acceptable manners. And she is striving to do right by a child that is not even her own. In my estimation, she is more than worthy of my company."

"I must admit, I am surprised by your tolerance."

"The world could use a bit more tolerance," she declared, snapping open her fan again. "It would certainly lessen the affliction on one's nerves."

Wylde chuckled. "Grandmother, you are an original."

"Indeed I am. But do not think this casts you out of the briars yet, my boy. What of these unpleasant rumors? If it is not you propagating these scandals, then who dares shame the name of Wyldehaven in such a manner?"

He tightened his jaw. "A pretender, Grandmother. A scoundrel who resembles me enough that he is able to present himself as Wyldehaven in order to commit this mischief."

"Dear Heaven!" The duchess's fan ceased in mid-wave. "Who is this vagabond?"

"I do not know. That is something else the runner is investigating. The imposter is the one who started the brawl at Fulton's and is also the one who scuttled Mrs. Colley's new carriage."

"And is he also the man who fathered Miss Fontaine's babe? She did seem convinced that you were the rogue who sired and then abandoned the child."

"I have begun to believe the same thing," Wylde admitted. "Which means that this fellow has been brewing his mischief for far longer than I suspected."

The duchess folded her fan again and leaned forward. "If the babe's sire was one of your father's baseborn sons, then perhaps he bears enough resemblance to you to cause this coil. I vow *he* is the imposter you seek."

"I will not know for certain until I find him." He reached for her tiny, wrinkled hand and kissed the back of it. "Until then, believe no stories you hear about me. The bounder is cunning and seems to be getting more impudent with each challenge."

The duchess patted his cheek. "See to it you put an end to this, my boy."

"I will, Grandmother. No one shall soil the name of Wyldehaven ever again, not as long as I breathe."

"I've never been to Bond Street, never in all my days!" Clad in Miranda's serviceable gray dress and straw bonnet, Annie bounced on her seat as she turned this way and that, trying to see all the shops from the barouche. "Goodness, look at all the fine ladies!"

Dressed in an elegant dress of pale blue with a matching bonnet, Miranda could not help but smile. "Remember, Annie, you work in a fine household now. Try to reflect the dignity of your station."

"Oh. Right. I mean, of course." Annie folded her hands tightly in her lap, but her gaze continued to dart back and forth, spurring a laugh from Miranda.

Upon reaching the linen-draper's, the barouche pulled out of traffic and in moments the footman had hopped down and was offering a hand to the ladies to descend.

Annie gaped at the fashionable women crowding the streets, servants burdened with packages scurrying after them. "It's like a circus!" she whispered.

"Indeed it is. Have a care to stay close lest we get separated in the crush." Head held high, Miranda began to make her way through the throng toward the doors to the shop.

Annie hurried behind her, muttering observations under her breath. "Heavens . . . how does that hat stay on her head? Is that a bird's nest? And sure as I breathe, that 'un stuffs her bosom, else I'll be called a three-legged donkey. Gad, look at this 'un's hair. That blond ain't from nature, not with those black brows . . ."

Miranda couldn't suppress a chuckle as she listened to the colorful musings. She would need to discuss with Annie her ability to whisper. Clearly she thought she was being discreet, but the occasional glare cast back at her by passersby told another story.

"Stop! Thief!" The shriek stopped the crowd in its tracks. Heads turned as an urchin raced past them, barreling through the crowd, a lady's reticule clutched in his hand. Miranda glanced from the overblown matron wailing about her loss to the disappearing boy. Silently, she wished him Godspeed.

A pair of servants took up the chase, sending the elegant shoppers scurrying out of the way as they shoved through the throng. Miranda found herself backed up against the wall of the shop as ladies shrieked and scrambled. She looked around for Annie and could just see the flowers on her bonnet not far away. The girl had pushed to the front of the crowd to better observe the thief's getaway—of course.

Miranda straightened her own bonnet and assured that her reticule had remained fastened to her wrist. She went to take a step toward Annie. Then someone jerked her back with a hand around her elbow. She had only a moment to glance up at her captor—he was dressed in livery, like a groom, with a hat that shadowed his face—before the sharp blade of a knife pressed against her side.

"In the alley—now."

She glanced around, frantically searching for Annie, but the girl had vanished from sight. The crowd still jostled about, the horde yammering about the thief and what had been stolen, craning their necks to see. The knife dug harder, enough for her to feel it even through her corset.

"Now. Or I can kill you right here. No one would even notice." He gave a tug, and she had no choice but to take a step backward. The crowd shifted around her, no one realizing that the man was slowly guiding her away from the safety of other people.

"What do you want?" she murmured. "I have no money."

"Shut your mouth," he snarled. "I want you to come with me. And keep that tongue silent. I wouldn't want to have to cut it out."

The utter certainty—glee, nearly—in his tone

made her realize he might well do it. Silently willing Annie to come looking for her, she had no choice but to allow the ruffian to back her away from the crowd and around the corner of the building. There, he abruptly spun her around and a dark, narrow alley stretched before her, the sun blocked by the huddled buildings. "Walk," he commanded, and gave her a shove.

She walked, knowing with each step she might never leave this alley alive. One step, two. Then she stumbled, surprising him, and gripped the wall for support as he muttered a curse.

"Damn it, you troublesome sow!" He grabbed her around the neck, making her whimper as the ribbons of her bonnet dug into her flesh, and tugged her head back with his arm beneath her chin to expose her throat. Cold steel pressed against her pulse. "One more stupid move like that and I'll cut you right here."

"I—I tripped," she rasped.

"Useless tart!" With one slice he slashed the ribbon of her bonnet, then threw the expensive piece of millinery up in the air. It landed on the roof of a nearby shed, only the ribbons dangling within sight. He clenched a fist in her hair, tilting her head back again until her spine could not curve anymore, and once more laid the blade just beneath her ear. "If I chose it, you would be dead in seconds and no one would ever know."

"What do you want?" she whispered.

"To give you a message. Now walk down this alley so I can give it to you proper." With a nasty chuckle that made her heart scream with fear, he urged her down the alley ahead of them.

With a soft nudge of her foot, she edged the reticule she had dropped a bit farther into the shadows, then allowed him to push her along, praying she had not just hidden too well the only clue someone might use to find her.

"They'll never find that 'un," Annie said with a chuckle, turning away from the scene where the little thief had effectively lost his pursuers. She looked around, searching for Miranda. But even as the crowd began to disperse, she did not see her.

The carriage was still stopped in front of the linen-draper's, since the coachman had not been able to move the team with all the spectators clogging the streets. She hurried over and grabbed the footman as he started to climb back onto the carriage. "Where is Miss Fontaine?"

The footman tugged away his arm. "I thought she was with you."

"I lost her in the crowd."

"Is she in the shop?"

"I didn't look."

"I will. You stay by the carriage." The young man darted into the shop, easily slipping between the wealthy patrons with their rich clothing and layers of skirts, disappearing from sight.

"Where can she have gone?" Annie said to herself. "We were both standing right here." She turned in a slow circle. Now that the excitement was over, the spectators had returned to their normal routines. Well-dressed gentry ambled along the street, trailed by servants. Horses and carriages hurried by, the low rumble of the wheels on the road nearly drowning out the calls of the street vendors. Nothing appeared to be amiss. But she had seen and heard enough in her twenty-two years to know that a normal scene could hide beneath it a twisted skeleton.

The footman emerged from the shop, his crest-fallen expression conveying his defeat.

"She's not inside?" Annie asked.

He shook his head. "How can we have lost our mistress in so short a time? We will all be discharged!"

The coachman leaned down. "Here now, Thomas. You and Annie walk down the street a piece to see if maybe Miss Fontaine went into another shop during all the hullabaloo. I've got to be moving the rig."

Thomas nodded. "Perhaps she did. Maybe the crowd—"

"What's that?" Annie darted toward the alley at the side of the shop. "Ho there! Wait a moment!"

A thin girl—barely more than a child—jerked her head up from the blue reticule she was examining. Clenching her fingers around her prize, she spun and ran in the opposite direction.

"That's Miss Miranda's purse!" Annie called to the men, and raced after the child.

"Wait! Wait!" Thomas the footman pounded after her and grabbed her arm.

"What are you doing?" Annie shook off his hold. "That little mite will be gone in a thrice!"

"She came out of the alley," Thomas said. He pointed back the way they had come. "Shouldn't that be where we start?"

Annie hesitated. Her blood demanded she pursue the little thief, but her real goal was to find Miranda. She gave a nod and whirled on her heel, heading back toward the alley at a trot. Stolid Thomas followed, easily keeping pace.

"What happened?" John the coachman asked as they approached. "Did you catch her?"

"We're looking down there." Thomas pointed at the alley. "Have you your pistol, John?"

"I do." Grim-faced, the coachman reached beneath his seat and withdrew the weapon. "Have a care. 'Tis loaded."

"Good." Gripping the pistol, Thomas met Annie's gaze. "Stay behind me, Annie."

"I won't," she snapped, both irked and flattered, then charged for the alley.

"Bollocks," Thomas muttered and hurried after her.

"What do you want?" Miranda whispered, willing her voice not to shake.

"Well, now, that's a question." Her assailant grabbed her around the waist and pulled her back against him. He smelled of stale beer and garlic, and his breath reeked enough to choke her when he leaned close to her ear. "What will you offer for your life?"

"Since I am not a fool, I will offer whatever you will take."

"And if I want to 'take' you?" He ground his hips against her bottom, and she realized he was aroused. Bile rose in her throat but she struggled to keep her head.

"You have a knife. I cannot stop you."

"That's right." He trailed the flat edge of the blade along her cheek. "And you're going to tell me how much you like it or else I'll cut that pretty face."

Her limbs began to tremble and she forced herself to breathe. "Why are you doing this? Robbery? Rape? What do you want with me?"

"Someone hired me. Said to snatch you and give you a message."

"You said that before." She could not suppress a shudder of revulsion as he slid the edge of the knife along her breast. "What message? From whom?"

229

"Leave London or die. That's the message." He rubbed the back of his hand against her breast, still clutching the knife. "You've got nice teats for a little thing. I always wanted to stick it to a lady, see what you've got that's so special under those skirts that other trollops ain't got."

She ignored the vulgarity and focused on the matter at hand. "Who sent you?"

"I don't know—I spoke to a servant. But I was told they don't care what happens to you, so long as you get out of London." He snickered. "Or die."

His obvious enjoyment of her fear nearly paralyzed her. There was no Lettie nearby with a chamber pot to save her this time. She would need to depend on her own wits.

"There is a busy street only a few yards away," she reminded him.

"I guess we'll just have to be quiet." He chuckled again, rubbing his groin against her bottom.

"I can assure you I will not be quiet. I will scream as loudly as I can."

"Then I'll kill ye." He lifted the knife to just beneath her chin.

"That will spoil your other plans for me, will it not? How will you have your way with me if I am dead?" She paused. "Unless you are one of those men who enjoys grave robbing for such a purpose?"

"Bloody hell!" He shoved her away. "What kind o' lady talks o' that? I don't dally with the dead!"

She shrugged, weighing her chances of bolting. "I am just trying to understand what you want from me."

"You're planning on screeching, are ye?" He grabbed her by the hair, arching her head back with a painful jerk. "Let's make sure that doesn't happen. This way we both get what we want."

He thrust her down on her knees, stuck the knife between his teeth, then began to unfasten his breeches.

Well aware of what he intended, she grabbed his coat with both hands and used his body as leverage to surge to her feet. The unexpected move sent him stumbling backward. Eyes blazing with fury, he bellowed with rage. The knife fell from between his teeth and clattered to the ground.

She jerked her skirts to her calves and bolted, streaking like lightning toward the sunshine at the end of the alley.

Two forms suddenly appeared, blocking that glorious sunshine—and her route of escape. But she did not even hesitate. Whoever they were, they could either let her through or get trampled.

Then she realized that one of them wore skirts. She could not let another woman fall into the trap she had just left behind.

"Run!" she screamed. "He has a knife! Call the watch!"

"Miss Miranda?"

Annie's voice. Her legs nearly buckled beneath her, but she did not slow her pace. Annie started running toward her, followed by a man.

"Annie, no, go back! He is right behind me!"

"I'll see to him. Annie, get the mistress." Before Miranda could identify the young man who spoke, he raced past her, a pistol clutched in his hand. She caught a glimpse of her own household's livery.

"Miss Miranda, what happened?" Annie reached her and grabbed her by the arms, jerking her to a stop.

Miranda clutched at her, gasping for breath. Her dratted corset just would not allow enough air to get into her lungs! "A man grabbed me, threatened to kill me."

"In full daylight? A cheeky bastard to be certain!"

Miranda gave a half laugh, all her tight laces would allow. "We must discuss your language at some other time, Annie, but I must say I agree with you."

"Hang my language, miss. You were nearly murdered right on Bond Street! What will His Grace say about that?"

"Nothing." She met Annie's gaze, held it. "You will not tell him about this, Annie."

"But—"

"I am not his responsibility. Please remember that."

Annie pursed her lips, eyes narrowed. "You live in his house and it's his footman who is chasing after the blackguard right now. How can we not tell him?"

Miranda closed her eyes, unable to maintain her bravado another moment. Her legs trembled so much they could very well fold beneath her at any moment. "Which footman?" she asked, trying to change the subject.

"Thomas. He's a good lad, just a bit too quick with ordering a body about. Come back to the carriage now."

Miranda gratefully accepted Annie's arm around her shoulders as the maid began to lead her toward the street, only paces away. The terror of her ordeal was starting to take its toll. "I thought the brigand was right behind me."

"Perhaps Thomas stopped him."

"Perhaps." Miranda halted just before stepping into the patch of daylight that would bring her back to safety. "But I did not hear the pistol, and this fellow had a knife."

Annie met her gaze, the concern Miranda shared mirrored in her eyes. "Should we go back and look for him?"

"I want to." Miranda cast a glance behind her into the shadows. "But at the same time . . . "

"We will send someone to fetch him," Annie decided. "For now we must get you home."

"I do not want to leave him—"

"Someone is coming!" Annie dragged her toward the sunlight. "Hurry, in case it is your attacker!"

"Annie!" Thomas's voice accompanied the sound of his running feet. He was panting as he reached them. "The bounder got away. Darted down a crack between the buildings, and I couldn't see to get a shot. But he's gone now."

But he's gone now. The footman's words seemed to release something inside her. Miranda's knees finally turned to water, and Annie caught her as she stumbled.

"That's the end of it. Let's take her home." Annie offered her shoulder, and together the two servants assisted Miranda to the carriage and away from the scene.

Chapter 13

Wyldehaven thumped on the door of Miranda's home with his gloved fist. The door opened, but rather than the butler, he found himself facing Annie. "How is she?" he demanded, striding into the house.

Annie closed the door behind him. "A bit rattled is all. The villain didn't hurt her none, just scared her."

"How can such a thing have happened, and on Bond Street no less?"

"Well, Your Grace, I'm thinking it wasn't just some snatch and grab. She says he was supposed to give her a message."

"What message?"

A servant appeared to take Wylde's hat and gloves. Glancing at the fellow, Annie said, "Perhaps we had better talk about this in the parlor."

"Indeed." Appreciating her sense of discretion, Wylde handed his hat to the servant. "Lead the way, Annie."

Once in the parlor, Annie closed the doors and took a piece of paper from her pocket. "Miss Miranda asked me not to say anything to you about what's been happening, but I found this in her things as I was putting away her clothing. And then the incident today . . ."

Wylde took the paper and read it. "Curse her! Why did she not tell me of this?"

"I don't know when she got it, but the bloke who grabbed her today told her the same message. Leave London or die."

"She is new to London. How can she have enemies?" He looked at Annie. "Where is she?"

"In the nursery with little James. Says he calms her."

"This cannot be allowed to go on." He crushed the note in his fist. "By heaven, does she not realize that I can protect her?"

Annie pursed her lips. "I said the very same thing to her, Your Grace, but she said she's not your responsibility and I shouldn't tell you about this. I figure she's just too stubborn to know when to ask for help. Some of the girls at Ball's were the same way."

Wylde's mouth quirked. "I am glad you had more sense, Annie."

She shrugged. "Like you said, this gig is easier than whoring. And I haven't forgotten who took me away from that."

236

He shoved the crumpled note into his coat pocket. "Where is the nursery?"

"This way." Annie opened the parlor doors and led him toward the stairs.

Miranda cuddled little James in her arms, tickling his chin with her finger. After the harrowing events on Bond Street, she had changed her clothing and immediately made for the nursery. Looking down on James's innocent face made the entire distasteful episode seem far away.

But even the calming influence of the baby's presence could not completely stop her mind from puzzling over recent events. Who had sent the brigand after her? Who wanted her gone so badly? Obviously whomever hired that thug had also sent her the anonymous note. At first she had thought it was Wyldehaven, but now she completely dismissed that notion.

Which meant that she had some unknown enemy who wanted her gone—perhaps even dead.

The thought chilled her. She had given a brief thought to bringing the issue to Wylde but stopped herself from taking such a foolish step. It was bad enough she was living in his house, bad enough that he now paid for the very bread that went into her mouth. But on the heels of the intimacies they had shared in the breakfast room . . .

No, the moment she started bringing her problems to his doorstep, he would take over. And then the next thing she knew, she would be in his bed. Under his control. And most probably in love with him.

That could not happen. She had been managing her own life since long before her mother died. The child of a drunkard learned early to hide her coins and stay out of the range of an angry hand, to do whatever she had to in order to survive. She had been successful at that; she would succeed here, too.

And even more so since Annie had told her of Wylde's problems with the imposter. With those tales had come the realization that Wylde could not be the cad who abandoned Lettie in her hour of need. Clearly the responsible party had been this look-alike who also committed the other misdeeds in his name. That said, how could she continue making Wylde pay for another man's mistake?

It was time to go. As soon as she completed the performances she currently had scheduled, she would take whatever money she'd earned and disappear to the country with James. Initially she had intended to stay in London, but that was when she thought Wylde was James's father, which was not the case now. The country was more affordable, and she would be able to live on her earnings as the contessa until she acquired some other sort of employment. It was better this way.

Especially for her heart.

The door to the nursery opened, but she did not look away from the baby. He was the focus of her life now, and she would do her best by him.

"A moment longer, Mrs. Cooper. I believe he is nearly asleep."

"Excellent. I will wait."

She jerked her head up at the deep voice. A thrill shot through her at the sight of the sophisticated Wyldehaven standing in the doorway of the domestic setting of the nursery. For some reason, she found the image more pleasing than seemed reasonable. "Your Grace, what are you doing here?"

He came into the room, closing the door behind him, but did not approach. Keeping his distance from the baby as always. "I heard of today's events."

"Oh." Her excitement deflated. "It was kind of you to come by, but as you can see, I am unharmed."

"Are you?" He meandered around the room, then stopped by an old wooden rocking horse and touched a finger to its head. The paint had begun to fade on the toy, but his gesture conveyed a reverence that surprised her. "This was mine. I named him Zeus. He and I had many a wild ride together when I was a lad."

"I did not know." Her heart melted a little at his wistful tone, her defenses weakening. "It was here when we got here."

"I imagine someone thought young James would enjoy it."

"If it was not supposed to be brought here—"

"No, it is fine." He held up a hand and smiled at her, but pain flickered in his eyes. "Had my own son lived, he would have enjoyed Zeus as much as I did in my youth. James is a Matherton. He should have all the benefits of being a member of the family."

"About that . . ." A downward glance revealed that James had finally fallen asleep. She got to her feet and moved toward his cradle. "Annie told me what you did for her. How you took her from that awful place." Carefully, she placed the baby in his bed, tucking his blankets around him.

"A lady should not hear such tales."

She straightened and met his gaze. "Wyldehaven, you and I both know I was not born a lady, though I do consider myself respectable."

"Nevertheless, your demeanor indicates you were raised as one."

"That is neither here nor there." The warm admiration in his dark eyes only resurrected the memories of scandalous pleasure in the breakfast room. She struggled to focus on the conversation. "You know very well I have seen things no lady should see. Let us say I am a woman of character who will do her best to live a respectable life."

"Very well." He gave a nod. "I also consider you a woman of good sense."

"Thank you." She clasped her hands in front of her, more pleased than she should be at such a compliment.

"Which is why I cannot understand why you did not come to me with this." He withdrew a crumpled paper from his pocket and unfolded it. She recognized it at once.

"Annie." She pressed her lips into a line. "I specifically asked her not to trouble you with this."

"Trouble me?" Despite his quiet tone, his eyes blazed. "Young woman, someone has been threatening your life. Did you not once consider asking for help?"

"Anonymous notes come from cowards." She shrugged. "I thought perhaps they would stop if I did not heed them."

"Apparently your brilliant plan did not work, since you were accosted today in the middle of a busy street!"

"I know." She wanted to glance away from the accusation in his eyes, but to do so would allow him to see her vulnerability. Instead she stiffened her spine. "But as you see, I am unharmed."

"By pure luck and the tenacity of your servants. I absolutely demand you stop performing as the contessa. It is unnecessary now, and it is putting you in danger."

"I will not."

He blinked. "I beg your pardon?"

"I said no, I will not." She put her hands on her hips, resolved to hold her ground. "We have discussed this before, Your Grace. You are not responsible for me. I came here because I believed you to be James's father. But I no longer believe that."

"Oh, really?" He shoved the note back into his pocket. "Now that I think back, I believe I did have a drunken bout after my wife died, and I recall taking advantage of the services of an accommodating little actress—"

"Balderdash! You and I both know that you are too honorable a man to dally with a woman so soon after your wife and child were laid in the grave. And if you did take up with Lettie, you would never have abandoned her if she was with child."

He said nothing for a long moment. "This is quite the change of heart for you, my dear. Just days ago you were determined to send me to Hades on the end of a pitchfork with your own two hands."

"I know you better now." He was watching her with a fondness that only fed the simmering desire deep inside her. "Ever since we met, I could never equate the honorable man I was seeing with the tales of the blackguard that I had heard from Lettie. But then Annie told me how she met the imposter herself. She swears he looks just like you, and suddenly your wild tales of someone impersonating you became fact rather than fiction."

"I shall have to thank Annie, as unfortunately my own word was not proof enough." A shutter had come over his face. "So you have decided that I am not James's father. Now what happens?"

"I will complete the performances that I have scheduled at this moment, and then James and I will leave London."

"What if I will not let you take him?" He shrugged when she gaped at him. "The child is definitely a Matherton. Why would you not leave James in my care? I am head of the family, after all."

"Because . . ."

"Because you want to raise him yourself?"

"Yes." She lifted her chin. "A child needs love, not nannies and boarding schools. You can barely be in the same room with him, let alone hold him or comfort him."

"Nonsense."

"It is not nonsense at all. Even now you linger on the other side of the room rather than come near the cradle. James has lost his mother and been abandoned by his father. I will not see him raised in the cold sterility of a boarding school."

"The boy deserves an education befitting a Matherton. It is what his mother wanted."

"True. But there are some seven years at least before he is ready for that, Your Grace. Who will care for him until then? A nurse? A governess? That is not the upbringing a mother would want for her child."

"Not so, Miranda." He came toward her, despite the proximity of the cradle. "Lettie wanted her son to have his birthright. That means living in a duke's house. Being raised by governesses and tutors. Being educated at Eton as all the Mathertons have been for generations." He laid his palm against her cheek. "It is you, my little soft heart, who wants more for him than that."

"He deserves more." She pulled away from his touch, silently damning her quickening pulse.

"What if I can give him more? What would be your argument then?"

"I would have none, obviously." Trapped, she met his gaze head on. "Go on, then. Pick him up, if you will. I would see if you can."

"A challenge, is it?" He glanced at the sleeping babe. "I should not wish to wake him."

"Perhaps you will not."

"Nonetheless—"

"You cannot do it, can you?" She gave him a sad smile, her heart torn by the conflict she could see in his face.

"I am certain I can, but it seems a shame to wake the lad." He took a step closer to the cradle, then stopped. He stared at the babe from a yard away, his fingers curling.

244

"It really is all right." She came to him, laid a hand on his arm. "This is why I believe he should stay with me. He is not your child, and Matherton or not, I do not believe a cold and austere home would be the best thing for him."

"You would have a Matherton raised as a country boy racing through the meadow?"

"Yes. He will be happy. Loved. Can you promise him the same?"

"Damn you." He turned away from the cradle to pull her into his arms. "You leave me nothing, do you? This child who reminds me of the one denied me. And you—a beautiful woman who makes me feel alive again." He rested his forehead against hers. "Stay with me. Share my bed, Miranda. You know we are good together."

"I cannot." Her whisper came out harsh and tortured. "We must leave London, James and I, especially with this lunatic who is sending me threats."

"I can protect you."

"You have your own enemies, Wyldehaven."

"Do you doubt me?" He turned her face to his with a hand on her chin. She wanted to purr like a kitten at the sensation of his fingers against her throat even as her heart slowly cracked in two at the decision she must make.

"I am a skillful lover, Miranda," he said. "And I want you badly. No other woman has stirred me like this, not even my wife. I would make you happy, and you and the baby would be safe."

He stroked his other hand down her back, and she could not resist leaning into him, just for a moment. "And where would we live?"

"What is wrong with here?" He bent his head, inhaled her scent.

"And when you return to your estate? What then?"

"There is a cottage on the grounds, just the right size for you and James." He nuzzled his mouth against her throat. "We would see each other frequently."

"Tempting, Your Grace." She eased away from him, her flesh tingling but her heart aching. "But no. I will be mistress of my own fate, not a nobleman's bed."

His expression darkened. "I care for you, Miranda. This is not just a duke's whim."

"You are asking me to give up the only control I have over my own life," she said quietly. "I do appreciate that you care for me, Wylde. But if I cross that boundary, I can never get back what I was."

"What you are? Miranda, you are a woman with no family, no dowry. I am offering you a life of comfort and ease, a safe environment in which to raise James."

She managed not to flinch at his blunt summation of her background. "In exchange for sharing your bed. And when you tire of me? What then? When I age and lose my looks? Will you take James from me and send me on my way?"

"How could you think I would do such a thing?" Anger roughened his voice. "Blast it, woman, I honor my promises, and I promise you that you will have a good life under my protection for as long as you wish."

"Again, I appreciate your offer." She laid a hand on his chest and offered a small smile. "But we will never be equals, Wylde. I will always be just another sort of servant, subject to your desires and changing tastes. At least on my own I can make decisions and not worry about being beholden to another."

"I do not understand you." He turned away from her, strode to the window overlooking the tiny courtyard of the town house. "Do you not realize that most women would give anything for the opportunity you are refusing?"

"I do. But as you said, Your Grace, I am not most women."

He did not turn around. "At least allow me to help you with this enemy you seem to have acquired. I cannot fathom how, but it might be tied to my own difficulties."

"Take the note," she said. "And I will be happy to give you a full description of the man who attacked me this afternoon. But I will not stop performing, Wylde. Tonight I am supposed to appear at the Oakley affair. I have three other performances beyond that, and then I am going to leave the city."

He bent his head, ostensibly studying the windowsill. "Oakley, eh? One of his famous musicales, I suppose."

"Yes, it is."

"And when is it you plan to leave? I would like to know so I can take care of matters with the house."

She studied his back, wishing he would look at her. "My last scheduled performance is on Friday."

"Five days from now."

"Yes."

"Very well." Finally he turned to face her, but she could not read his expression. "I will contact you after I have spoken to my man of business." He started for the door.

"Wyldehaven." She stopped him at the doorway with a hand on his arm. "I want you to know this was not an easy decision for me. You are a very attractive, generous man."

"I understand your reasons, Miranda. I just wonder if you do." With that, he opened the door and exited the nursery, leaving her to contemplate his meaning.

Chapter 14

⟨ ∽◯◯∽ ⟩

The Oakley musicales had become something of a tradition over the years, and not because of the musical talents of the four Oakley sisters. More because Mr. Oakley, a gentleman by birth but a wealthy man by skill, tended to share investment advice with select guests during the intermission. For most men, tolerating the sisters' caterwauling was more than enough sacrifice for the chance to add to the family coffers. And for Mr. Oakley, imparting a bit of his vast knowledge was more than enough payment to have won a husband for three of his four daughters. Only the youngest, with the unfortunate name of Ophelia Oakley, still remained unwed.

Though not for long, if Mr. Oakley had aught to say about it.

Miranda arrived to find a small group—only twenty or so—gathered in the music room. While not the only performer, she was certainly the main attraction. The young debutantes who were in attendance would carry the balance of the evening with their various talents.

Mrs. Oakley greeted her warmly and with some enthusiasm, as did Mr. Oakley. Young Ophelia—barely seventeen—blushed and stammered and eventually retreated into the corner with the other girls her age. Miranda spotted Lord Arenson in attendance, but her brief concern about the elderly gentleman's roving hands was quickly relieved when she saw that his wife was also present.

Mrs. Oakley stood before the pianoforte and clapped her hands together. "If everyone would please take your seats, we are ready to begin."

The guests shuffled and murmured, and then finally all were seated in the chairs the Oakley servants had arranged. Miranda noticed a familiar looking blond girl seating herself with the Arensons, but before she could think much about it, the door to the music room opened.

"The Duke of Wyldehaven," the liveried servant announced, then stepped aside so Wylde might enter the room.

"Your Grace!" Mrs. Oakley hurried over to the duke, who stood in the doorway, and her husband rose from his seat in the audience to follow her. "I am so pleased you could join us!" Mrs. Oakley gushed.

"The pleasure is mine, madam," Wylde said with

a brief bow. He turned to greet Mr. Oakley, then followed his host and hostess into the room and allowed himself to be led to a seat.

Right next to Ophelia Oakley, of course.

The young girl blushed and glanced away from him, but Wylde did not appear to notice. He spotted Miranda standing to the side of the room, awaiting her cue. Their gazes met for a long moment.

What in heavens was he doing here? Miranda wondered, fighting the urge to twist her fingers together, feeling as if frogs were leaping about in her innards. She thought they had settled things earlier. Come to terms with the end of their relationship.

Apparently not.

Mrs. Oakley took her place before the pianoforte again. "Welcome, Your Grace," she said publicly to Wyldehaven, then looked out over the rest of her guests. "And now, I am pleased to introduce a talented performer who is fast becoming the rage of London. The Contessa della Pietra!"

Miranda stepped forward to gracious applause, but she was only conscious of one person, one set of eyes. A dark, heated gaze that seemed to look right into the deepest parts of her. With effort, she kept her composure as she seated herself before the pianoforte.

But as she lifted her hands to the keys, she knew

that despite the others in the room, she played for one person tonight. One man. Emotion flooded her, begging for release, and she knew that this performance would be different than any other. For as she struck the first note, the power of her feelings took control, quivering in each chord, yearning with each measure.

Through music, she gave herself to Wyldehaven—completely, exquisitely, mournfully.

In the only way she ever could.

The performance shook him as if he were a wet rag, wrung out and left to dry by the fire in the hearth. Her voice caressed him; her hands on the keys might have been fingers on his flesh. She wrapped him in music, soothed the wounded places of his heart, stroked the battered remnants of his soul. When she finished, he dared not move, lest he tremble like a puppy caught in the rain, desperate to be near her warmth.

With her performance, Miranda had touched places deep inside him that only composing had ever exposed to the light of day. He felt naked. As if they were already lovers.

But during the intermission, as he lingered just outside the small conversational groups, he watched her. The way the sapphire silk moved with her graceful body, the way the candlelight danced on her hair. And every curve of her mouth, every sway

of her hips—even the delicate bend of her elbow—
reminded him forcefully that they were *not* lovers.
That, in fact, she intended to leave him within the
week.

How could he let her go?

"Wyldehaven, you blackguard, you have some
cheek showing your face here."

Wylde turned toward the harsh whisper, his coldest glare in place. "Good evening, Arenson."

The old earl scowled at him, but it was clear he
was trying to remain discreet. "Had I known you
would be here, I would never have attended. Have
you no honor, man? No shame?"

Wylde stiffened, old memories of his father rising
to the fore at the disdain of the old man's words. "I
am at a loss, Arenson."

"The devil you are." Arenson took a glass of
champagne from the tray of a passing servant and
gulped a swallow. "How did you know she would
be here? Is it your wont to crow over your victory in
the face of your victims?"

"I truly do not know what you are talking
about."

"The card game. The way you shamelessly
bilked young Alonso out of the bulk of his inheritance!"

Wylde maintained his stoicism with effort.
The imposter again. It had to be. "Refresh my
memory."

"Refresh—" The earl's fingers tightened around his champagne flute. His kindly blue eyes hardened to glittering gemstones. "If Miranda were not here, you young cur, I would plant you a facer!"

"Miranda?" Wylde glanced toward Miranda, who was chatting with Mrs. Oakley.

"Look at me when I speak to you!" The earl's voice remained low, but the growl of anger was unmistakable. "Do you see her there, sitting with my wife? She all but swooned when she saw you enter, and not because of your pretty face. Had we known you were invited to this musicale, we would never have attended."

Sitting with . . . Wylde turned his gaze toward Lady Arenson. A pretty blond gel in debutante white and pearls sat beside the lady, her gaze focused on the hands folded in her lap. "Forgive my ignorance, Arenson, but who is Miranda?"

"Rothgard's daughter," Arenson snapped. "As if you did not know. Rothgard loves his Shakespeare. Why else would he name his children Miranda and Alonso? From *The Tempest*."

"And what am I supposed to have done?"

The earl's face reddened. "You know damned well you swindled young Alonso out of thousands of pounds at Maynard's card party the other night!"

"You are mistaken, Arenson. I do not attend Maynard's gatherings."

The earl sucked in a sharp breath, and for a

moment Wylde was certain the old man would expire on the spot from sheer apoplexy. "The apple does not fall far from the tree, does it?" he spat. "You are indeed your father's son."

Wylde managed not to flinch, and fisted his hands at his sides. "Have Rothgard contact me so we may clear up this misunderstanding."

"Oh, he *will* be contacting you. You are lucky he has chosen to keep the matter quiet." The earl raked a contemptuous glare over him. "You are a disgrace to your title, Wyldehaven, even more so than your father. Rothgard will see to it you get your comeuppance." He spun on his heel and stalked away.

Moments later Arenson and his wife and Rothgard's daughter—Miranda—walked past him and took their leave of the Oakleys.

Wylde glanced over to where Miranda—*his* Miranda—had been standing talking to one of the guests. Just the sight of her soothed the sting left by Arenson's contempt. The bloody imposter must have targeted Rothgard's heir, and now restitution had to be made. His mischief was escalating from annoying debts and seducing women to fleecing young lordlings and generating events that cast a shadow on the Wyldehaven honor. Perhaps Rothgard would be willing to listen to reason.

His Miranda moved, her sapphire dress sweeping along with her graceful stride and distracting him again. He pushed the matter of Rothgard to the back of his mind and focused instead on Miranda's enemy. That's why he was there, wasn't it? To keep her safe?

As he watched, she bent down behind the pianoforte, affording him a brief but memorable view of her posterior, and stood again, her reticule in her hand. Then she turned and left the room.

Was the woman feather-witted? She should not be going off alone. What if the madman struck while she was out of his sight? His blood surged with the scent of the chase, and he started after her.

As soon as he escaped the room, he caught sight of Miranda climbing the stairs to the second floor. He hurried after her and reached the landing of the next floor just in time to see her duck into a room down the hall and close the door quietly.

He followed her in. A fierce look sent the chamber maid scurrying from the room.

Miranda whirled around as he closed the door behind the servant, sealing them both alone in a small bedchamber. "For heaven's sake, Wyldehaven, what are you doing?"

"You should not be going off alone. It is not safe." He glanced at the bed that dominated the room, then back to her.

Her cheeks bloomed pink. "You are a danger all on your own, Wylde. Please leave. I came here for privacy."

"You keep trying to shut me out of your life," he said, approaching her. "Am I such a monster?"

"No, you are a rogue."

"Untrue. I have always treated you with respect." He stopped only inches away.

"Your definition of respect is different than mine. There were times when you treated me as if I would pilfer the silver."

He gave a reluctant nod. "True. But now that I know better, you cannot have any complaint. I wish you would reconsider your decision."

"I cannot." She fixed her eyes on his chest. "It must be like this. I am sorry."

"I will be happy to provide for James. See him educated."

"Oh, unfair, Wyldehaven!" She jerked her gaze to his then, her own eyes glittering with emotion. "You want me in your bed, and you will say anything to get me there."

He stiffened. "I am not some cad to force you, my dear. You want security for James, and I can provide that."

"Certainly . . . *if* I share your bed. There is a name for women who agree to such a bargain, my dear duke, and I refuse to accept that designation. Now if you will excuse me . . ." She glanced at the Chinese screen in the corner, then raised her brows at him in expectation.

He frowned, nonplussed. How was a man supposed to charm a woman when the chamber pot beckoned? "I will wait outside this room, Miranda, and we will continue this discussion."

She huffed a breath of frustration. "By God, Wyldehaven, you are a stubborn beast!"

He gave a little bow. "Agreed."

She pointed at the door. "Leave."

"I will be just outside," he reminded her, smothering a chuckle with effort. By Zeus, she was charming even in her ire.

She folded her arms and waited until he opened the door. He gave her a little salute before stepping out into the hallway. As he turned to close the door behind him, he caught a flash of sapphire skirts as she ducked behind the screen.

He lingered in the hall, imagining her fumbling with her clothing. He thought about her small hands peeling aside each garment, revealing her beautiful flesh inch by inch. He'd undressed many women in his time, and had no problem visualizing what she might look like naked and warm in his bed, her thighs spread in welcome . . .

Voices distracted him. Three ladies came up the stairs—Ophelia Oakley and two other debutantes—chattering like magpies. They cast him questioning glances as they reached the landing. Not wanting to be thought a lech, he nodded to the ladies, then wandered away from the doorway and down the hallway. The girls glanced after him, giggling and whispering, then hurried into the same chamber from which Miranda had not yet emerged.

What was it about women, he wondered, that made them travel in flocks like a gaggle of geese?

After what seemed an eternity, the door opened. Miranda emerged, her face pale, her green eyes wide with distress. She clutched her reticule with white-knuckled fingers.

He reached her in three long strides. "What is it? Did one of those chits treat you poorly?"

She only looked at him, her expression utterly lost. "No. They ignored my existence, as always."

Regardless of the chance they might be seen, he took her chin in his hand, caressing her delicate skin with his thumb. "Then what has put this look on your face?"

"It is nothing." She shook off his touch.

He let his hand fall away and took her arm instead. "I am not a fool. Something has happened."

She tugged, but he would not release her. "Let it be, Wyldehaven. It is not your concern."

"*You* are my concern, Miranda, whether you admit it or not." He led her unwillingly down the hall and into an alcove he had spotted earlier. "Now, tell me what has put that look on your face."

She looked at him for a long moment, until he wondered if she had truly closed him out. Then she gave a sigh and pulled her arm free so she might open her reticule. Every sense in his body jerked to alertness as she pulled out a folded piece of paper. "Another note?"

She nodded, her shoulders slumped with weary defeat. "How does he manage this?" she whispered. "We were in a room full of people."

He took the paper from her, gently unwrapping her fingers from around it. Her hand trembled, and the sight of it cut him deeply. Miranda had never been afraid, not even when going toe-to-toe with him on behalf of James. He placed her hand back on his arm, and she clung as he slowly opened the paper.

DEATH AWAITS YOU IN LONDON.
LEAVE NOW OR FACE THE CONSEQUENCES.

He arched a brow. "Rather dramatic," he commented.

"Perhaps he felt as if he had not already made his point," she managed, but the humor fell flat. "It was in my reticule, Wylde. How could this be? We were all right there in the music room. We should have seen him."

"You are correct, we should have. It could have been anyone. A servant, or even one of the guests. Unfortunately, I was not paying attention. I could not take my eyes from you."

"Flatterer." A wisp of a smile curved her lips.

"You have trapped me in your web of charms," he murmured, lifting her hand to his lips.

"Do you never cease the seduction?" She no doubt meant the words as chiding, but instead they came out with the slightest undertone of longing.

"I am a stubborn beast," he reminded her. "And I am going to insist you take your leave now. Someone here is your enemy."

He saw the flash of rebellion in her eyes, but then she pressed her lips together and nodded. "I have finished the performance I agreed upon."

"I shall see you home." He held up a hand when she made to speak. "Not a word of argument."

Her nose wrinkled, and she looked so endearing that his heart ached.

"I am not a fool, Wyldehaven. I admit I would feel safer if you followed me home."

He extended his arm, and she tucked her hand into his elbow. "Generally a man dislikes being thought of as safe," he drawled as he began to walk her back toward the staircase, "but in this case I am honored to be your champion."

Miranda walked back into the music room with Wyldehaven as her shadow. She had insisted on disengaging from his hold and rejoining the crowd under her own power, even though someone in that room had probably slipped the threatening note into her reticule. She looked each of them in the eye, somehow thinking she would know who it was with just a glance. But no one sprouted devil's horns or otherwise revealed themselves. She took her leave of her hosts, then walked alone to the foyer on the ground floor. A single footman manned the door, as the musicale was not scheduled to end for some hours yet. She requested that he summon her carriage.

He hurried to obey. As she waited, she could hear the murmur of conversation coming from upstairs, the plinking of keys as some neophyte plucked out a melody on the pianoforte. The foyer seemed huge and silent, despite the distant sounds of civilization. A chill danced over her skin, but not from cold.

Footsteps on the stairs behind her made her heart quicken. She glanced around, half afraid of whom she might see. But it was Wyldehaven.

Her heartbeat settled down into a calm, easy rhythm again.

He called an order to the servant, requesting his coach be brought around. Then he stood beside her, hands folded behind his back, studying an oil painting of a summer lake scene, acting as if they were barely acquainted.

But she knew better. It was all she could do to maintain her facade of indifference, to not to turn into his arms and let his comforting strength soothe her. Wyldehaven, with his inborn charm and subtle persistence, was proving to be a nearly irresistible oasis of sanity in a world of increasing madness.

Which was very dangerous in her current state of vulnerability. Someone wished her ill, and she had no idea who it might be. To her knowledge, she had wronged no one. But the threatening missives and the ruffian who had accosted her just the other day indicated differently. Someone wanted her gone from London.

Maybe she should oblige them.

The fees she would collect for her last two performances would go a long way toward providing for James, but it might be safer for both of them if she forgot about them and took what she had earned thus far and fled to the country. She could contact Thaddeus later for the rest of her mother's money.

And yet how hard it would be to walk away from the man standing beside her.

Annie arrived, summoned from belowstairs with the news that her mistress was departing. She cast Miranda a look of puzzlement, but Wyldehaven shook his head just the barest bit. As Annie came forward, he bent his head to speak low and quickly near her ear. She nodded, her eyes troubled as she listened. Her gaze flicked to Miranda once, then twice. Fearful. Concerned.

Outside, Miranda's carriage arrived, distracting the footman at the door.

Wylde looked at her. "You will ride in my carriage with me," he murmured, his voice so low she could barely hear it. "We will send yours on ahead and hopefully distract anyone who might seek to follow you. Give Annie your cloak."

The quiet command in his voice made something deep inside her soften. She had always noticed that while he was never cruel to any of the servants, no one ever doubted who was in charge of matters. Before, that authoritative tone would have gotten her back up. But now . . .

Now it just made her feel safe.

Wordlessly, she slipped off her cloak and passed it to Annie. The maid handed Miranda her own worn garment in exchange, and Miranda gratefully donned it. Both of them pulled the hoods up to hide their identities as Wylde whispered further instructions.

When the footman looked back at them, the deception was complete.

"Allow me to escort you to your carriage, Contessa," Wylde said, offering Annie his arm. She nodded, silent, and let him lead her forward. Miranda hurried after them, a servant, an afterthought.

She lingered in the shadows as Wylde made a show of helping Annie into the carriage. Then, as John the coachman coaxed the team into motion,

Wylde gestured to her. She hurried forward, grasping his outstretched hand as he strode to his own coach, his coat of arms on the open door. With a strong tug, he nearly heaved her into the carriage, moving quickly to urge her inside as he scrambled into the vehicle himself.

She landed on the seat across from him, her heart pounding and her breath coming in pants. The door snapped closed, and he tapped on the roof of the coach with his knuckles. The well-sprung equipage surged forward.

They were safe.

"Hopefully that will be enough to confuse your enemies," he said, his voice warm and soothing in the dimly lit coach. She caught a glimpse of his teeth as he flashed a smile.

In this insecure world, he was the only certainty. A man whom she at first believed a cad, but had proven himself a gentleman of honor and compassion. He would protect her if she allowed it, wrap her in soft silks and keep her safe in a comfortable home. She would want for nothing.

Except the permanence she could never have.

But still, she was moved to act on her feelings, to show him her gratitude, that she did not dismiss him as lightly as he believed. So she shifted forward to the seat beside him. And when he looked at her in inquiry, she leaned up and kissed him.

Chapter 15

Her innocent kiss sparked an inferno.

He hauled her into his lap, his mouth hungry. Demanding. She closed her eyes and released her defenses. She needed him to hold her, to touch her with those talented hands. Just once more she wanted to relish these swirling, delicious emotions. She already knew she was in love with him. It didn't seem so wrong to steal just a few moments of pleasure in the face of a lifetime of living without him.

He clenched his hands in her skirts, edging them up enough to slide his hand beneath them, along her stocking-clad leg. Everything inside her urged her to lay back, open to him, give him all that she was.

The street lamps flashed briefly through the windows of the carriage, casting an odd veil of unreality over them. His mouth on her throat, his teeth nipping just enough to make her insides bubble. His hand on her breast through her clothing. His other hand inching up beyond her garter to the sensitive, naked flesh of her upper thigh.

She did not hold back either, boldly meeting his tongue with her own. She slid her hands over those strong, broad shoulders, reveling in his male body. When he flicked his thumb over her surging nipple, she gasped, and he caught the sound in his mouth.

How she longed to once and for all give herself over to him. Would it be so wrong? She loved him. Surely that must make it right.

His hand edged higher beneath her skirts, brushed her inner thigh.

She ached. Just once she wanted to cross that bridge between them, go with him to a place where they could enjoy each other and just *be*.

They reached their destination far too soon.

Dimly, she was aware of the coach slowing, for he gradually pulled away from their kiss and cupped her face in his hands, resting his forehead against hers. "We have arrived."

She wanted to cry. Too soon. She wanted more, needed more. But perhaps this was for the best. In another moment she would have tossed all her principles into the Thames in order to have just a few more moments in his arms. She nuzzled her cheek into his hand. "Thank you for seeing me home."

"It is not—"

The coach door opened and Miranda quickly slid out of his lap onto the seat beside him. A footman in the Wyldehaven livery peered into the vehicle, his expression impassive. "Good evening, Your Grace."

"And to you, Benjamin." Wylde got up and moved into the doorway.

Stunned to realize they had arrived at Matherton House rather than her own, she could do no more than yank the hood of her cloak back over her head to hide her identity. Why were they here? What was he doing?

He stepped down to the ground and turned to hold out his hand to her. She hesitated, seriously considering the ramifications of staying where she was and demanding to be taken home. Should she give the servants something to gossip about with such a scene? He waited patiently while she wrestled with the notion, and in the end she decided to handle the matter between them alone. The staff did not need any drama for their entertainment.

She took his hand, dutifully ignoring the sweet thrill that curled in her belly at the mere idea of spending more time with him. He helped her from the carriage, then led her briskly up the steps where the butler stood holding open the door of the house.

"Good evening, Your Grace."

"Good evening." Wyldehaven removed his hat and handed it to the balding man. "Dismiss the servants for the evening, Travers. I do not wish to be disturbed."

"Very good, Your Grace." Without revealing a flicker of emotion, the butler closed the door and left the elegant foyer, his master's hat in his hand.

Wyldehaven glanced at Miranda, his dark gaze hot with passion. "Come with me, my dear. I have something I want to show you."

She did not move. "Why are we here? This is not my home."

"No, it is mine."

Regret left a bitter taste. He was acting like any other man. She had allowed too many liberties in the coach, and he'd obviously taken that to mean . . . "I have not changed my mind about sharing your bed," she said quietly, aware of how sound could echo in the cavernous house. "I should not be here with you."

"And in the coach?"

"Gratitude." She held his gaze with effort.

His mouth quirked into a crooked grin. "A buss on the cheek is gratitude, Miranda. What we shared is more than that."

"A moment of madness," she whispered. Tears stung, but she refused to shed them. "Please, Wylde, do not make this harder than it needs to be. Summon the coach back and send me on my way."

"I know you want me," he murmured.

"True." She fiddled with the strings of her reticule. "If I were seeking a lover, you would be the man I would choose. *If* I were seeking one."

"Not the sort of thing to tell a man you are attempting to discourage."

She squeezed her eyes shut. "I know. I am trying to be honest."

"You want certainty. A guarantee. But my dear, there are no guarantees in this life. If there were, my child would still be alive."

"So would Lettie."

"Indeed. Instead there is just us." He stroked the backs of his fingers along her cheek. "I shall never force you, dear girl. If you decide to accept me as your lover, all you need to do is say so. In the meantime there is something here I would show you. Something no one else has witnessed. Will you come?" He gave her that crooked grin again. "I promise you will maintain your modesty the entire time."

He looked at her with genuine affection in his eyes, his touch tender. Time and circumstance had always been against them, so how could she refuse this last opportunity? She nodded, then allowed him to take her hand again and lead her toward the curving staircase.

Of all the wonderful rooms in his home, she had not expected him to take her to the music room.

She could tell from the look of it that it was his private sanctum. The decor was darkly masculine, with rugs the shade of fir trees and well-polished instruments gleaming in the glow of the lamps scattered throughout the room. A graceful harp curved near the window, and a violin sat mounted on what looked like some kind of custom rack on a table. A Broadwood grand pianoforte—such decadence!—had been polished to a shine. A desk crowded near the wall, papers scattered over it. A comfortable looking armchair sat near the hearth with a small table, perfect for a late night meal.

"The servants know that I tend to work on my music at night," he said, closing the door behind them. "Sometimes I am here until dawn if the muse has caught hold of me."

"Such a wonderful room." She drifted near the harp, entranced by the majesty and elegance of the instrument.

"That was my mother's," he said. "She remarried some years ago and lives in Italy. No one has touched it since."

"That is a shame. Such a beautiful harp deserves to be played often."

"I have always thought so." He came to her and tugged at the ties of her cloak. Her lips parted and she darted her surprised gaze to his as he swept the garment from her shoulders. His own eyes gleamed with mischief as he said, "Do not scold me. You have

271

made it clear that this is the only garment that will be removed this evening."

Her heart did a funny little flip, and she struggled to keep her expression stern. "Mind your manners, Wyldehaven."

"Of course." He bowed, sweeping a hand toward the armchair. "My lady's throne awaits."

"Such fustian." She marched over to the chair and sat down. "Are you satisfied, Your Grace?"

He straightened and folded the cloak over his arm like the finest manservant. "Hardly, Miss Fontaine, but I shall not allow that to spoil my surprise for you."

She scoffed at his foolery but waited patiently while he went to drape her cloak over the desk chair. "I cannot stay long. I must get back to James."

"Annie and the others will take good care of him." He fussed with the papers on the desk, sorting through them until he found whatever he was looking for. Gripping several sheets in his hands, he turned to face her. Paused.

The uncharacteristic hesitation grabbed her attention more than a shout would have. "Is something wrong?"

"Not at all." He let out a long breath, then went to a corner of the room and grabbed a music stand, easily lifting it with one hand so he might bring it to the middle of the room. He arranged his papers on it, and she caught a glimpse of distinctive lines and notes, handwritten.

Music.

Surely he was not about to play one of his compositions for her? Such an honor caught the very breath in her lungs. She did not deserve such a gift.

He smiled a bit unsteadily, then went to the table and removed the violin and bow from the rack. He brought the items back to the music stand, plucking the strings of the violin and making minor adjustments to the pegs. This went on for several minutes.

What kind of fool was she, to become so aroused just watching him tune the violin? Her pulse skittered in her veins, her skin flushed with warmth. She could not take her eyes away from his fingers, so competently caressing the strings.

Finally he lifted his gaze to hers. "This is a part of the opera I have been writing since my wife died. It is an aria sung by a young woman who has just lost her child. No one has ever heard it but me."

She laid a hand over her thundering heart. "I am honored you would allow me to listen."

"You might be the only other person I know who would appreciate it." He lifted the instrument to his chin, then winced. "I beg your indulgence, Miranda, but I cannot play this way."

"Oh, no, do not think upon it another moment." She stood, disappointed beyond words—not that she would let him see it.

"No, no, sit down." He gestured at the chair with the hand holding the bow. "I merely must make an adjustment."

She sat down again, and he went to the desk and put down the violin and bow. Then he shrugged out of his coat. Her mouth dropped open as he peeled the garment free and laid it on the desk, revealing his impressive form in nothing but the snowy linen shirt. Then he tore at the simple yet elegant knot of his cravat, finally unwinding it and discarding it atop his coat. Taking up the violin and bow again, he returned to the music stand.

Oh, wicked, wicked fate. Without his Weston coat and stylish cravat, Wyldehaven looked . . . wild. His white shirt emphasized his masculine physique—broad shoulders, slim waist. And his tight breeches—she had to glance away, lest she look too long and too hard at something about which she was entirely too curious. When she found herself stealing yet another peek, she jerked her gaze upward. A lock of jet black hair draped over his forehead, and without his cravat, she could study every detail of his throat, which for some reason suddenly fascinated her.

Laying the bow on the music stand, he tucked the violin under first one arm and then the other so he might roll up each of his sleeves, exposing strong forearms. Her mouth watered as she watched him, as if he were a tasty pastry prepared just for her.

"That should take care of things." He took the violin by its neck in one hand and picked up the bow with the other. He started to lift the instrument to his chin, then paused. "I should have asked your permission to remove my coat, Miranda. I apologize. I do tend to be rather single-minded when it comes to my music."

"Not at all," she managed. "As a fellow musician, I understand completely. Please do not give it another thought."

"I appreciate your indulgence." The smile he gave her was so sweet, so boyish, she could barely believe this was the same man who had brought her to climax on her own breakfast table.

But with the first hum of the bow across the strings, she knew she was in the presence of a master.

The violin crooned of love, of a mother and child. Wailed of the agony of loss and desperation. Wept of hearts broken and lives shattered.

The music swept her along like the strongest of tides and whisked her on a journey of aching denial, frustrated guilt. Terrible, dark pain that never stopped throbbing. Duty and suffering. The torture of living. She could not help drowning in it, getting lost in it.

Then, a glimmer of light. Of hope. Of love, renewed.

By the time his bow stroked the strings with the last note, tears were trickling down her cheeks.

He opened his eyes—having closed them during the performance—and looked at her. She fumbled with her reticule, searching for her handkerchief. The tiny bag tumbled from her hands. In a moment he was kneeling in front of her. Placing the violin on the floor, he picked up the bag and handed it to her. But still her hands could not navigate the strings.

Gently, he pushed aside her fluttering fingers, then opened the drawstring and withdrew her handkerchief. But instead of handing it to her, he used it to dab at her cheeks.

His tenderness ripped aside her lingering control. She raised a trembling hand to cover his. "That was the most heart-wrenching thing I have ever heard. It was beautiful."

He ducked his head for a moment, focusing on the carpet. "Thank you."

"So tragic," she murmured. "To lose your wife and unborn child at the same time. Was there an accident? An illness?"

"No. Nothing like that." He pressed her handkerchief into her palm and dropped her reticule in her lap. Then he stood and walked over to set the violin back on its display rack.

She clutched her belongings, undone by his stiff posture and awkward movements. "Will you tell me what did happen?"

He said nothing, merely came back to fetch the music stand. He took his pages in one hand and the stand in the other, carrying the stand back to the corner. Then he turned to his desk, shuffled through the pages of his opera, and shoved those he had played back into the stack.

"Wylde? Please answer me."

He stiffened, rested his hands on the desk and bowed his head.

Silence weighed on the room like a woolen cloak in summertime. Heavy. Stifling.

Miranda rose from her chair, placing her handkerchief and reticule on the seat, and made her way across to him. She paused before hesitantly touching his arm.

He shook her off, then glanced at her. His dark eyes shone with unshed grief, his mouth grim. He looked dangerous, unpredictable.

Tortured.

Distress radiated from him in nearly visible waves. She could not resist the call. Bravely, she stepped closer, laid her hand on his chest. His heart thundered against her palm. So vibrantly alive. Everything he did, he did with such passion.

He stood very still, his breath flaring his nostrils.

"Something terrible happened," she whispered.

"I can tell. It is so horrible you cannot even speak of it."

He closed his eyes, shuddered.

"Wylde." She stepped closer, wrapping her arms around him and laying her head against his chest. "I am so sorry you were hurt."

A sound escaped him—a sob, a laugh, a cry of pain. Perhaps all three. He wrapped his arms around her, crushing her tightly within his embrace as if simply holding her would banish his anguish.

She clung to him, trying to absorb his pain. How could she have ever thought he was the type of man to get a woman with child and then abandon her? He felt everything so deeply. He would never discard a person as less than nothing.

He buried his face in her hair. His hands stroked over her back, not in a way meant to arouse, but as if he were trying to assure himself that she was really there. She just kept whispering assurances to him, hoping to lend him enough strength to come back into the present.

"She killed my child," he murmured.

Shock jolted through her, though she struggled not to show it.

He straightened and met her gaze. Anguish etched lines into his face. "She killed my child," he repeated, "and in doing so, ended her own life."

"Oh, Wylde."

"It was a marriage of convenience." He released

278

her and bent to open a cabinet beside the desk that she had not noticed. He pulled forth a bottle and a glass, then held up both and lifted a brow.

She shook her head. "No, thank you."

"I hope you will not be offended if I indulge." Without waiting for her reply, he opened the bottle and poured some of the liquor into the glass. "The marriage was arranged by our fathers. She was very beautiful and, I discovered, quite vain." He looked down at his liquor, then took a swig. "So vain that she did not want my child deforming her beauty."

"Oh, no." She covered her mouth.

"She went to a local woman who gave her some herbs, promising it would rid her of the child."

"Surely she knew you would require an heir."

"She did not care. The prestige of being a duchess and her own fine looks were her only concerns. She went a bit mad when she discovered she was expecting my child. I thought it was simply a natural fear about the birth or some such thing. I did not pay enough attention, I suppose. I was giddy at the thought of being a father." He tossed back the rest of his drink. "So she died, and the babe with her, no thanks to me."

"You could not know she intended to do herself harm."

"Herself? No, she had no intention of injuring herself. Just the child." He set the glass on the desk. "Just my child."

"How horrible." Her throat tight, she wrapped her arms around her middle. "I understand now why you avoid James."

He rubbed a hand over his eyes. " 'Tis true the lad reminds me all over again of what I lost."

"I am so sorry I barged into your life and forced him on you."

"What?" He jerked his head up and glared at her. "Do you not understand what you have done to me, Miranda Fontaine? I was dead inside, and then you arrived on my doorstep with your high-minded principles and stubbornness and brought me back to life."

She shook her head. "No, I made matters worse for you by foisting James upon you."

"You did not." He took her face in his hands and forced her gaze to his. "I was lost in my music, in the past. Tortured by memories. You brought me into the present. And I thank you for that." Reverently, he pressed a kiss to her lips.

Her will melted away like shaved ice in the sun.

He pulled back, his lips curved in a smile, his eyes gentle. The house was quiet, the servants abed. His instruments surrounded them like guardians, gleaming in the lamplight. Tomorrow she intended to cancel her remaining performances, and then she and James would leave London.

But tonight . . . Tonight was her one chance to steal a few moments of happiness to treasure for the rest of her lonely days. For she knew she would never meet another man like Wylde. He had opened his heart to her. Perhaps it was time she did the same.

"What is your given name, Your Grace?" She took a step back, slowly unbuttoning one of her gloves.

His gaze fixed on her hands. "Thornton."

"Thornton Matherton, Duke of Wyldehaven?" She peeled the glove from her hand.

"Thornton Alistair Edward Gideon, actually." He did not look away as she leisurely undid the other glove.

"I am Miranda Katerina." She smiled and set the gloves on his desk. "Mama was fond of Shakespeare."

She reached up to take the pins from her hair. The ebony locks slipped down around her shoulders, tumbling down her back. She placed the pins on the desk beside her gloves and shook her head, her straight hair gleaming like jet in the lamplight.

"Miranda," he said in a hoarse whisper, "what are you doing?"

"Changing my mind." She took his hand and placed it over her breast.

Her soft flesh beneath his palm lit the fuse on his carefully banked desire. He hooked his arm around her waist and pulled her into his embrace, her womanly figure molding to his. Her lips parted and her eyelids drooped. Beneath his hand her nipple swelled.

"Do not play games with me, Miranda," he warned, nearly dizzy from the scent of her. "I want you too badly."

"This is no game." She slid her arms around his neck, easing closer to him. "I want you to make love to me, Thornton."

"You said you would be no man's mistress." He buried his face in her throat, nipped the flesh there.

"And I will not." She arched her neck, allowing him more access. Her dark eyes, sultry with sin, slid to his. "There can only be this night, Thornton. If you cannot accept my terms, I will go."

"Can you leave so easily?" He tugged at the bodice of her evening dress, laved his tongue along the exposed curves of her bosom.

Her breath caught with a surprised little squeak that made him smile. He slipped his fingers into her décolletage. Found and rubbed her nipple with the backs of his fingers.

"Can you let me go so easily?" She gasped as he stroked a particularly sensitive spot. "Please say yes, Wylde. Please say we can have this night."

"We can have this night." He took her mouth in a kiss that had her fingernails digging into his shoulders, had her rubbing against him. He pulled back from the kiss, catching her lower lip between his teeth. His brain had fogged; his blood thundered in his veins, demanding he take her. Here. Now. "Tomorrow," he muttered, "we will talk."

"Talk. Yes. Now kiss me before I go mad."

He covered her mouth with his, crushing her into his embrace, one hand tangled in that black, Gypsy hair. She arched against him, silently demanding closer, harder, faster.

And he never disappointed a lady.

Chapter 16

H e removed her clothing with a skill that left her breathless, leaving her clad only in her shift and stockings. The rest of her garments he cast aside willy-nilly, his movements quick and sure, his face taut with urgency. She sagged in his arms, knees weak, content to let him do with her what he would. He backed her up against the pianoforte, capturing her nipple in his mouth right through the delicate cotton of her chemise. She whimpered as the pleasure exploded through her, grasping his hair in her hands as he cupped her bottom in his palms and rubbed against her.

She should have been frightened. She was a virgin. But she had seen and heard too much in her years to be undone by maidenly modesty. Secretly she had always wondered what it felt like to be bedded. Clearly it could not be painful—except for that first time, she had been told—or else women would never tolerate such behavior. And she trusted Wylde—Thornton—to be kind.

He nuzzled his face between her breasts, then took the neckline of her shift in his teeth and tried to tug it down. She squealed in surprise, and he let go of the material, grinning at her.

She grabbed his shirt and attempted to pull the edges from the waistband of his breeches, though she was only half successful. "What think you of that, wicked man?"

"You want wicked?" His reckless grin both thrilled her and made her nervous. He yanked the shirt over his head, popping ties along the way, then tossed the garment on the floor. Before she could do more than goggle at his naked torso, he leaned over and closed the lid to the pianoforte. The snap of the wood made her jump, and then she let out a small yelp as he grabbed her around the waist and seated her on top of the instrument.

She sat with her face on a level with his, her heart nearly pounding out of her chest. He held her gaze for a long moment, then slid his hands beneath the edge of her chemise, stroking over stockinged calves and frilly garters before his hands swept over her bare thighs. She said nothing, just watched. Just felt. Her lips parted.

His thumbs brushed over her mound before he grabbed her bottom in both hands and tugged her forward, shoving the chemise to her waist as he did so.

"Oh my!" She grabbed his shoulders, then pinkened as he looked down at her exposed womanhood. She nearly squirmed away, but the expression of appreciation on his face held her captive. Slowly, he raised his gaze to hers.

"*This* is wicked," he whispered, leaning in to kiss her with lazy deliberation. As if he had all the time in the world to enjoy her mouth, tease her tongue. Meanwhile he stroked her dampening folds with his fingers. She whimpered, leaning into his kiss, spreading her legs a little more.

"And this." He dipped his head down to her breasts, took the hard nub of one nipple between his teeth. And still his fingers lingered between her legs.

Her head fell back, her eyes slid closed, and she clung to him with both hands.

"And this," he murmured, easing her down to lie flat on top of the pianoforte. Then he ducked his head and touched his tongue between her legs.

She jolted, nearly sitting up again. But he laid a hand on her chest, gently easing her back down, and proceeded to make her head spin with the insane pleasure of his mouth.

How could she have known such bliss was possible? Awash in overwhelming sensation, she dug her nails into his shoulders and hung on tight. She was so aroused that her body responded instantly to his demands. He urged her up and up and up until she arched her pelvis toward his mouth, begging him in whispers to end her torment. Then he did, and pleasure exploded through her like Chinese fireworks.

Her body sagged on the pianoforte, his hands on her hips holding her fast so she did not slip to the floor in a puddle.

"Sweet girl," he murmured. "Do you want more?"

She lolled her head to the side and opened her eyes. He was watching her with that intent gaze, the utter picture of a man holding on to his control with slippery fingers.

"I want *you*." She undulated her hips. "Please God, finish it, Wylde. Take me before I go mad."

"Be certain," he warned in a guttural tone, tearing at the fastenings of his breeches.

"I am certain." She smiled as he managed to shove his clothing down, baring that part of him she had never seen, only imagined. And her imagination had not done him justice. His manhood thrust forward as if leading the charge, hard and swollen.

For an instant panic fluttered in her belly. "You are larger than I expected."

He gave a chuckle as he slipped his hands beneath her bottom and tugged her to the very edge of the pianoforte. "Do not fear, Miranda. Man and woman were designed by God to fit together—like a key in a lock."

"I trust you not to hurt me." She grasped his forearms and clung.

"A maiden's first time involves a bit of discomfort," he said, urging the head up against her female folds. "I shall endeavor to be gentle."

"Thank you," she murmured, then moaned as he pressed his hot flesh forward in slow, unrelenting increments.

He filled her near to bursting, working his manhood into her untried body. She winced at the sting as he forged inexorably forward. When he was fully seated inside her, he leaned over to kiss her lips.

"Hold on," he advised, then began to move.

She had thought his fingers talented back in the breakfast room. She had thought his mouth to be the zenith of heaven only moments ago. But *this* . . . this transformed her body and sent her senses spinning, the epitome of anything she had ever felt before.

"That's it," he murmured, lifting her leg beneath the knee and curving it around his waist. "Hang on to me, love. Let me take you places you have never imagined."

"Dear God, what are you doing to me?"

He ground his hips against hers, his hardness rubbing against sensitive spots deep within her that she'd never imagined she had. "Making you mine."

"Oh, God." Her eyes slid closed as it began again. She clung to his neck blindly as he bent over her, laving her nipples with his tongue, driving them both mad with desire. If anything, he seemed to grow bigger inside her, moving faster, harder. More urgently.

"Hold on to me," he commanded, then thrust once, twice. Then he slipped out of her and stiffened, his eyes closed and neck muscles bulging. A long, low groan slipped past his lips as his climax swept over him, his fingers clenching around her limbs as he spilled himself on her thigh. Then he relaxed, over her, around her.

She toyed with his hair as he laid his head near her shoulder, breathing as if he had run for miles. A small smile curved her lips. "So that is lovemaking."

He opened one eye. "Give me a few moments and I will show you more, perhaps even in a bed this time. I am afraid that was over more quickly than I intended." He closed his eyes again, then reached up a hand to lazily fondle her breast. "I wanted you too much. I cannot imagine *not* wanting you, ever. Even when we are both in our dotage."

She tried not to read too much into his comment. "I never imagined you as a lecherous old man."

"I imagined you all the time." He stroked his hand lazily over her nude form. "Just like this. Naked. Mine."

She was flattered by his desire, but her heart ached for what he did not offer. She had succumbed to her passions and given herself to him, but nothing had changed. And nothing would. She would never have his love or the right to stand at his side as his wife.

"I am yours for tonight," she whispered. She only hoped she had the strength to walk away when the time came.

"Well, Wyldehaven, we are waiting. Show the cards."

Daniel Byrne raised a regally sardonic brow. "Are you implying something, Rothgard?"

"Perhaps I am." Lord Rothgard tapped the edge of the short stack of cards on the table. "No one has that much good luck."

Byrne shrugged. "Lady Luck is not with you this evening, Rothgard. Or perhaps it is your skill that is in question."

Rothgard surged to his feet, green eyes blazing. "Have a care with your words, Duke."

"Not every man has a head for cards." Byrne smirked. "Perhaps it is a family trait."

The men watching the game murmured with alarm as the tension in the room rose.

"What are you implying, Wyldehaven?" Rothgard demanded.

"Simply an observation that not all men have the

logic—or the temperament—for gaming. Like your son, for instance."

"You leave my son out of this!" Rothgard slapped his cards facedown on the table.

"I must admit it was my pleasure to beat him. His cattle will make a wonderful addition to my stable." Byrne also laid down his cards. "Do you concede this game, Rothgard? Or is this drama merely a way to avoid paying your losses?"

The earl stiffened. "Tread carefully, Wyldehaven."

"I am simply wondering if this is a new tactic employed by the men of your family, to cause an incident at the tables when your luck is not going well. One could almost call it cheating . . . or dishonorable at best."

Rothgard jerked to his feet, his chair toppling over. "You dare call my honor into question? I accept that from no man!"

"So vehement." Byrne toyed with his pile of winnings, a smile playing at his lips.

"I demand satisfaction."

"At your pleasure," Byrne said with a nod.

"My seconds will contact you." Rothgard leaned forward, his hands flat on the table. "And stay the hell away from my son." He jerked away, storming from the room.

"Well then, that was a bit of excitement." Byrne slid his gaze over the spectators. "Would anyone else care to play?"

* * *

A warm and tender hand slid along her belly, up her ribs, and closed gently around her breast.

Foggy with sleep, Miranda instinctively pressed herself into the palm of that hand, arching her back. Her bare buttocks came into contact with furred skin and something hard and hot. Her body recognized it before her mind could wake, and she rubbed her bottom against the delicious hardness.

"That's it," a voice whispered in her ear. "Show me what you want."

"Wylde," she murmured. A hand slid between her legs from behind, parting her feminine folds. Then his hard cock slid between her thighs, not penetrating, just resting snugly close to her heat.

Her eyelids drifted open. Sunlight trickled in through the window, gleaming off the elegant pitcher and bowl on the bureau. Heavy bed hangings kept most of the light at bay, sheltering them in a cocoon of shadow. She was wrapped in Wylde's arms, one of his hands kneading her breast and the other splayed across her belly, holding her fast against his aroused body.

Her own hunger shocked her with its intensity. Her nipples peaked like pebbles and dampness slicked her inner thighs. Desire spiked when he began to lazily suck on her neck, as if she were a candy to be savored. She moaned, curling backward into him, wanting him.

"Can you take me again so soon?" he asked. The hand on her belly drifted lower, one finger slipping between her folds.

"I want to," she replied, parting her thighs, aching for his touch. "But it is morning."

"That just means we can see what we are doing." He moved from her breast and lifted her leg with a hand beneath her thigh, opening her up to him.

"What are you doing?" she gasped, startled by his manhood rubbing more firmly over her damp sex.

"Something new." With his other hand, he reached down and adjusted himself, and then she felt him slide into her from behind. "Tell me if I hurt you."

Hurt her? She groaned at the deliciously new, yet familiar, feeling. There was something scandalous about allowing him to make love to her this way, facing away from him. He curved one arm firmly beneath her, his hand splayed on her belly, guiding her in time with his slow, steady movements. He held her leg aloft with the other hand. The hand on her belly dipped lower, and he searched for and found her center again, rubbing the sensitive bud with his fingers. Passion roared through her. She pressed her bottom back against him, encouraging his thrusts while his fingers drove her wild.

She had learned during the night how to tell

when he was near release. So many times he had allowed her to reach her climax first, then followed later when she was limp and sated, always spending outside her body. But not this time. This time she wanted to give something to *him*. She wanted to make him so wild that he would explode inside her. The drive to do that overwhelmed her. When she felt his muscles clench in preparation of pulling back, she tightened her inner channel around him.

"Sweet Jesu, Miranda." He hesitated, then thrust into her again. And again.

"I love how that feels," she whispered.

"It feels incredible." His hips stilled but he kept stroking her with his fingers, kept building the fire.

Her mind spun with escalating desire. He was going to do it again, give her pleasure and then satisfy himself afterward.

Not this time, she thought.

She reached down, halted the hand that was caressing her loins. And rocked her hips, caressing his cock with her slick passage. She heard his quick, indrawn breath, felt the tension in his body.

"Come with me," she whispered. "Do not make me go alone."

"God." He took her hips in both hands, burying his face in her neck as he pulled her back onto his hard shaft, then slid her forward. Again. And again.

She clenched her hands in the bedding and closed her eyes, giving herself over to him completely.

His thrusts grew stronger, more demanding. His fingers dug into her hips, but she did not care. Her mind spun with glee that he had relinquished control. That he was so hungry for her. The pressure built inside her as his movements grew less practiced, more urgent. More frenzied.

He nipped her neck. Fire shot through her, straight to her loins. She rocked her hips in rhythm with his thrusts, determined to urge him onward. Faster. Harder. Whatever it took to send him past the point of sanity. Then she felt him stiffen. He gave a harsh groan and plunged inside her one more time and held there, shuddering, as his seed poured into her.

His climax pushed her over the edge, and her world exploded into multicolored starbursts, leaving her limp and panting and utterly, completely satisfied in his arms.

Already he was relaxing, his softening cock slipping out of her. She slowly pulled her leg from his grasp. He curled his arm around her waist again, pulling her back more snugly against him so her bottom cradled his loins. His breathing sounded ragged and his heartbeat thundered against her back. They lay together in silence, perspiration slowly drying on dampened hair and skin. Gradually, his arm grew heavy across her waist; his respiration eased.

He was falling asleep.

She stroked his arm, listening to his breathing as the sun rose higher above the horizon. Finally she knew she could linger no longer. She gingerly slid from beneath his arm, easing from the bed so as not to wake him. He mumbled something and dragged the pillow closer, burying his face in it. Then he settled.

She stood for a moment, naked in the morning sunlight, drinking in his magnificent body. Any woman would be thrilled to have a man like this as a lover. As hers. But she knew well enough that even though he had become her lover, he would never be hers to keep. Men like him did not wed women like her—nobodies with dubious parentage.

This night, this memory, was all she would ever have. It would have to be enough.

Silently, she gathered her clothing. It was time to go home to her child.

Chapter 17

"**W**ylde!"

The shout, followed by a shove to his shoulder, woke Wylde from a sound sleep. He swiped at the hand shaking him. "'Tis the bloody middle of the night; let me sleep."

"It is nine o'clock in the morning, you fool, and there is much to do."

Wylde opened his eyes, squinting in the morning light. "Who opened the draperies?" He scowled at Wulf, who stood beside his bed. "What are you doing here?"

"Late night, was it?" Wulf asked, his sarcasm in full form.

"Is he sotted?" Darcy's voice came from somewhere behind Wulf, where the sunlight was the brightest.

"I am not sotted," Wylde snapped, closing his eyes against the blinding glare.

"'Tis the only thing that makes sense to me,"

Darcy said. "What other explanation is there for what happened last night?"

Last night . . .

Wylde sat straight up in bed, bunching the covers around his waist. He glanced around the bedchamber. But no trace of Miranda remained. She was gone.

"Blast it," he muttered, then scrambled from the bed, dragging the coverlet with him.

"That's the spirit," Darcy said. "There is still time to fix things."

"Not too late at all," Wulf agreed.

Ignoring their nonsense, he jerked open the bedchamber door. "Phillips!"

A passing housemaid turned to look at him, squeaked in alarm at his near nudity, then reddened and scurried down the hall.

"Fetch Phillips!" he called after her, then shut the door, leaning back against it. His friends watched him steadily from their places beside his bed. "And what the devil are the two of you doing here again?"

"We're your seconds," Darcy said. "At least I assume we are. We did not ask Kit."

"Seconds? What the bloody hell for?"

Wulf frowned. "Your duel with Rothgard."

"My *what* with *whom*?" The door opened behind him, nudging him in the back. He glanced over his shoulder and through the opening to see his valet peering back at him. "Ah, Phillips. Excellent. I must dress immediately."

"Yes, you must," Darcy agreed as Wylde opened the door wide so the valet might enter. "The sooner we tender your apologies to Rothgard, the sooner this might all be forgotten."

"I do not know what the two of you are babbling about," Wylde said, then addressed his valet. "When did Miss Fontaine leave?"

"Miss Fontaine?" Wulf cast a questioning look at Darcy, who raised his eyebrows.

"I believe it was shortly before eight o'clock, Your Grace. Travers sent her home in your carriage." The servant lowered his voice. "The ducal crest was covered for discretion."

"Excellent. At least I know where she is." He clapped Phillips on the back. "Good man. Now fetch me some clothes. I must catch her before she flees London."

The valet darted for the wardrobe, and Wulf rose from his seat. "Have you not heard a word we have said, Wylde?"

"No, and I do not have time—"

"Stop." Wulf held up his hand. "Make the time. Last night the Duke of Wyldehaven insulted the Earl of Rothgard during a card game at Maynard's home. Rothgard has issued a challenge. Pistols at dawn tomorrow in Hyde Park."

"I was not at Maynard's last night. I was—"

"You were here," Wulf finished for him. "With someone named Miss Fontaine, apparently."

"Oh, I see," Darcy said to Wulf. "It must have been the imposter at Maynard's."

"What?" His attention caught, Wylde blindly accepted the drawers Phillips handed him. "Curse that bounder! He has insulted Rothgard?"

"And caused Rothgard to challenge Wyldehaven," Wulf clarified.

"Bloody hell. I shall go to Rothgard and explain."

"Explain what?" Darcy arched his brows. "That you have a mad twin running about London wreaking havoc in your name, when 'tis well known you are an only child? Well, that is an explanation I would believe, don't you agree, Wulf?"

"Oh, indubitably." Wulf crossed his arms and nodded.

"Besides, as your seconds, we should be the ones to tender your apologies," Darcy said.

"No, the imposter is my cross to bear, so I shall endeavor to handle the matter. What was the insult over?" Wylde allowed Phillips to shoo him into the dressing room, but he kept the door cracked open and raised his voice to be heard. "Cards, was it?"

"The false Wyldehaven impugned the earl's honor by intimating that Rothgard was attempting to cheat," Darcy explained, raising his voice to be heard. "Naturally that provoked a challenge."

"Which he will leave you to face, I have no doubt," Wulf said with a snort.

"Unless you apologize for the slight," Darcy added. "In which case Rothgard might accept your apology, though I doubt it after what happened with young Alonso."

"Alonso?" Wylde emerged from his dressing room clad in breeches and his shirt and stockings. Phillips hurried after him, a fresh cravat dangling from his fingers. "Hold a moment. Arenson said something to me about that at the musicale last night."

"Arenson and Rothgard are friends from their school days," Wulf said. "I am certain Arenson is privy to the family secrets."

"Your Grace, please sit," Phillips said. "I must tie your cravat." The valet waved the piece of linen. "You cannot go anywhere until you are appropriately garbed!"

Wylde pulled a wooden chair away from a small table and sat in it. "A simple knot today, Phillips. I am leaving in a few minutes."

"But, Your Grace—"

"I am sitting, Phillips. Get on with it." He glanced at his friends. "Darcy, what do you know of this business with Alonso?"

Phillips gave an aggrieved sigh but came forward and began to loop the cravat around Wylde's neck.

"The scandal has been hushed up," Darcy said, moving to stand where Wylde could see him around the valet. "Luckily, I tend to frequent certain establishments that cater to clientele of a somewhat lower social class. Some of these fellows were at Maynard's during the incident with Alonso."

"What do they say happened?"

"The false duke cleaned Alonso out of most of his inheritance. The earl was out of town at one of his northern estates. When Rothgard returned and discovered what had occurred, he got himself invited to Maynard's next gathering and challenged the devil he thought was Wyldehaven to a game. I do not know if he intended to win back his son's wealth or simply confront the man who had taken it, but the next thing we knew, accusations were made and the imposter called Rothgard's honor into question."

"And now there is a dawn appointment for tomorrow morning," Wulf said. "But I doubt the imposter is going to show for it."

"Which would put *your* honor on the block," Darcy said. "A challenge has been issued. You can apologize—"

"Which Rothgard probably will not accept, not after what happened with young Alonso," Wulf pointed out, as Darcy had moments before.

"Or you can meet him at dawn," Darcy said. "Now we know you are a crack shot—"

"But if you kill Rothgard, you may have to flee the country," Wulf concluded.

"And if Rothgard kills *you*, well, none of us want that." Darcy frowned. "And if you do not show up at all, the honor of Wyldehaven will be questioned."

"There was enough of that in your father's time," Wulf said. "So the best solution would be to find this imposter and march him up to Rothgard to prove your story about a look-alike."

"But we have been looking for him since you came back to London and are still unable to find him, so we cannot count on taking that tack," Darcy said. "Now if you had some other way to prove to Rothgard that you were not at Maynard's last night . . . "

"Such as a witness who can vouch for you . . ." Wulf raised his brows in meaning.

"I have no witness," Wylde said as Phillips finished the last knot on his cravat.

"What about Miss Fontaine?" Wulf asked. "Might she vouch for your whereabouts?"

"Out of the question." Wylde stood as the valet darted back to the dressing room, only to reappear moments later with a bottle green coat. Wylde held his arms out to the sides and allowed the valet to garb him in the impeccably cut Weston creation. "I will not drag a lady into this."

"Oh." Darcy and Wulf exchanged looks. "Since she stayed the night with you, we assumed—"

"Assume nothing. And forget about Miss Fontaine. She will not be a part of this."

"But—" At Wylde's sharp look, the words died on Darcy's lips.

"I will go to Rothgard and attempt to placate him," Wylde said, standing still as Phillips checked the fit of his coat. "He is a reasonable man."

"I pray you are right," Wulf said. "But we will stand as your seconds until the matter is resolved. In the meantime, we will continue to look for the imposter in hopes of dragging him before Rothgard."

"Agreed." Wylde waved the valet away and turned toward the door. "I will send a note around to the two of you and let you know if your services will be needed. Hopefully, they will not be."

"What kind of madness is this?" The Earl of Rothgard stormed into the drawing room where Wylde awaited. A tall, lean man with dark hair heavily streaked with silver, his sharp features included thick brows, a blade of a nose, and glittering green eyes. Despite his age—somewhere near fifty, Wylde guessed—the earl still possessed a powerful force of presence that might have made a less confident man cower. Especially now that fury came off him in waves, like steam on the walkway after a hard rain.

"I have come to offer my apologies for the misunderstanding last night," Wylde said, getting to his feet.

"Misunderstanding?" Rothgard pointed a finger. "How dare you insult my honor and then expect me to forgive all with a few pretty words? Someone needs to put you in your place."

"I know my place." Determined not to give in to his own temper, Wylde reminded himself that this man had been ill-used by the imposter and had every right to be angry. "I am the Duke of Wyldehaven, and I have come to apologize and offer restitution."

"Restitution? Your insult might have been forgiven with restitution," Rothgard said. "But what you did to my son was unconscionable."

"I am prepared to make amends—"

"Amends! You drained the boy of a year's allowance, then took ownership of his stables and sold his favorite team at Tat's. How the devil will you make amends for that?"

"If you simply provide me with a figure . . . "

"'Tis not about the money, you scoundrel, 'tis about the honor of my family. And that has no price." Rothgard raked a scornful gaze over him. "Except perhaps your blood. Now get out of my house."

"I have my honor, too," Wylde said, deciding to show all his cards. "And it is being stained by another. Someone is blackening my name, someone who looks very much like me."

"Are you drunk? What kind of nonsensical story is this?"

"It is the truth. I was not at Maynard's last night, Rothgard. Or the night your son lost everything. This fellow looks like me and is calling himself Wyldehaven and causing me no amount of trouble."

Rothgard stared for a long moment, then burst out laughing. "You expect me to believe such a wild tale?"

"It is the truth."

"Indeed? And is there anyone who can vouch for your whereabouts the night my son lost all? Or last night for that matter?"

"My servants will testify that I was home on both nights in question."

"Your servants?" Rothgard chuckled. "Your servants depend on you for their living, so of course they will say whatever you require them to say. Is there no one else? Someone who is *not* dependent on you for their living?"

Wylde thought briefly of Miranda. "No. There is no one."

"Then we have nothing to discuss. I will meet you tomorrow at dawn. I hope your affairs are in order."

"See to your own." Jaw tight, Wylde strode out of the drawing room.

* * *

With a heavy heart, Miranda wrote the last of the notes to cancel her performances. She could stay in London no longer, not after having spent the night in Wylde's arms.

She was not worried about scandal. Rather, she feared for her heart. She knew if she stayed, she would end up back in his bed again, no matter her resolve. And she would never want to leave.

Part of her wondered if that life would really be so bad. To be cared for by a man like Wylde, a man who would never treat her with disregard, even if their liaison came to an end. To live a comfortable life raising James while enjoying nights of passion in Wylde's bed. So tempting . . .

But to depend on him for every crust of bread, every piece of clothing? To be subject to his will in the matter of raising James? No, she did not want any of that. She wanted to be regarded as an equal, not a hireling. She wanted his respect, not his money. She wanted him to value her as a person, not a possession. But the Duke of Wyldehaven was too far above the touch of Miranda Fontaine from Little Depping, however convincing a contessa she made. The only position she could ever hope to attain would be mistress; her birth precluded her from anything more honorable than that. She had once sworn to herself that she would never stoop to such a position, and she intended to keep her promise.

No matter how difficult it might be.

There was no more to be done now. It was best if she took James and returned to the country. She had collected her belongings as well as the baby's. As soon as Thaddeus arrived with the last of her inheritance, she would take James and purchase a seat on the next mail coach out of London.

To stay longer, to be tempted by what she could not have—it would tear her heart in two.

The knocker sounded at the front door. As the servants saw to the caller, Miranda carefully addressed each missive, genuinely sad to have to cancel the engagements. For all that she had initially resisted the idea of performing, she had to admit she seemed to have a talent for it. She truly enjoyed singing in front of a crowd, though she had no ambition to tread the boards of the London stage. That life brought her mother nothing but misery, and so as the contessa, she had been content with smaller, private gatherings.

If only things were different, she would have continued to perform as long as Society would have her.

The footman announced Thaddeus, and she glanced up as her friend entered the room. Then she gasped and jumped to her feet. "Good heavens, Thaddeus! What happened?"

He tried to smile, despite his swollen lip. "Mint and Barney had a word with me last night."

"My goodness!" She assisted him into a chair, then hovered over him, scanning his battered face. "You must be mad to associate with such people!"

"I agree with you. And I shall endeavor to do better." He paused, then withdrew a pouch from his coat pocket. "Beginning with this."

"Oh, good, you brought the money." Miranda opened the pouch, looked inside, then gasped. "Good heavens, Thaddeus, this is too much!" She raised her gaze to his. "I shall not accept a sou more than what is mine. You must take the rest of this back."

"It *is* all yours." He cleared his throat, and his face reddened, but he did not look away. "I told you that your investments did not do well, that you had lost half your dowry because of it. But the truth of the matter is, *I* took the money."

"What?" She could only gape at him, her mother's dearest friend. "You took the money? Whatever for?"

He indicated his bruised face. "Gambling. The moneylenders were after me, and I felt I had no choice. I borrowed it." He tightened his jaw. "No, I *stole* it. I told myself that I would repay it, yet I never did. But then you arrived in London asking for the money, and I panicked."

Her heart heavy, Miranda sank down in her chair. "How could you?"

"I know it is unconscionable, and your mother, God bless her, would probably roast me alive had she been here to see it. I cannot tell you how deeply I regret betraying your trust."

"Oh, Thaddeus." Saddened, disillusioned, she closed the pouch and clenched her hands around it. It was appearing more and more to the best that she leave London. "Perhaps you should leave now."

He tried to smile, but it did not touch his eyes. "I do not blame you for that. But the money was not my only reason for paying this call. Have you heard the latest?"

"The latest what?"

"Gossip," he confirmed. "Rumor has it that Rothgard has challenged Wyldehaven."

"What?" She gaped at him. "When? Why?"

"Last night Wyldehaven insulted Rothgard's family name across the card table. And after what the duke did to Rothgard's son, I can hardly blame the man for calling Wyldehaven out."

She dropped the pouch on the table. "You had better tell me—slowly—what happened. I can hardly conceive that Wylde—Wylde*haven*—got himself into such a position." She knew it had to be the imposter. After all, Wylde had been otherwise engaged last night—with her. But no one else would know that. To the world, it would indeed look like he had impugned Rothgard's honor.

"As I said, it started with Rothgard's son. Alonso lost a year's allowance and his entire stable to Wyldehaven in a game of whist a couple of nights ago. I suspect Rothgard went looking for a confrontation with the duke, and it resulted in a challenge."

"Of course Wyldehaven refused." She met his gaze, hoping he would agree. "Naturally he would explain to Lord Rothgard. Apologize."

Thaddeus hesitated. "You cannot simply refuse a duel, my dear. Honor is at stake."

"But he is innocent of the crime. You know of the imposter, Thaddeus. Surely it was him, not Wyldehaven, who did these things."

"Pah! I do not believe that Banbury tale, and I thought you did not either. Then again, perhaps your *tendre* for the duke has changed your mind about his character."

She scowled at him. "Do not patronize me, Thaddeus. You are in no position to cast stones. Facts have come to light that make me believe without a doubt there truly is an imposter who is trying to blacken Wyldehaven's name."

"I see." He sent her a look of pity. "As you wish, my dear. But I felt you should hear the news from a friend."

"When is this duel to take place?" she asked, deliberately ignoring the reference to himself.

"Tomorrow at dawn. I am certain I can learn the location."

"No, thank you." She stood, and courtesy demanded he stand as well. "I appreciate your assistance while I was here in London. But I have much to do, and—"

He held up a hand. "I was on the stage for over thirty years. I can tell when the audience has lost interest."

"I am sorry." His downcast expression tugged at her heartstrings, but she could not ignore the fact that he had lied to her. Stolen from her. "Be well, Thaddeus."

"And you." He took her hand and pressed a kiss to the back of it, then laid his other hand over hers, meeting her eyes. "Your mother would be proud of you."

Her cheeks pinkened and she slowly tugged her hand free. "Thank you, Thaddeus."

"Farewell, fair one." With a bow, he turned and left the room.

Miranda waited until she heard the front door close behind him before she scooped up the money and followed. When she reached the foyer, she told the butler, "Summon the coach. And send Annie to my chamber."

"Yes, miss."

Then she turned toward the staircase. She had intended to leave London immediately, without seeing Wylde, her heart closely guarded. But now . . .

By the time she reached the top of the stairs and

made her way to her bedchamber, Annie was already waiting for her.

"Summon Mrs. Cooper to watch over James," she told her. "Then help me change my clothing. We are paying a call."

Chapter 18

❧

"**W**hat do you mean the duke is not at home?" Miranda glared at the gray-haired butler. "Where has he gone?"

"I am not at liberty to say, miss. Would you care to leave your card?"

"No, I do not wish to leave my card. I wish to wait for the duke's return."

A pained expression crossed the servant's face. "I do not know when that will be, miss, so it is better if you leave your card with me."

"I bet he's in there," Annie said. "He just doesn't want to come out."

The butler drew himself up, his features rigid. "I assure you His Grace is not at home. I shall inform him of your call." And he closed the door.

Annie gaped at the closed door. "Rudesby!"

"Calm yourself, Annie." Miranda began to descend the stairs toward her coach, which stood at the curb. "Perhaps I should have left my card, but I forgot them in my hurry to get here."

"The duke knows who you are. That stiff-rump will get his."

"Now, Annie." Even through her distress, Miranda smiled at the girl's loyalty. "I have every intention of speaking with the duke today, no matter how many servants try to block the way."

"That's the spirit!" Annie grinned, then nodded at the street. "And you might get your chance. I think that's the duke's carriage."

"Oh." Miranda paused on the sidewalk as the elegant equipage came to a halt behind her own vehicle. When the duke stepped down from the carriage, her heart leapt and tumbled in giddy response.

He paused when he saw her standing on the sidewalk, then came to her, his strides eating up the sidewalk. He stopped right in front of her—rather abruptly, as if he'd changed his mind about something at the last moment—then gave a bow. "Miss Fontaine."

She bobbed a curtsy. "Your Grace."

"Have you been here long?"

"No." Out of the corner of her eye she was aware of the butler opening the door, of the footmen standing by to wait on the duke. But she could not look away from him, away from those velvety dark eyes that even now simmered with barely restrained passion.

"Do come inside." He extended his arm, and she took it, allowing him to accompany her up the stairs. Annie followed behind. "You should not have come here so boldly," he murmured as they stepped into the safety of his home. "The gossips will talk."

"Let them." She lifted her chin. "I rather believe there is a more tasty tidbit for them to nibble on today."

He handed his hat to the butler. "So, you have heard."

"I have. Why are you doing this?" She searched his face for answers. "You know as well as I that you were nowhere near Rothgard last night."

"Not here." He swept an arm toward the hallway. "Let us adjourn to the drawing room. Annie, make yourself comfortable belowstairs. And Travers, will you see to tea?"

"Yes, Your Grace." The butler turned to carry out the order as Miranda accompanied Wylde to the drawing room.

"You do realize," Wylde said as they entered the room, "that you have risked your reputation by coming here today."

"I do not give a fig. I am leaving London anyway."

"I hate that you say that so easily."

"I have no choice. You know I do not." Alone with him in the drawing room, she laid a hand on his

316

arm. "Tell me you are not so foolish as to meet Lord Rothgard at dawn tomorrow."

"You are well informed."

"Thaddeus told me. I understand that you feel the need to pay the tradesmen and make other amends for the actions of the imposter, but risking your life? Is that not too much of a sacrifice?"

"It is complicated."

"No, it is not." Frustrated with his calm acceptance, she propped her hands on her hips. "I see the choice here. If you do not meet Rothgard, your honor is in question. If you do, you might die or, in the best of circumstances, be forced to flee the country."

"That is about the sum of it." Wylde nodded at the servant who entered the room with a tray of tea and biscuits. "We are not to be disturbed," he told the man.

"Yes, Your Grace." With a curious glance toward Miranda, the fellow bowed out of the room, closing the doors behind him.

"Closed doors? Really, Your Grace. What will the servants say?"

"Hang them." He pulled her into his arms. "I have been thinking about this since I opened my eyes this morning and you were gone." He lowered his head and took her mouth in a kiss that made her head spin and brought back every memory of their night together.

By the time he released her, she needed to cling to him for balance. "Good heavens."

He rested his forehead against hers. "I woke up, but you were not there. I hated that feeling."

"We talked about it." She stroked his cheek. "This is for the best, Wylde. I cannot live as your mistress."

"And as a wife? Would you stay then?"

Her breath froze in her lungs. "What are you asking me?"

"Nothing. I am just trying to understand you." He let out a long sigh. "I want you with me, that is all."

"I see. You only said that to get my attention." Disappointed, she struggled to explain. "It is not that I do not want to be with you. I do. But I cannot in good conscience share your bed in exchange for food and shelter. No matter how fancy you dress up the situation, it always remains the same—I would be a whore."

"So a wedding band makes all the difference."

Stung by the dry tone, she stepped out of his embrace. "Yes, because it means I have value to you beyond a warm body in your bed. It means that you trust me to bear your name and your children, to stand beside you in good times and bad."

"I do trust you." The tenderness in his voice was almost enough to convince her. *Almost*.

"Apparently not enough." She blew out a frustrated breath. "This gets us nowhere. What are you going to do about the duel?"

He took her change of subject in stride. "There is nothing to do but meet Rothgard at dawn."

"You are *not* considering such madness! You were not even there. You were with me."

"I remember." The heat in those dark eyes, the roughness of his voice, told her without a doubt that he *did* remember.

"Then tell that to Rothgard. Or let me tell him. I am the only person who can prove that you were not at that card game last night."

"No." He shook his head. "I will not sacrifice your reputation to save my honor."

"My reputation is not worth your life."

"Your reputation is worth everything, and I will do anything to protect it. The imposter is my problem, and this duel is a result of that. If the resolution is to meet Rothgard at dawn, so be it."

She stepped closer, lowering her voice to drive home her point. "Listen to me, Thornton. You cannot let this imposter beat you by luring you into this duel. If you die, then he wins."

"And if I do not appear, he wins as well. My honor would be worthless."

"But if you just explain—"

"I tried to explain. Rothgard laughed in my face." He set his jaw. "No one treats Wyldehaven with such disrespect."

"Now you are just being stubborn!"

"No more so than you." He raised his brows. "You refuse to be a man's mistress because of what happened to your mother. Well, I refuse to allow my honor to be insulted. My father did enough of that for a whole generation of Mathertons."

"I refuse to be a man's mistress because I want more than what my mother had. I want to matter to someone."

"And I want to be known as a better man than my father, not to be considered just like him. Yet that is exactly what this imposter is doing—making people believe I am just like my father. No honor."

"And if I stay here," she said softly, "I *will* be just like my mother—a mistress. A possession. An employee to be dismissed."

"If that is what you think, why did you stay with me last night?"

She stared at him a long moment, hollowness filling her chest where her heart had been. "Don't you know?"

"No, I do not."

"Perhaps it was a bit of madness. Curiosity." She blinked rapidly, fighting back the sting of moisture. "Please do not allow this duel to happen."

"If Rothgard will not accept my apology, there is nothing I can do."

She sniffled, then ignored his searching look. "That is all you need to do—apologize?"

"As long as he accepts it, which he did not. So there is nothing left but to face him."

"You could simply not appear."

"And be branded a dishonorable scoundrel? I would rather die."

"You very well might."

"I am a crack shot."

"So you would rather kill him than suffer dishonor? Why are men so ridiculous?" She dug in her reticule and pulled forth a handkerchief, then dabbed at her eyes. "I am not crying over you," she informed him in her haughtiest tone. "I believe I have dust in my eye."

"Of course you do." He tugged her unresisting back into his arms and cuddled her close. "Darling girl. If only things were different."

"Then make them different." She crushed the handkerchief in her hand and thumped her small fist on his chest. "You are a duke, are you not? Can you not put an end to this madness?"

"Only by meeting Rothgard at dawn."

She dropped her hand to her side. "Do not expect me to be at your funeral."

"I have made arrangements for James," he said. "You only need to consult Barstairs, my man of affairs—"

"I do not want your money. I never did." She sniffled again, distraught to realize the tears had begun to trickle down her cheeks. "Since you insist on pursuing this foolishness, I will pray for you." She took a step back, out of his reach.

"Miranda—"

She cast up her hands. "Leave me be. You have made your choice, and I have made mine. James and I will be leaving on the afternoon mail coach. If you survive—" She sucked in a shaky breath. "If you survive this foolishness, do not look for me."

"But—"

She stepped forward and pressed a kiss to his cheek, then gazed into his eyes. "Good-bye, Wylde. Know that you take my prayers with you." Pressing her handkerchief into his hand, she turned and left the room.

Wylde watched her go. Everything inside him demanded that he call her back, that he entreat her to stay. But he could not.

He crushed her handkerchief in his fist, the gentle scent of rose water clinging to his fingers. His choices in this were either to die or be dishonored, and neither was a situation to which he wanted to expose Miranda. He cared for her too much.

No, he realized. It was more than that. He had fallen in love with her.

Miranda with her proper ways and steadfast morals and generous passion and stubborn independence. She would have made a hell of a duchess. But how could he ask her to join her future to his?

If he did not appear to face Rothgard at dawn, he would bear the taint of dishonor all his days. How could he ask her to share that? To bear that? And how could he ask her to be his wife, only to make her a widow before she was a bride?

Better she leave him now, before she knew what they might have had together. Better to let her go and leave him to shoulder the blame for what was to come on his own.

He lifted her handkerchief to his nose and let the aroma linger in his mind. And considered what might have been.

Dawn came quickly when death was imminent.

Wylde sat in his coach, looking across the green at Rothgard's carriage. The seconds gathered together in the middle of the meadow, wisps of fog curling around their ankles as they examined the dueling pistols and spoke in hushed tones.

The curtains of Rothgard's carriage twitched. Wylde watched with a bone-deep calm as the earl peered out. Their gazes met briefly, then his opponent disappeared back into his carriage.

Wylde glanced down at the handkerchief in his hands. He wound the dainty white square around his fingers, each twist teasing more rose water scent from the bit of linen. The white material had softened with age, and in some spots the cloth was nearly transparent, though the tiny blue flowers along the edges retained their color. An elaborate *F* graced one corner, a blue long-stemmed rose functioning as the middle line through the letter.

F for Fannie?

It would be just like Miranda to keep Fannie's handkerchief as a memory of her mother. Just like he was keeping it to remember Miranda.

He wasn't certain how long he sat there, but then the door to his carriage opened and Darcy stood there, his face grim. "We are ready."

Wylde tucked the handkerchief into his coat sleeve, then climbed out of the carriage.

Rothgard waited by his seconds, one of which was Arenson. His other second bore the case with the dueling pistols. The physician, Dr. Morse, lingered nearby. Rothgard watched Wylde with flinty eyes.

Foolishness. Wylde paused on the green, surveying the tableau. Was there no hope for cooler heads in this insanity? Was there no possible peaceful, reasonable outcome?

The imposter would win, curse him. Unless he was able to convince Rothgard that they could work this out without bloodshed.

"Will you not accept my apology, Rothgard?" he called out, approaching his opponent.

"Apology?" Rothgard scoffed. "Was it not you who spun me the tale about your evil twin brother who is running about London causing all sorts of scandal? What sort of apology is that? According to you, you are innocent and this other fellow is the blackguard." His cronies chuckled and cast pitying glances at Wylde.

"I suspect, Rothgard, that you will accept nothing at all from me."

"After what you did to my son? I bloody well will not."

The last of his hopes for a peaceful reconciliation died a short and final death.

"He is telling the truth," Wulf said. "There really is a fellow who looks like him causing all this trouble."

"You are as mad as he is," Rothgard scoffed.

Wylde laid his hand on his friend's shoulder. "There is no reasoning with him, Wulf. Let us get on with this."

Rothgard shed his hat and coat, leaving him in his shirtsleeves. Despite his age, the man looked as physically fit as Wylde. He waited with disdain on his face while Wylde handed his hat to Darcy. Then Wulf helped Wylde strip off his immaculately tailored coat. Miranda's handkerchief slipped from inside the sleeve and fluttered to the ground.

"Blast it." Wylde had barely managed to extricate himself from the garment when Arenson swooped forward and scooped up the bit of lace.

"And what is this, Wyldehaven? A token from your ladybird?"

Wylde held out his hand. "Please return that."

Arenson sniggered and waved the handkerchief. Then his expression sobered and he held up the square by its corners so he could better see the embroidery. He glanced at Rothgard. "Look at this."

Rothgard snatched the handkerchief from his friend and glanced at the pattern, then froze. "Where did you get this?" he asked, his voice hoarse.

"It belongs to a friend. Please return it."

Rothgard's fingers clenched around the bit of cotton and he raised it to his nose and sniffed. "Attar of roses," he breathed.

"It looks like—"

"I know what it looks like," Rothgard snapped, cutting off Arenson. "But it seems impossible." He fixed his gaze on Wylde. "A friend, you say?"

"A dear friend." Wylde continued to extend his hand. "If you would . . ."

"Where is she?" Rothgard demanded. "How do you know her?"

Wylde frowned at Rothgard. "I do not see how this is any business of yours."

"Shall we get on with the duel?" Darcy asked. "Before someone comes and reports us to the watch?"

"Never mind that," Arenson said. "Where did you get Fannie's handkerchief?"

"Bollocks," Darcy muttered, glancing across the park. "We are too late. Someone is coming."

All of them turned toward the approaching carriage. Rothgard's second closed the pistol case and signaled to one of Rothgard's footmen to come and take it back to the coach.

Wulf shaded his eyes. "That looks like one of your rigs, Wylde."

"Bloody hell. What the devil is she doing here? Excuse me, gentlemen, while I handle this bit of business." Even as the carriage stopped close to the combatants, Wylde was striding forward. "John, are you mad for bringing her here?"

The coachman looked just as unhappy as Wylde. "If I hadn't, Your Grace, they were going to hire a hack."

"Blast that woman. This is no place for her."

Young Thomas the footman hopped down and opened the door to the carriage. Annie scrambled out. "We've come to stop you from killing yourself," she announced cheerfully.

"Annie, you should not be here. Now take your mistress and return home."

Miranda appeared in the doorway. "I am not going anywhere," she announced. He refused to step forward, to help her from the coach, but she climbed nimbly down with Thomas's assistance. Once on the ground, she glared up at Wylde. "I refuse to sit at home wringing my hands, Wylde, when I can put an end to this foolishness."

"This is no place for a woman." He took her arm,

tried to urge her back into the carriage. "Leave. Now."

"I will not." She jerked her arm from his and looked behind him at the assembled party. "Which one of you is Lord Rothgard?" she called, striding forward.

"I am Rothgard." The earl stepped forward, his face arrested with fascination.

"Contessa," Arenson said. "What are you doing here?"

"Setting matters straight." She focused on the earl, who studied her face with something akin to wonder. "Lord Rothgard, the duke is innocent of the crimes you lay at his door. There is someone who greatly resembles him going about London causing no amount of mischief. We suspect this miscreant is one of the former duke's by-blows amusing himself at the duke's expense."

"Wyldehaven said as much in his apology," Rothgard said, his tone kind. "However, miss, you must understand how fantastical that sounds."

"I do. But my maid has seen this fellow with her own eyes and can attest that he does exist."

"That I can!" Annie said.

"Enough of this," Wylde growled. "There is supposed to be a duel taking place here."

Miranda sent him a look of disbelief. "Are you so eager to die, Your Grace?"

He glared. "Your confidence in me is astounding."

"Contessa, how did you come to be here?" Arenson asked.

Rothgard shot a meaningful glance at his friend. "Arenson, will you not introduce me to this lady?"

"This is the Contessa della Pietra, Rothgard. Remember, I told you about her? She is the wonderful songbird who so resembles Fannie Fontaine."

The earl took Miranda's hand and brushed a kiss along the back. "You do look remarkably like our old friend Fannie," he said. "You must forgive our stares."

"Actually," Miranda said with an apologetic smile, "Fannie was my mother."

The earl's hand spasmed around hers. "What did you say?" he rasped.

"Fannie Fontaine was my mother." Gently, she tugged at her hand, which the earl finally relinquished. "My lord, you must understand that you have made a mistake in challenging the duke. He was otherwise engaged the evening you issued your challenge. I stand as witness."

"Enough." Wylde took her arm. "Miranda, you should go home. This is men's business."

"Did you say Miranda?" Arenson whispered. He traded glances with Rothgard.

"Stop," Rothgard said when Wylde would have led her away. "Perhaps I have been too hasty in rejecting your apology, Wyldehaven."

329

"What?" Wylde frowned in confusion.

Wulf leaned forward. "Do not question it, Wylde."

"I was angry over what was done to my son," Rothgard said. "But if you were not the perpetrator of that misdeed or the man who insulted me over cards, then I have no quarrel with you." He looked back at Miranda. "When did your mother marry, my dear? Was your father a kind man?"

Miranda stiffened. "My mother never married, my lord."

"I see." He studied her, his gaze sliding from her hair to her face and back again. "Might I ask your age, Contessa?"

"Actually, my name is Miranda Fontaine. The Contessa della Pietra is a name I use when performing."

Rothgard sucked in a breath. "What is your full name, my dear?"

"Miranda Katerina Fontaine."

"*Miss Fontaine,*" Darcy whispered with a nudge at Wulf.

"And your age . . . ?" Rothgard prompted again.

"I am twenty-two years old."

"And your birth date?"

"For pity's sake, Rothgard," Wylde intervened. "This is not an inquisition! Miss Fontaine has nothing to do with our issue. Allow me to put her back in her carriage and return her home."

"I beg your indulgence," Rothgard said, raising a hand. "Tell me your birth date, Miss Fontaine."

"The twenty-ninth of December," she replied, exchanging a puzzled glance with Wylde.

"And you stand as witness that Wyldehaven was not at Maynard's the night before last?"

"I do. And my maid stands as witness that there truly is a man who is pretending to be the duke and looks very much like him."

"The game where the insult occurred was in the wee hours of the morning," the earl said with a kind smile. "So as much as I admire your attempt, I fail to understand how you can stand as witness—"

"I was in the duke's company the entire night." Her cheeks flamed at the gasps of the gentlemen around them, but she did not shrink away.

"Blast it, Miranda." Wylde turned her to face him, but when he saw the stubborn loyalty in her eyes, the blistering lecture he had intended to give faded away. He gently stroked her cheek. "I did not want this for you," he murmured.

She gave him a warm smile. "I could not let you pay the price for something you have not done. Not this time."

Rothgard sent a seething glare at Wylde. "Damn you, Wyldehaven. Just when I was prepared to accept your apology, you give me perfect reason to go through with the duel!"

"For pity's sake, Rothgard. What could I possibly have I done in the past five minutes that would have injured you enough to challenge me?"

"Wyldehaven, if what I suspect is true . . ." The earl gazed at Miranda. ". . . I believe you may have compromised my daughter."

Chapter 19

I t was a stunned group that adjourned to Wylde-haven's house to discuss the new developments. Rothgard had withdrawn the challenge, and Miranda's head spun at the thought that she may have actually found her father.

They sat in the breakfast room—Wyldehaven, Miranda, Rothgard, Arenson, Darcy, and Wulf—and enjoyed a piping hot breakfast as they tried to sort through the unexpected surprises of the day.

Arenson stabbed at a piece of sausage and glowered at Rothgard. "I cannot believe you did not tell me about you and Fannie. It has been over twenty years!"

"I apologize," Rothgard said. "I was in a difficult position. I was expected to offer for Penelope, and yet here I was falling in love with Fannie. We decided to keep our love secret until I could extricate myself and offer for her properly."

Miranda set down her fork. She had been swirling her food around on her plate rather than eating, her mind spinning with the implications of the morning. "You mean you intended to marry my mother?"

"Indeed." A wistful smile crossed his face. "Fannie was like no one else. I did not care that she was a poor country girl and an actress, while I was a new earl. I would have married her without hesitation."

"Why didn't you?" Wylde asked.

"She disappeared." Pain flickered across his face. "Vanished from London. I tried to find her, but my Fannie was no fool. She covered her trail well enough that I was never able to locate her, despite years of trying."

"You kept trying to find her?" Miranda whispered.

"Of course." Rothgard sighed and picked up his cup of coffee. "At first I was angry. I decided she had never really loved me, and so I went through with my marriage to Penelope. But as time went on, it continued to bother me that she would run off like that. Running away was not Fannie's style. She would choose to stand fast and fight the archangel himself for her place in heaven rather than run and hide. Something must have happened to send her away." He sent a tender glance to Miranda. "I can only assume that something was you."

"Perhaps she was afraid you would not wed her if she were with child," Wulf said.

"Bah! Fannie?" Arenson hooted with laughter. "More likely she would march right up to Rothgard and demand he do right by her."

"She was not one to be set aside, that is for certain." Rothgard smiled, but then the expression faded. "I am distressed to hear that she has passed away. When I heard that you were her daughter, I had hoped . . ." His voice broke and he looked down at his plate of untouched food.

Miranda hesitated, then reached out and touched his hand. "Why do you believe you are my father?"

Rothgard looked at her, turning his hand beneath hers so their palms met in a brief squeeze. "Your mother was a loyal woman. As long as we were involved, she would never betray me with another man. I told her I intended to wed her but I had to extricate myself from the expectations of Penelope's family first. She was willing to wait for me. We met at Christmastime 1792, and our affair lasted through the winter months and into the majority of the following Season."

"I was born in December 1793."

"Which means you were conceived around April 1793, the height of my affair with Fannie."

"She disappeared around June of that year," Arenson offered. "Rothgard and I were both mad for her, and we mourned. I had no idea the depth of their relationship."

"You look like your mother," Rothgard said. "Your face is nearly identical, and your voice sounds just like hers."

"Mama was a blue-eyed redhead. I always wondered where I got black hair and green eyes. My skin is darker than hers was as well. Mama was very fair."

"We have a Spanish gentleman a few generations back in the family tree. Periodically his darker coloring appears in our offspring. But your green eyes come from me, a noted trait in our family."

"It seems odd to me that I have family. All I ever had was Mama."

Rothgard grinned. "You have a brother and sister. Alonso is my heir, a fine boy, though apparently foolish at the tables." He raised a brow at Wyldehaven, then looked back at Miranda. "And you have a sister, also named Miranda."

Miranda gaped, and Darcy said, "A wild coincidence, I'd say."

"Not really," Rothgard replied. "Fannie knew I was mad for Shakespeare, especially *The Tempest*. I had always planned to name my first child either Alonso for a son or Miranda for a daughter. I am touched that she remembered that and named you as I would have." His voice broke and he glanced away.

Miranda stared down at her plate. She had siblings, albeit half siblings. Legitimate siblings.

Unlike her.

"What are you going to tell them?" she asked, the question nearly choking her. How awful it would be to finally find her father but never be able to acknowledge him in public! She reminded herself that he had been as surprised as she was. What if he planned to keep her existence a secret? What if he chose not to acknowledge her at all?

"I must speak to my wife and children and break the news gently. I have no intention of ignoring your existence, my dear. But you do understand this is a delicate matter."

"Of course." She nodded with ladylike calm, but inside, her heart was dancing with joy.

"And you, Wyldehaven." Rothgard fixed Wylde with a hard stare. "We will discuss your relationship with my daughter in some detail."

"I intend to marry her," Wylde said.

"What!" Wulf dropped his toast.

"Marry?" Darcy set down his cup with a hard click.

Miranda gaped at Wylde, then looked at her father. "He only says that because he feels my reputation is at risk. Please pay no attention."

"Your reputation *is* at risk. I am gratified he intends to do something about it."

"I love you, Miranda," Wylde said, reaching across the table toward her and snagging her fingers. "I did not tell you before because I thought I

337

might die or at the very least suffer horrible scandal. I did not want that for you."

"What about what I want?" she demanded. She stood, pulling her fingers from his. "I have never intended to marry."

"Nonsense," Rothgard said. "Of course you will marry. And I will dower you."

She sent him a startled look, torn between longing to be accepted by her father and maintaining her independence.

"What about James?" she challenged, turning to Wylde. "You cannot even bear to be around him."

"Who is this James?" Rothgard demanded.

"Her child," Wylde replied. "And yes, I can bear to be around him. It will simply take time."

"Her child!" Rothgard slammed his hand on the table. "Someone explain. Now."

"It is my friend's child," Miranda said. "She died in childbed, and I have elected to raise him as my own."

"Oh." The ire faded from his face. "Very well, then."

"The boy is a Matherton," Wylde said.

Darcy choked on his eggs. "He is?"

"He will be raised as one, just like Lettie wanted," Wylde continued. "But he will also be raised with love, as you want."

Miranda opened her mouth to protest more.

"I love you, Miranda. I love you, and I love him. Already he feels like mine."

"Oh." She closed her mouth, saw the truth in his eyes. "You are an impossible man," she said, sitting down and picking up her fork. "And I have no idea at all why I love you."

Wylde grinned. "I shall remind you later. Lord Rothgard, I would like to formally ask for your daughter's hand in marriage."

"Done," Rothgard said, then took his first bite of food.

"Well, Rothgard," Arenson said. "Leave it to you to become a father, a father-in-law, and a grandfather all within one breakfast."

"I have ever been an efficient fellow," Rothgard said.

"Where are you going, Linnet?"

Kit jumped at the sinister voice coming from within the depths of the stall. His horse, Satan, shuffled and snorted, indicating an intruder. Kit drew out the small pistol he carried for such events; this section of London was not the best even in broad daylight.

"Who is there?" he demanded.

After several long moments Daniel Byrne stepped out of the shadows. "'Tis I, Kit. Your good friend 'Wyldehaven.'"

Kit did not relax his grip on the weapon, but he

did lower it. While the intruder was not a random thief, Daniel Byrne was far from trustworthy. "What the devil are you doing here? How did you find me?"

"I have ways, as you should know. I received some distressing news. Wyldehaven is *alive*." He spat the last, his lip curling with disgust.

"What do you mean? Of course he is alive. Why would he not be?"

"Because I went through great trouble to arrange matters so that Lord Rothgard challenged him to a duel. But something went wrong, and my sources tell me that instead of blood on the green this morning, Rothgard *and* Wyldehaven *and* all their seconds *and* that mistress of his have all returned to Matherton House for breakfast. Breakfast! Not a shot was fired!"

"Mistress?"

"That fetching Italian wench. Wyldehaven has provided a house for her, as well as a carriage and servants. Perhaps I will pay a call as Wyldehaven and give her a go." He leered.

"I do not know what you are talking about. I know of no mistress."

"Apparently, he does not include you in everything, does he, Linnet?" Byrne chuckled. "This morning, after my disappointment over the duel, I went to the wench's house and spied on her. And I discovered something wonderful."

Kit eyed him, wondering if he could possibly knock Byrne down, mount his horse, and escape before the fellow got up again. But Byrne would track him down. He knew an amazing network of informants, and London was not that big a city to someone with those connections.

"Tell me what you discovered," he said, hoping it would satisfy the madman and send him on his way.

"Wyldehaven's mistress has a child," he gloated. "Only months old. She must have whelped in the country while he was in exile with his bloody music."

Kit's jaw dropped with surprise before he could think to hide his expression.

"Ah, you did not know. He is a quiet one, that darling duke, I must give him that. No doubt he sent for her once he decided to stay in London."

"He only stayed in London because of your exploits," Kit replied. "Otherwise he would have returned to the country right after Michael's funeral."

"And I would never have known of this new weakness! Think of how he mourned the death of his wife and the brat she carried. I must admit, I am surprised he took a mistress so quickly. I did not credit that saintly Wyldehaven would bow to the same physical needs as the rest of us. But he did and the results are there for the taking." He rubbed his hands together.

341

"For the taking?" Dread crept over him with icy fingers.

"Wyldehaven is going to take his little baseborn son for a ride in the park—at least as far as the servants know. Think of how marvelous it will be when he discovers that I have slipped away with the child and will trade the babe's life for his!"

"Trade . . . you would kill an infant?"

"Only if it becomes necessary. Do not fret, Linnet. You know as well as I that Wyldehaven will charge to the rescue."

"I cannot allow that." Kit raised the pistol again and pointed it right at Byrne's heart. "This has gone on far enough. I will not be party to innocent deaths!"

"Well." Byrne's wild green eyes narrowed with menace. "Then I suppose you shall not be."

Byrne shot out his hand, jerking Kit's wrist skyward and squeezing. The pistol fell to the ground. Kit countered by kicking Byrne in the gut, sending him sprawling into the straw. Then he shoved his foot into the stirrup, flung his leg over the saddle, and kicked Satan into motion.

He had gotten only a few feet beyond the stable when he heard the report of the pistol. Fire tore into his shoulder and the pain nearly blinded him. The world tilted. He struggled to hold on, to remain mounted.

Darkness crept into the edges of his vision.

* * *

"Say you will marry me," Wylde said.

Rothgard and his seconds had left Matherton House. The earl intended to inform his family of Miranda's existence immediately; he wanted to lose no more time as her father. Darcy and Wulf had also taken their leave, discussing among themselves the need to locate Viscount Linnet and inform him of the amazing events of the morning.

Which left Miranda alone with Wylde in the gardens.

"Say you will marry me," he repeated. They sat on a stone bench surrounded by rosebushes, with Annie wandering the paths several feet away for the purposes of propriety. Wylde had agreed to pay a call on Rothgard on the morrow to officially discuss his marriage offer, but Miranda still hesitated to accept him.

"Last night was my gift to you," she said. "Please do not feel forced to offer marriage simply because I have a father now."

"I have not been forced into anything. I want you for my wife." He tilted her chin and pressed his lips to hers.

As always, his touch sent answering sparks all through her body. She wanted nothing more than to lose herself in his arms and let him take care of her forever. But there was something inside her that held back.

She pulled out of the kiss. "I want to continue to perform."

"We do not need the income." He grinned, a boyish expression that lightened his whole face. "But if it means that much to you, I have no objection to you performing whenever you want. It will be every hostess's honor to have the Duchess of Wyldehaven singing at her affair."

Some of her defenses melted at the sincerity she could hear in his voice. "What about James?"

He took her hand and ran his thumb over her fingers. "He will be raised as the son of the Duke of Wyldehaven. He will never be able to inherit; I cannot change the law. But he will be as treasured as any other child our union might produce."

She could not help speaking the thought that was uppermost in her mind. "But how can you treasure him when you cannot even make yourself hold him?"

He let out a long sigh. "The pain at losing my own child fades more every day, but it may take my heart some time to heal. Eventually I will be more at ease with him."

"I hope so." Uncertainty lingered.

"You know I love you." He entwined her fingers with his. "I could not say it yesterday when I thought I might be going to my death, but now I am free to shout it from the rooftops."

"But my mother was—"

"I do not care."

"And while my father is an earl, he was not married to—"

"It does not matter."

"But that makes me—"

He placed his finger on her lips. "That makes you the woman I love. The woman who took a duke to task on behalf of an infant that was not even hers. A woman who was determined to do anything, to make whatever sacrifices were required, to assure that justice was done and those she loved were taken care of. A stubborn, smart woman who will give me stubborn, smart sons and never, ever bore me."

She cocked her head to the side, somewhat hopeful at the talk of more children. "What about daughters?"

He chuckled. "I am certain our daughters will be just as beautiful and stubborn and smart as their mother."

A smile slowly curved her lips. "If I become a duchess, I want to organize a charitable house where women who are in the family way and were abandoned by their lovers can stay and begin to rebuild their lives."

He was silent for a long moment. "I agree that such a place is needed, but perhaps we had best call it a foundling house for the sake of the sticklers of society."

She narrowed her eyes, but saw no resistance in his expression. "You are willing to help me create such a charity?"

"I am." He bent his head and kissed her fingers. "I simply want to avoid the criticism of the narrow-minded."

She stared at him for a long moment. With this man at her side and the power of a duchess, she would be able to help so many like Lettie, who had been abandoned by those who professed to love them. Taking his face between her hands, she kissed him with all the love bubbling inside her. "Yes," she murmured against his lips. "Yes, I will be your wife."

He wrapped his arms around her and kissed her with a passion that stole the breath from her lungs. And she closed her eyes and kissed him right back.

Long moments later footsteps sounded on the pathway.

"Your Grace."

Wylde took his time breaking the kiss. Never looking away from Miranda's radiant face, he said, "You must wish me happy, Travers, as Miss Fontaine has agreed to be my wife."

"Excellent news, sir."

Miranda heard the troubled tone at the same time Wylde looked at his butler. "Is something the matter, Travers?"

"Viscount Linnet is here, Your Grace. He has

346

been badly injured and is most insistent he speak to you."

"Good God." Wylde jumped up from the bench, pulling Miranda along with him. "Where is he?"

"We have installed him in his usual chamber."

Mouth grim, Wylde strode inside, Miranda hurrying beside him.

Kit looked paler than the white sheets he rested upon. Phillips was just stepping away from the bed with the viscount's bloodstained coat, which had clearly needed to be cut away. Kit's neck cloth had also been removed.

"He was shot," the servant said. "We have sent for a physician."

Wylde nodded, then stepped to the side of the bed. "Gad, Kit, what the devil happened to you?"

"Wylde . . . had to tell you."

"Tell me what?" Wylde dragged a chair near to the bed and indicated that Miranda take another nearby. "This is no time for deathbed confessions, Kit. I am certain you will be right as rain."

Kit managed to slowly shake his head against the pillow. "Coming for the baby."

"What? Whose baby?"

Kit glanced behind him at Miranda.

"James," she whispered in horrified realization.

Wylde leaned forward to hear better. "Who is coming for the baby?"

"I . . . am sorry. Bad friend."

"I do not understand. Is someone after James?"

"Yes." He nodded slightly. "Baby. James."

"Who?" Wylde clasped his hand around Kit's good shoulder as if he could will his own life force into the man. "Who is coming for him?"

"You. But . . . not you."

"Me but not—blast it, Kit, are you trying to tell me the imposter wants the baby for some reason?"

"Yes." Kit nodded. "Hates you. Wants to kill you."

A horrible suspicion bloomed in his mind. "Do you know who he is, Kit?"

Grief twisted Kit's features. "I am sorry."

"Dear God." Wylde pulled his hand away from Kit's shoulder. "You have been helping him, haven't you?"

Slowly, Kit nodded. "He is mad," he rasped. "Jealous . . . of you. Wants to be the duke."

"I will not even begin to argue that bit of lunacy."

"Byrne," Kit managed. "Daniel Byrne."

"That is his name?"

"Yes." Kit sucked in a shuddering breath. "Hurry."

Wylde rose from his chair and strode out of the room, leaving Miranda to scurry after him.

"What are you going to do?" she asked, trying to

keep up with his long-legged stride as he headed down the stairs.

"I am going to bring the baby here so he will be safe."

"But Kit said this fellow is mad. What if he hurts James?"

He stopped in the middle of the staircase and turned to where she halted a step above him. Taking her hands in his, he looked deep into her eyes. "I will make certain nothing happens to James. But we must move quickly. This Byrne may have already stolen the child."

"Does he think he can simply walk into the house and take the baby?" Miranda asked, keeping pace as Wylde continued down the stairs. "How can he even believe such a thing?"

"Simple." They reached the ground floor and headed for the foyer. "He is me, remember?"

"Oh, my God. He can simply pay a call and as the duke no one will question him."

"Indeed." Wylde caught the eye of his butler. "Have the coach brought around, Travers. And be certain my pistols are loaded. I shall need them."

"Yes, Your Grace." The butler immediately began directing the servants to fulfill his master's request.

"I am going with you."

"No, you are not." He placed his hands on her shoulders. "This fellow may be dangerous, so it is best if you are not in the area. I will stop him and collect James and come right back here."

"But—"

"It needs to be this way," he said. "I cannot allow you to be in danger." Two footmen hurried over with a brace of pistols and his hat. He donned the hat and tucked the pistols away beneath his coat. Taking Miranda's hand in his, he pressed a passionate kiss to the back of it. "Wait for me," he said, his dark eyes gleaming with promise and purpose. Then he turned and strode out the door.

She watched him go, panic tearing at her insides. He was brave, to go face this madman all alone. Yet still she feared for him. This imposter had led them a merry dance for months now. What made this time different?

Because for the first time, she realized, they had advance notice about where the villain was going to be.

And Wylde expected her to stay behind while he charged in? He was mad if he thought she would meekly hide when her child was in danger. And she was not about to lose her future husband before he had a chance to say the vows.

"Summon my carriage, please, Travers."

"I am sorry, miss. The duke has instructed me not to allow you to follow him."

She drew herself up to her haughtiest height.

"For your information, I am not following the duke. I have an appointment with Lady Rothgard."

"If you will give me her direction, I will pass it to the coachman."

"Thank you," Miranda said. "Please send Annie back to my home; I will be safe enough with a footman at Lady Rothgard's." *And perhaps Annie would be able to escape with James before the worst happened.*

Chapter 20

W hen Miranda arrived at Rothgard's town house, she had not even considered that she might be turned away. But Lord Rothgard would recognize her name, and it was he she asked to see. Apparently someone was at home, for she was requested to come inside and was shown to a drawing room to wait.

She had been there several minutes, roaming the room and studying the lovely Chinese decor, when the countess entered. Lady Rothgard's manner was cool, hesitant, yet curious as she said, "Good afternoon, Contessa. What a surprise that you have come to call."

"Good afternoon, Lady Rothgard." Miranda bobbed a curtsy. "I had hoped to speak to your husband. Is he at home?"

"No, he has been out all morning." The countess sank into a chair. "May I ask why you are looking for my husband?"

From the countess's calm acceptance of her, Miranda assumed that Rothgard had not yet had the opportunity to talk to his family about the morning's events.

"Mrs. Weatherby suggested I speak to his lordship about a presentation of *The Tempest* she would like to see performed," she lied. "I believe she is seeking patrons to donate funds."

"Oh, a play." Lady Rothgard nodded. "And *The Tempest* is his favorite. I will certainly give him the message when he returns."

"Thank you." She had to get home, to get back to James. Rothgard could not help her. "I have another appointment, so I shall take my leave . . ."

"My husband is inordinately fond of the theater." The edge in Lady Rothgard's voice halted her exit.

She looked back. "Everyone must pursue their passions."

"Indeed." The countess glanced down at her folded hands. "Are you one of those passions, Contessa?"

Miranda blinked in surprise. "I beg your pardon?"

The countess stood. "You did not come here to solicit donations for the arts, did you? You have some personal interest in my husband."

Miranda edged closer to the door, anxious to escape. Perhaps Wylde had fetched James without incident. Perhaps Kit had been wrong and the imposter did not threaten her child. But she doubted it.

Coming here had wasted precious time. "Please tell Lord Rothgard that I came to call."

"I knew this would happen. You look just like her. The first time I saw you, I knew."

The urgent hiss of the other woman's voice put her on her guard. "Lady Rothgard, you have me at a disadvantage."

"How could he resist? A woman who bears such a striking resemblance to his beloved Fannie. Of course he would seek you out. Anything to have her again."

Her voice grew shrill. Miranda hurried back to the countess, cursing herself for coming to Rothgard in person She could have sent a message. But the idea of a father was still so new, she had wanted to see him again. "Lady Rothgard, you have the wrong idea."

"Have I? Are you going to stand here in my own drawing room and deny that you are having an affair with my husband?"

"Indeed I am," Miranda said. "Listen to me, Lady Rothgard. Fannie Fontaine was my mother."

"Your mother!" The countess paled. "Dear God, no wonder you look so much like her."

"You really should discuss this matter with the earl," Miranda said. "I should never have come. I *must* take my leave, right now."

"No!" Lady Rothgard grabbed her arm. "You cannot leave me here wondering. What is my husband to you? Why are you really here?"

Miranda sighed, wanting to be anywhere but here, looking into the countess's pain-filled countenance. "He should be the one to tell you."

"Then there *is* something to tell." Her fingers dug into Miranda's arm.

"Nothing of consequence. Good day to you, my lady." She tried to pry the woman's fingers away, glancing up to lock gazes with her as she did so.

Suddenly the countess gasped and jerked free. "Those eyes. Dear God. Not a lover. You are his daughter, aren't you?"

"Lady Rothgard—"

Miranda held out a pleading hand, but the other woman's eyes rolled backward, and then she collapsed in a dead swoon.

"Oh, no!" Miranda managed to catch her before she hit the floor. With some effort, she dragged the Countess to the couch and laid her sprawled halfway on the sofa. As she struggled to lift her legs up onto the cushions, she heard a footstep in the hall. "Help!" she called. "In here!"

The door was slightly ajar and swung open to reveal Rothgard's daughter, the other Miranda. Pale, blond, and shy—

"What have you done to my mother?" she snarled, then leaped at Miranda like a tigress.

* * *

Wylde walked in the front door of Miranda's house, alert to anything out of the ordinary.

A maid came down the hall. "Goodness, Your Grace, I thought you were in the nursery! Has Mrs. Cooper returned?"

"Not yet." Wylde glanced at the staircase. "I am going back up to look in on James."

"Very well, sir." Humming a tune to herself, the maid continued down the hallway.

Wylde crept up the stairs, quietly drawing one of the two pistols he'd brought from his pocket. He reached the nursery without incident and eased open the door.

"Come in, Thornton, old boy. 'Tis about time we met."

Wylde paused, then pushed the door fully open. A man sat in a chair in the middle of the nursery, rocking the cradle with the sleeping infant in it with his foot. A pistol rested across his lap. The grin that spread across his face was the same one Wylde saw in the mirror every morning. His build, his hairstyle—now Wylde could understand why his own servants had been fooled. Except for the green eyes and the madness glittering in them, the imposter was his duplicate.

"I assume you are Daniel Byrne." Wylde shut the door behind him.

The look-alike's face lit up. "So Kit survived, did

he? I was counting on that." He tapped his pistol. "I decided in the end I wanted to kill you myself. Much more satisfying."

"I admit I am at a loss," Wylde said, keeping his own pistol out of sight with his leg. "I have never met you before, nor even heard of you. How can it be you bear me such enmity?"

"Justice." Byrne's foot slipped from the cradle with a thump. "I was the firstborn, you know. Our father was supposed to have married my mama, but your mother seduced him and trapped him into wedlock."

"As I recall, my parents were betrothed from birth."

"As you recall? You were not there, you nitwit! How could you recall something you did not witness?"

"My grandmother told me the tale."

"As if she can remember anything clearly at her age. No, my mama told me how I should have been the Duke of Wyldehaven." Byrne tilted his head, a grin playing about his lips. "Then I met dear Viscount Linnet, and the whole plan came together in one beautiful symphony. You should appreciate that."

"What is your intent?" Wylde eased closer to the cradle. "Why have you gone through so much trouble to blacken my name?"

"Part of it was pure entertainment. But truly,

I intend to see you dead and then I will take your place. I am, after all, the elder brother."

"I cannot see how such a thing would work," Wylde said. "If I were to die, it would be quite public, and then everyone would know you are not the true duke."

"I am the true duke!" Byrne roared, rising to his feet. The baby began to wail. "Quiet, you hell spawn!" He pointed the pistol at the cradle.

"No!" Wylde leaped forward and smacked Byrne's hand upward. The pistol fired into the ceiling.

Byrne drew back his fist and hit him in the jaw. Wylde's head snapped back as pain exploded in his skull. He tried to bring up his own pistol, but Byrne wrenched it from his hand.

"One pistol fired and only one left." Byrne sent him sprawling across the floor with a hard kick to the abdomen. "Shall I kill the father or the son?" He swung the pistol back and forth between Wylde and James.

"Your child," Wylde managed, gasping for air. "Lettie's child."

"Lettie? Good God, that whore who fancied herself an actress?" He laughed. "So this is her get, is it? She was the first to believe that I was Wyldehaven."

"You will never be Wyldehaven." Wylde could feel the other pistol beneath his coat, digging into his side.

"I already *am* Wyldehaven. And soon the ton will know it, too." The wails of the baby grew louder, and Byrne cast an annoyed look at the cradle. "Does that squalling blob of human flesh ever stay quiet?"

"You woke him."

"Silence!" Byrne shouted at the child. "I said silence!" He kicked the cradle.

"He is your son," Wylde said.

"As if I care about some puling brat. Though perhaps when I am recognized as duke, I shall help myself to a piece of that ladybird you have been keeping. Plow her until she is with child." He laughed, but then the baby hit a shrill note, screeching loud enough to shatter windows. "Damn you," he thundered, raising his weapon at the cradle. "I said silence!"

Wylde pulled out his second pistol, swore as it caught in his coat. Byrne cursed at the child, taking careful aim.

A shot rang out, and the baby's cries abruptly stopped.

Miranda fought off the wild termagant who flew at her with nails extended like claws. "Calm yourself! She has swooned! Your mother swooned!"

"What did you do to her?" The girl grabbed a hank of Miranda's hair and pulled.

"I did nothing." Miranda grabbed the girl's wrist and squeezed hard.

Rothgard's daughter screeched and let go of Miranda's hair. "I told you to leave! Why could you not just leave London, leave us in peace?" She slapped at Miranda's hand.

Miranda did not relax her grip, only shook the girl. "I said calm yourself! Have you any hartshorn for your mother?"

"Just leave London." The blond girl sniffled, tears welling in her eyes. "Why did you have to come here? Everything was perfect before you came."

"What the devil is going on?"

The thunderous, furious male voice had both girls jerking their heads around. Lord Rothgard stood in the doorway, hands on his hips, a crowd of servants gathering behind him.

"Lady Rothgard has swooned," Miranda said even as Rothgard's daughter cried out, "Papa, she has injured Mama!"

"For pity's sake." Rothgard signaled to one of the maids. "Fetch Lady Rothgard's vinaigrette." The maid rushed off. Rothgard looked at Miranda. "My wife is prone to the vapors. Please release my daughter. She is just seventeen and somewhat excitable."

Miranda let her half sister loose, and the blond girl stumbled sobbing to the sofa where her mother slumped. "What have you done to Mama?"

"Hush, now, my sweet. She will be right as rain as soon as Bridget returns with the vinaigrette."

Rothgard looked up at the sound of running feet. The little maid returned, panting. He took the vinaigrette from her and walked over to the sofa, where he flicked over the tiny silver box and waved it beneath his wife's nose.

The countess gasped, sniffled, then jerked awake. "Heavens, what happened to me?" She looked around, saw Miranda and paled.

"Oh, Mama!" Rothgard's daughter threw her arms around her mother, then glared at Miranda. "I told you to leave London. Why could you not listen? Do you not see how much you hurt her just by being here?"

"What do you mean, you told me to leave London?" Miranda asked.

"You got my notes," the girl said.

"*You* sent those?"

"The first time Mama saw you at Mrs. Weatherby's, she swooned. And I know why. It is because you look like *her*."

"Her?"

"Your mother. Fannie Fontaine."

A stricken look crossed Rothgard's face, and he dismissed the servants, handing the vinaigrette to one of them. "Off with you now. Back to your duties." As they scattered, he closed the doors to the drawing room, then strode around to the sofa where his daughter sat with his wife. "Miranda, tell me what this is about."

"As I said—" Miranda started.

"She—" Rothgard's daughter began.

"Silence." Both girls quieted, and Rothgard looked from one to the other. "This is going to be quite confusing with the two of you possessing the same name." He pointed at the younger girl. "You, Randa. What is the problem?"

"Her," the girl snapped. "Just seeing her breaks Mama's heart. I want her to go away and leave us alone."

"I have been receiving threatening notes warning me to leave London," Miranda said, choosing not to reveal the physical attack in the alley. "Apparently your daughter sent them."

"I am appalled at such behavior!" Rothgard said. "You should be ashamed of yourself, Randa."

"She does not belong here." Randa pointed a finger at Miranda. "Her mother was a whore who tried to take you away from Mama!"

Stunned at the attack, Miranda could only stare at the younger girl, cold anger firing in her belly. With effort, she refrained from spewing forth her own venom.

"Miranda! How dare you say such a thing!" The countess gaped at her daughter with horror.

"Where did you ever hear this tale?" Rothgard gritted out.

"From Papa Stone."

"My father?" Lady Rothgard gasped.

"He told me the story while he was so sick, when I was the only one he had to talk to. He told me how that *actress* tried to lure you away. He took care of her, though. He paid her to disappear, her and her brat."

"Miranda Juliet Titania Evers!" the countess exclaimed. "I am appalled to hear such filth come from your lips!"

"It is the truth." Randa sent Miranda a scathing glance.

"So that is what happened." Rothgard looked at Miranda. "I never knew why Fannie left so abruptly. But if my father-in-law was involved . . . well, he was a ruthless man."

"He paid her to go," Randa said. "And told her he would have her killed if she did not leave London and never return."

"Dear God in heaven." The countess sank back against the cushions. "I can believe this of him; he was determined we would wed, Stephen."

"I know." Rothgard's face looked to be carved from granite. "Randa, Penelope, this young lady is Miranda Fontaine. She is my daughter, and I intend to acknowledge her as such."

"Papa, no!"

The countess gave a gracious nod. "As you wish, Stephen."

"She will also become engaged to the Duke of Wyldehaven, once the appropriate documents are signed. That could be advantageous for Randa."

"Sister to a duchess." The countess contemplated the notion, anxiety fading from her eyes, replaced by a gleam of excitement.

"I will not say she is my sister!" Randa folded her arms across her chest, her expression mutinous.

"You will welcome her as your sister," Rothgard warned, "or you will spend the rest of the Season in the country."

Randa's mouth dropped open, but she said nothing more, just sat with arms crossed and a pout on her pretty face.

Sensing the danger was past, Miranda claimed Rothgard's attention. "My lord, I came here to ask for your help; however, it may already be too late."

Her distress must have echoed in her voice. "What is it? What is the matter?" he demanded.

"This morning we learned the imposter was going to try and abduct James—or something worse. Wyldehaven has gone to stop him. Alone."

"Curse these young hotheads! Where is Wyldehaven now?"

"At my home." She bit her lip. "I fear for the worst, for I have lingered here too long."

"There cannot be a worse time for Cheltenham tragedies," he grunted, with a baleful look at his wife and daughter. "Randa, I will deal with your abominable behavior later. And Penelope . . ." His voice grew tender. "I regret any pain or embarrassment this may have caused you."

Lady Rothgard's face lit up, and Miranda realized that she truly did love her husband. And for all that Rothgard had never forgotten his first love Fannie, he appeared to care a great deal for his wife.

"It is a shock," the countess agreed. "But we will weather the storm." She visibly gathered herself, then offered Miranda a tentative smile. "Welcome to our family, my dear."

"Thank you."

"We will continue this later." Rothgard lifted his wife's hand to his lips. "A child's life may be in danger, and time is of the essence."

"Go," Lady Rothgard urged. "My prayers go with you."

"Thank you," Miranda whispered.

"Come," Rothgard said. "We will take my carriage."

When they arrived at Miranda's house, Rothgard indicated a rig parked to the side as they descended from the carriage. "That is the surgeon's coach."

"Dear God." Miranda gathered her skirts and ran up the steps.

"Do not panic, my dear." Rothgard easily caught up with her just as she lifted the knocker.

She tried to calm herself, but looked up hopefully as the door opened. "Travers, is all well?"

"Miss Fontaine, please do come in. Sir, may I take your hat?"

"This is Lord Rothgard," Miranda said as her father doffed his hat and handed it to the servant. "Where is the duke?"

"I believe he is still in the nursery." He reached out a hand as she raced for the stairs. "No, miss! Wait!" The butler turned back to Rothgard. "You may want to accompany her, my lord. It is no sight for a lady's eyes."

Even as she raced up the stairs, Miranda heard the butler's comment to Rothgard. Fear tasted bitter in her mouth, and her heart pounded so loud she was certain everyone could hear it. "Please," she whispered as she halted outside the nursery. Hesitantly, she pushed open the door.

The room was empty. But blood had sprayed the walls, pooled on the floor.

Splattered on the cradle.

Where was James?

A harsh, hiccuping sob escaped her lips. She could not tear her gaze away from the baby's blood-smeared bed. Her knees weakened and she leaned against the doorjamb, slowly sliding down toward the floor, not wanting to know. And desperate to know. *Was James—* Her world tilted and threatened to go black.

"Goodness, Miss Miranda. What are you doing here?" Annie came up in the hall behind her and helped her to her feet. "This is no fit place for you."

What happened? She thought she spoke, but she could not form the words. She allowed Annie to support her, unable to rip her gaze from the bloody scene.

"Miranda, what has happened?" Rothgard caught up with her, blanched at the sight of the nursery.

"She came up here before we could clean up the mess," Annie said. "Miss Miranda is a gentle one. This must have scared her to death."

"What happened here?" Rothgard demanded.

"That imposter fellow came visiting, pretending he was the duke. I was with Miss Miranda, or I would have told that stiff-rumped butler not to let the blighter in here. But then after the real duke came, that fake duke got himself shot."

"What about James?" Miranda forced the words past stiff lips. "Where is he?"

"Now don't you fret about him." Annie patted her arm. "The duke took him out to the garden. The little mite was all worked up with all the gunshots and whatnot. His Grace thought the flowers would soothe him."

"He is all right? They are both all right?"

"Right as rain."

Miranda sucked in a deep breath. Then another. James was all right. Wylde was all right.

"And the imposter?" Rothgard asked.

DEBRA MULLINS

"Dead as can be. The surgeon has the body down the hall."

"I must go to him. I must see for myself." Miranda pulled away from them and raced for the stairs.

"I've got to find those chambermaids to help me clean up this mess," Annie muttered.

She started to walk away, but Rothgard caught her hand. He rubbed his thumb over the black smear of gunpowder on the pad of her thumb. "Thank you for helping him."

Startled, she slowly nodded, then continued about her duties.

When Miranda burst into the garden, she saw Wylde immediately. He sat on a small stone bench, his head bent toward the blanket-wrapped bundle in his arms.

All at once her world righted on its axis. The sky was blue, the air was warm, and the flowers smelled sweet.

"Is everyone all right?" she asked, walking toward him.

He glanced over and smiled at her. "Right as rain, as Annie would say."

"And James?"

"He was yelling fit to wake the dead. Mrs. Cooper had stepped out to the market, so I am attempting to keep him calm until she returns." He shifted on the bench, showing that the babe gnawed and sucked with vigor on one of his fingers. "I do not believe he has yet figured out that this is not the teat he wants."

A startled laugh escaped her throat. "Let us hope he remains in ignorance a bit longer." She sat down on the bench beside him, then rested her head against his shoulder. "I see you have overcome your aversion to children."

"I was never averse to them." He leaned over and brushed a kiss to the top of her head. "I adore children. When I lost mine—" His voice broke, and he cleared his throat. "I lost my child before I even got to hold him. It was the fiercest, most desperate agony I have ever felt. I thought that by avoiding this baby, I would never feel that again."

She reached out to stroke her finger along the child's downy head. "I take it something changed your mind."

"Byrne was going to kill him, shoot the babe right in front of me, and all that horror rose up again. I had never held this child, tried to pretend he did not matter. Did not exist. And again a babe in my care would be taken away. Again I would fail."

"You did not fail," Miranda said, smiling up at him.

"I might have, if not for Annie," Wylde corrected. "My blasted pistol was tangled in my coat. She had recognized the imposter and helped herself to my weapons chest. She fired just as I freed my pistol and did the same. One of us killed him; I do not know which."

"Even if you did not fire the fatal shot, you did your best to save James."

"Yes," he agreed. "At least this time I had the chance to try."

"You will make a very good father."

He smiled down at the infant. "I hope you are right."

"Remind me to tell you about my visit to Rothgard's home," she said. "By this evening it will be an amusing tale."

"Why not tell me now?"

"Later." She bent forward to kiss the top of James's head, then turned to Wylde and pressed her mouth to his in a soft, lingering kiss. "We have the rest of our lives."

"We do," he agreed, then tilted his head to the sky to watch the clouds drift by.

The sky was blue and the air was warm, and the duke's heart was healed at last.

*Next month, don't miss these exciting new
love stories only from
Avon Books*

Desire Untamed by Pamela Palmer
They are called Feral Warriors—an elite band of immortals who
can change shape at will. Sworn to rid the world of evil,
consumed by sorcery and seduction, their wild natures are
primed for release. And Kara MacAllister has just realized she
is one of them.

Surrender to the Devil by Lorraine Heath
Frannie Darling wants nothing to do with the men who lust for
her. She can take care of herself and feels perfectly safe on her
own—safe, that is, until *he* strides into her world, and once
again it becomes a very dangerous place indeed.

Four Dukes and a Devil by Cathy Maxwell, Elaine Fox,
Jeaniene Frost, Sophia Nash, and Tracy Anne Warren
Fall in love with the unpredictable and irresistible dukes (and
one dog named Duke). Join five bestselling and award-winning
authors for tales of noble danger and devilish desire.

For the Earl's Pleasure by Anne Mallory
They were once cherished companions, until a scandalous
secret tore them apart. Now Valerian Rainewood and Abigail
Smart are the fiercest of enemies. But when the earl is viciously
attacked, Abigail's distress tells her that something still binds
her to the wild Rainewood.

Unforgettable, enthralling love stories,
sparkling with passion and adventure
from Romance's bestselling authors

IN BED WITH THE DEVIL   *by Lorraine Heath*
978-0-06-135557-8

THE MISTRESS DIARIES   *by Julianne MacLean*
978-0-06-145684-8

THE DEVIL WEARS TARTAN   *by Karen Ranney*
978-0-06-125242-6

BOLD DESTINY   *by Jane Feather*
978-0-380-75808-1

LIKE NO OTHER LOVER   *by Julie Anne Long*
978-0-06-134159-5

NEVER DARE A DUKE   *by Gayle Callen*
978-0-06-123506-1

SIMPLY IRRESISTIBLE   *by Rachel Gibson*
978-0-380-79007-4

A PERFECT DARKNESS   *by Jaime Rush*
978-0-06-169035-8

YOU'RE THE ONE THAT I HAUNT   *by Terri Garey*
978-0-06-158203-5

SECRET LIFE OF A VAMPIRE   *by Kerrelyn Sparks*
978-0-06-166785-5

Avon Romances
the best in
exceptional authors and unforgettable novels!

At Avon Books, we know your passion for romance—once you finish one of our novels, you find yourself wanting more.

May we tempt you with . . .

- **Excerpts** from our upcoming releases.

- Entertaining **extras**, including authors' personal photo albums and book lists.

- Behind-the-scenes **scoop** on your favorite characters and series.

- **Sweepstakes** for the chance to win free books, romantic getaways, and other fun prizes.

- Writing **tips** from our authors and editors.

- **Blog** with our authors and find out why they love to write romance.

- **Exclusive content** that's not contained within the pages of our novels.

Join us at
www.avonbooks.com